9

The House of Cavendish

OUTROADS

Malcolm Brocklehurst

Eloquent Books

Eloquent Books
An imprint of Strategic Book Group
P.O. Box 333
Durham CT 06422
www.StrategicBookGroup.com

ISBN: 978-1-60860-307-7

Printed in the United States of America

Book Design: Rolando F. Santos

Contents

Also by Malcolm Brocklehurst
The Secret History of Christianity
ISBN 978-1-84529-763-3

I would like to dedicate this book to my Grandfather;
the late Arthur Storey without whose legacy of research
into our family history back to 1734,
this novel would not have been written.

Acknowledgments

I wish to thank my family and friends who supported and encouraged me, especially my wife who suffered through the difficult birth throes of this book. She has been a part of the bequest left in the legacy from the moment I received it.

I would like to thank Edna Sharrock; an old Palatine school friend, who has been a continuing source of assistance into family research and without who's help, parts of this book would not have been written.

Grateful thanks to the Cleveleys' Writers and in particular to Ivan McKeon, Victoria Copeland and Pam Ford for their help and support during the construction of this book and to David Neal for his critique when reading draft manuscripts. To all of them I extend my appreciation.

I especially want to thank my editor, Doug Watts of the Jacqui Bennett Writers Bureau, for his editorial comments combined with kind critiques and generous gifts of time and advice.

My gratitude must be given to the staff at Cleveleys' Library for their help in researching and obtaining reference books.

Thanks to the staff at Hardwick Old Hall Office for invaluable information on Bess of Hardwick and Hardwick Hall and my appreciation also goes to Andrea Hill, the Visitor Operations Manager at the English Heritage for Bolsover District & Nottinghamshire for providing local information relative to the area.

Thanks to James Hester a researcher at the Royal Armouries Museum, Leeds for information on muskets and flintlocks pistols.

Malcolm Brocklehurst

A thank you to Ian Dickinson, general manager of Yesterday's World, Gt Yarmouth. Ian provided valuable information of the price of tobacco in the seventeenth century.

With grateful appreciation I thank Ashley Lister who provided invaluable help on editorial matters. Ashley is an English tutor on Blackpool Palatine Campus and like myself an *'old Palatine boy'*

To all these named persons and to the many unnamed persons whom I have telephoned and requested information, I extend my grateful thanks.

Author's Introduction

When my grandfather Arthur Storey died in 1943, he left behind a legacy of family intrigue and a paper trail to a lost unproven will with bequests that are valued at ten million pound by today's standards. Grandfather traced the will through the family tree back to the early eighteenth century when Elizabeth Cavendish, daughter of a wealthy Derbyshire family, fell in love with William Clarke her coachman, who was a man below her station in life. Eventually the couple eloped and possibly married in 1734. In 1743 they had a son named Robert Clarke

Elizabeth's family owned estates in Derbyshire, England and their associated inheritances were left dormant but even so, when the disinherited Elizabeth died she left £95.000 to her son Robert and the continuance of that story is for a sequel to this novel.... but to give some historical credibility as to where the money may have originated, and before I publish the history of the family legacy 1734 to 2000, I decided I must write a novel giving a fictitious source of the estate's wealth interwoven with factual historical characters that may have entered the family stage during the sixteenth century during the creation of Elizabeth Cavendish's ancestry.

It all began five generations previously, when Henry Cavendish the genuine elder son of 'Bess of Hardwick' fathered at least four illegitimate sons. To give some historical background to my novel and to explain were my grandfather's legacy may have originated; and without making claims on the Cavendish estates of Chatsworth House, I had to create a fictitious account of what could have been a fifth illegitimate son. This novel is the story of Henry Cavendish's descendents who resided at Ufton Manor in the Derbyshire parish of South Wingfield up to 1730.

Descendants of William Cavendish

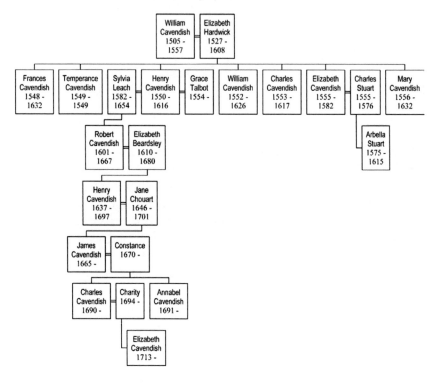

Preface

The parish of South Wingfield lies eleven miles south of Chesterfield in the county of Derbyshire. The village of Oakerthorpe, known in ancient times as Ulkerthorpe, also lies in this parish. In the nineteenth century, within Oakerthorpe and near the Peacock Inn lay the ruins of Ufton Manor. In the middle of the sixteenth century the chapel of Limbury adjoined the old manor house. Some ruins of the chapel could still be seen as late as 1800.

The Peacock Inn situated near the Alfreton-South Wingfield crossroads dates back into the eleventh century and is reputed to be the oldest inn in the county of Derbyshire.

The inn is mentioned in the Domesday Book when it was known as Ufton Barnsand. It was rebuilt in 1613 and has a most interesting history; legend has it that Dick Turpin one of the most famous highwaymen in English history stopped off at the inn on his ride to York.

An underground passage in the bottom of the cellar in the Peacock Inn is reported to lead to nearby South Wingfield Manor. Exploration through the tunnel leads to a large cave where there is a deep pool of water over thick mud. The tunnel is around five feet high and about four feet wide with parts bricked up - most of it is excavated through living rock.

It was at Wingfield Manor were Mary Queen of Scots was imprisoned in 1569 then again in 1584 when her attempted rescue by Anthony Babington ended in disaster. His plan was to lead her down through the tunnel to the cellar at the inn where horses were waiting to take her to safety. Babington went down through the tunnel from Oakerthorpe but he got caught. For his crime he was beheaded at Lincoln's Inn in 1586. Mary was taken to Fotheringay and beheaded the same year.

Another legend associated with the Peacock tells that in the eighteenth century a respected churchwarden at the chapel and the landlord of the Peacock Inn was Peter Kendall. He had a beautiful daughter named Ann who wore such fashionable wide hooped dresses that she had to enter the church doorway sideways. The local church, which figures quite largely in the following tale, is called South Wingfield, although it is on the Oakerthorpe side of the River Amber.

Ann Kendall was courted by a young local farmer who seems to have remained anonymous in the records. The farmer seduced Ann and she fell pregnant. The farmer then deserted Ann and left her to give birth to a daughter. The disgrace so weighed upon poor Miss Kendall's mind that she died on fourteenth of May 1745 of a broken heart. Just before she died she asked for Psalm 109 to be read at her funeral. Since that time, at churches within the district Psalm 109 is known as "Miss Kendall's Psalm"

> *"For the mouth of the wicked and the mouth of the deceitful are opened against me: they have spoken against me with a lying tongue. For my love they are my adversaries: but I give myself unto prayer."*

It was an old custom in several Derbyshire churches to carry a special garland at the funeral procession of a young man or maiden. These garlands were made of wooden hoops decorated with rosettes, ornaments of white paper and ribbons, and sometimes a pair of white gloves. They were hung up in the church after the funeral, many lingering for centuries. Such a garland was carried at Ann Kendall's funeral and was still hanging in South Wingfield in the 1870s, in spite of previous offers to purchase the curio. That is not however the end of the story, nor the reason why it has lived on in the memories of the local inhabitants. Shortly after the funeral, the man who had betrayed the maid was riding past South Wingfield church; suddenly the bells crashed out, the horse reared and the rider was thrown to the ground, breaking his neck. Of course people said that the judgment of God had fallen upon him... There was another funeral. Legend does not recount if there was a garland this time. Nor are we told if the lovers lie together in peace nor if the bell ringers were in the church at the time of the accident. Maybe supernatural hands were at work that day...

Or maybe the bell ringer was Miss Kendall's father, but then I maybe a cynic.

Prologue

It was the third Saturday in the hot long June of 1381, and the peasants were in revolt over the implementation of new taxes. Sir John Cavendish, the king's chief justice, was running for his life, pursued by a mob, some wielding scythes others armed just with sticks.

He reached St. Mary's church door and with a last gasp grasped the handle, "Take care, you scoundrels," he called, "In the name of our Lord, I claim sanctuary in this house of God."

Jack Straw, the leader of the mob, prised the hand of Sir John from the door handle and the angry mob fell onto the kicking struggling knight of the realm.

The mob dragged their prisoner behind a cart all of the seventeen miles to Bury St Edmunds. Five hours later the exhausted chief of justice was led into the market place and after a brief mock trial his accusers found him guilty of acts against the rebels; namely that as a representative of the king, he was responsible for the judiciary's cancellation of all charters granted to the rebels by Richard II.

Jack Straw and other leaders forced Sir John to his knees and then by the use of a woodsman's axe he was brutally decapitated.

Sir John had taken his name from his ancestral home in the Suffolk village of Cavendish.

This story is based on incidents and actions of two of his descendents, Sir Thomas and Sir William Cavendish.

Sir Thomas Cavendish was born in the Suffolk village of Trimley St. Martin in 1560. At the age of fifteen he attended Corpus Christi College at Cambridge but left two years later without taking a degree. The next eight years he squandered his inheritance on rakish, raucous living. After short terms in Parliament he sought to renew his fortune by purchasing a small ship named *Elizabeth* and joining Sir Richard Grenville's flotilla when it sailed to Virginia in 1585. It was whilst in Virginia that Sir Thomas made the discovery that by dipping tobacco leaves in sugar, the leaves produced a milder and mellower smoke, a discovery that proved worthless in improving Sir Thomas's fortune and only established the Cavendish name as a brand of tobacco.

Sir Thomas now returned to England to obtain his own "letters of marque" to act as a privateer. Having observed the benefits that Sir Richard had obtained as the leader of a flotilla, Sir Thomas now planned his own voyage as a "legal pirate" in command of his own flotilla. With some of the profits he had gained with his investment in Sir Grenville's voyage, Sir Thomas bought a new ship, which he named the *Desire*, and his flotilla of privateers set sail from Harwich on the twenty-seventh of June 1586. It was a voyage that at the age of twenty-seven was about to make him a very rich man, most of his wealth coming from the looting of the seven hundred ton Spanish galleon the Santa Ana, a capture that was to become the richest haul of prize money ever recorded from a Spanish galleon.

It was the morning of Saturday, the fourteenth of November 1587, the sun had risen and a stiff offshore breeze blew off the Californian coast. The breeze filled the main sail as the helmsman on the *Desire* moved the wheel two points to starboard. As the ship responded, the topsails of an enemy ship were seen on the horizon. The two ships closed, the crew of the *Desire* cleared their decks for action aware that all other ships in the Pacific were enemy. Meanwhile the other ship, a Spanish galleon named the *Santa Ana* under the command of Captain Tomás de Alzola, was sailing on a south-south-easterly course towards Acapulco and on an interception course with the *Desire*. Arrogantly the Spanish captain assumed that the Spanish had total command of the Pacific, but that assumption was about to be challenged when his lookout saw the topmasts and sails that were between them and the California shore. The lookout assumed that the other ship was the *Buena Esperanza, a* sister ship that had sailed with them from the Philippines.

The two ships closed. Through his telescope the lookout saw the red and white flags on the *Desire* signifying its English sovereignty. Alzola raised the alarm, issuing swords and arquebuses to all able-bodied hands.

The *Desire* came alongside and several swashbuckling Englishmen leapt aboard the *Santa Ana.* Fierce hand-to-hand fighting took place as the Spaniards fought and repulsed the initial attack.

"Save yourselves," yelled Jack, a young midshipman, as he leapt into the sea.

The *Desire* by this time was two cable lengths off the Spaniard's port bow and Cavendish ordered two of his cannons to open fire.

On the cannon's recoil a few deckhands lowered ropes into the water and all but two of the swimming sailors clambered back aboard their ship. The two remaining sailors were splashing and struggling in the water to reach the *Desire*. Both had been wounded and as they swam in the water, weakened from loss of blood from their wounds, lookouts on the *Desire* saw the fin of a shark circling the two hapless swimmers. The fin cut through the water then disappeared from view. Moments later, Jack the midshipman screamed as his body was jerked with violent, hesitant tugs by the attacking shark. Jack's screams fell silent.

A bloodstain patch of water expanded. The surviving swimmer found a renewed source of energy, boosted no doubt by adrenalin he grabbed a rope and was pulled from the sea. He hastily scrambled up the rope and fell sobbing on the deck of his ship. The Spanish meanwhile had observed the incident and recognized the fate that awaited them, if their ship sank off shore. The *Desire* came alongside the *Santa Ana* for a second attack, but the Spanish ship was now in trouble, cannon fire had holed her below the water line and she was listing. English sailors boarded her once more. Amid fierce hand-to-hand fighting two English sailors climbed the rigging, cut the mainsail and the Spaniard lay listless, at the mercy of the currents and tide. After a six-hour sea battle the *Santa Ana* was captured with 400,000 silver pesos and

600 tons of booty.

Cavendish and his crew rigged the sails and the galleon sailed slowly into shallow waters. The Spanish crew were put ashore onto the Californian coast. After a week spent picking through the finest merchandise of the booty, Sir Thomas was only able to add the silver pesos and forty tons of merchandise to his already heavily laden ships. The *Santa Ana* was set afire and sank with the bulk of the abandoned merchandise before Cavendish and his flotilla set sail for the Philippines where they arrived on the fifteenth of January 1588.

After two months in the Philippines Sir Thomas departed for Africa, arriving at the Cape of Good Hope on nineteenth of March, from were he sailed into the south Atlantic and arrived at St. Helena on the eighth of June at the same time that the Spanish Armada was setting course to attack England.

Cavendish finally reached the coast of England on third of September, where he learned that the English and Dutch navies, led by Drake and Hawkins, had defeated the Armada.

Sir Thomas's privateer slipped almost unnoticed into Plymouth Sound on the tenth of September 1588, his exploits ignored in the aftermath of the great English victory.

The second descendent of Sir John Cavendish was Sir William Cavendish who was at court during the reign of Henry VIII and gained great wealth from his position in the exchequer and also from acquiring assets that derived from the dissolution of the monasteries.

Sir William married Bess of Hardwick with whom he had eight children. The eldest son was Henry Cavendish who first saw the light of day on a cold December morning in 1550.

His mother Bess of Hardwick requested that Princess Elizabeth and John Dudley, Earl of Warwick, would honour her by becoming godparents to the infant Henry. At the age of ten, Henry attended Eton College and was later admitted to Gray's Inn. In 1567 Henry was sent on the "grand tour" to broaden his outlook and explore great cultural cities of Europe.

On his return he entered into an arranged marriage with Grace, who was the eight-year-old daughter of George Talbot, sixth earl of Shrewsbury. When Grace reached maturity, and the marriage was consummated their union proved to be childless and a disaster. Later in life and without justification Henry often referred to her openly as a "harlot". Bess eventually became un-impressed by Henry's inability to produce a legitimate heir and perpetuate the family line, although it is factual that Henry did father at least four illegitimate sons and four daughters. What follows is a fictitious account of what was rumoured to be a fifth illegitimate son and the story of his descendents.

The Meeting

Spring quarter day twenty-fifth of March 1598 started as any other day at Hardwick Hall. Henry rose early, breakfasted then summoned a groom to saddle Dudley, his favourite stallion. The stallion had been surreptitiously named Dudley after the first Earl of Leicester, who was Henry's god father and, more to the point, the queen's favourite. Henry would deny his jocular pun, but he liked to think he had cocked a snook at society. Henry was going about family business with the family solicitors in Derby and with the Dean of Derby Cathedral.

The country lanes were dangerous places, so Henry had armed himself with his rapier and a brace of Wheelock pistols holstered on his saddle. The pistols he had acquired back in '78 during his service with William of Orange. Back in those days he had been an adventurer and had raised a regiment of some six hundred men from his own estates to join the army. By March of '79, he had lost the stomach for the gruelling nature of the Dutch war of independence from Spain that was to rage on for seventy years. He abandoned his regiment and came home to Derbyshire. His war was just a memory.

Today he was dressed for the weather in riding britches, with a coarse linen shirt under his doublet. To protect him from foul wind and rain he had a plain casaque cape over his shoulders. The cape, cut with two fronts, two backs and two shoulder pieces gave Henry fast access to his pistols or rapier if he was set upon by ruffians or robbers. On his head he wore a capotain hat with its tapered crown and wide brim, a fashion imported from the continent, where it was stylish in Spain and now the mode in London.

About mid-day, having passed the cart track up Winfield Manor where, at times, his late step-father, the Earl of Shrewsbury, had been guardian to Mary Queen of the Scots, he paused for refreshment at the old Peacock coaching inn by the village of Oakerthorpe located on the old pack horse track into Chesterfield. After partaking of a bowl of quail potage washed down with a flagon of ale, he remounted Dudley, kicked the stirrups and rode on for another mile where he soon found himself alongside a lichen-covered churchyard wall.

Looking over the wall from his mount, Henry saw a graveyard with unlevelled and hummocky ground adorned with a mix of grave slabs, chests and crosses. Shade and foliage was provided by two large ancient yews located near the south-east corner of the church and a large oak was located on the north-west side. Henry noticed that in recent years more yews had been planted along the northern boundary wall. His military eye, such as it was, allowed him to take all this in at a glance. He noticed the churchyard cross set central on the path up to the church door. The cross was a slender octagonal red sandstone shaft on an octagonal base that provided steps up to the cross.

Henry's eyes drifted towards the church gate. At that moment he saw her, she was opening the old church gate. The dappled spring sun shone down through the trees and highlighted the maiden's auburn locks that poked provocatively from under her white linen cap.

Henry, never one to pass up a chance for a lady's company, drew rein, leaned forward in the saddle and addressed the girl, "Good day, fair mistress, are you visiting the grave of a dear departed relative, or seeking some solace in the tranquillity of God's house?"

"Why, no, sir, I am on an errand for my father, he is vicar of All Saints. Today I am to sweep the church, dust the pews and make ready for the Sabbath."

"And I trust you have a diligent day, mistress..." He paused "But here I am forsaking my goodly manners. I am sorry I do not know your name as we have not been introduced."

"My father is Reverend Charles Leach and I am Mistress Sylvia."

Grasping the brim of his hat Henry said, "Mistress Sylvia, I shall bid thee a joyful farewell and trust we shall meet again." He pulled on the reins; Dudley's head turned and with a gentle thrust of Henry's thighs, the horse and rider moved off down the lane.

Indeed we shall meet again, thought Henry.

Weeks passed until at the end of May, Henry had cause to venture again along the packhorse lane that traversed the peak district from Chesterfield to Derby. This time he did not dally at the Peacock Inn but rode on to draw rein at the churchyard gate. Dismounting swiftly he tethered Dudley on the verge to allow him to graze. He opened the gate and proceeded towards the church porch.

Removing his rapier from the frog on his breeches belt, Henry left his weapon in the porch, then removing his capotain hat, he ventured into the church. All trappings of its Catholic historic past had long disappeared to be replaced by the more fashionably austere Protestant interior. The long familiar statues of the virgin and the old fragrances of burnt incense had gone. Now his nostrils picked up the faint dank odour always associated with old cold buildings.

Dipping into the font, Henry automatically crossed himself before proceeding down the aisle, and then he saw Sylvia removing dead flowers from the sanctuary. Not wishing to approach her unannounced, Henry sat in a pew towards the rear of the church and bent his head for a few moments in silent prayer. Sylvia paused in her work glanced to the rear of the pews and saw a person in devout prayer. She thought she recognized the person as the handsome rider who had spoken to her a few weeks previously.

Henry raised his head from his prayers and sat upright and caught Sylvia's gaze.

"Good day, Mistress Sylvia, and how are you today?"

"Oh, sir, you took me unawares," she whispered as she stepped back from the sanctuary table, "You have me at a disadvantage now, sir," she uttered in sweet delicate vocal tones as she walked down the aisle towards Henry, "You may well know my name but I do not recall that you gave me yours."

"I am Henry Cavendish, my family home is Hardwick Hall and my mother is Bess of Hardwick, but I am pleased if you would address me as Hal, for that is what my friends call me when we are being informal. This is a beautiful church that you keep so clean and tidy. Why, in all my travels in Italy and the Low Countries it is second to none. Your father should be proud to have such a diligent child." Hal was trying to put Sylvia at ease with his platitudes and idle banter.

"What do you do besides looking to your father's needs? Have you no mother?"

"Mother died when I was born," responded Sylvia, "but I keep busy with housekeeping duties and some embroidery."

For the next hour, the pair talked in whispers, both aware of the sanctity of the place but neither wishing to halt the conversation.

"I have been on the road these last three hours, and I have not eaten since breakfast. Would you care to partake of refreshment down at the local hostelry, I believe the Peacock coaching inn provides good fare?"

"Oh, sir, you take me for a trollop. Me, I am a vicar's daughter and you want to escort me to an ale house," Sylvia responded with a touch of coyness in her voice and facial expression.

"Oh, I am sorry, Sylvia…" Henry faltered, "I was not suggesting anything improper, merely some company whilst I partake of a small dinner. Methinks I shall stay over tonight to continue well rested on the morrow, but, ah well, if you so refuse, Mistress Sylvia, may I bid thee farewell."

Henry was turning to leave when Sylvia interjected, "Sir, I had no wish to offend thee also, but a poor maiden has to look to her reputation. However I am well known in the village for I am the vicar's daughter and I am sure no impropriety will be suggested or shall take place, so let us partake of some refreshment, but nothing that will spoil my appetite at father's supper table this evening, and I must be home by the hour of four."

Sylvia followed Henry out into the fresh air, turned and closed the door of the church behind her while Henry retrieved his rapier from the porch, although he did not replace his hat in the presence of a lady. With a spring in his step, he escorted Sylvia to the lane where Dudley was still grazing contentedly from the lush grass on the verge outside the churchyard. Leading his horse by the rein, Henry and Sylvia walked casually the short distance to the Peacock Inn. Henry tethered his horse and the pair entered the wooden-framed alehouse. The floor of the inn was strewn with straw, the wattle and daub walls covered in a white lime wash. Henry lowered his head slightly to avoid the oak beams as he escorted her to a scrubbed oak bench.

The pair seated themselves. Henry sensed Sylvia's apprehension and assumed she was worried to what her father would term her waywardness.

"A quart of your best wine landlord, two mugs and a portion of your pigeon pie," ordered Henry. When the wine was served and they had eaten, he enquired as to the availability of accommodation for himself as he was weary and wished to travel no further that day.

Sylvia and Henry spent the remainder of that afternoon in conversation and by the time Sylvia was to take her leave, she felt comfortable and happy in his company. The couple rose from the table. Outside Henry unhitched Dudley and walked Sylvia back to the church.

Raising his hat in farewell, he mounted his horse saying, "I shall pass this way on the next quarter day when I have business in Derby, until then, fair mistress, I must leave you."

Henry wheeled Dudley and cantered off down the lane to the Peacock Inn, leaving Sylvia with her thoughts to wander the short walk home.

Opening the parsonage gate, Sylvia saw her father still working in his glebe, the land that the church gave to the vicar to supplement his stipend, "You've tarried a while, my child," he said, by way of greeting, "Was there so much to do in the church?"

Sylvia knew she must tell her father, but she feared the consequences of his wrath when he learned of her dalliance.

"Father," she began, "we had a visitor in the church today, he came by last quarter day on his way to Derby and again today. First he came into the church to offer up a prayer. Later we had a conversation about the church and some of his ancestors whose earthly remains lie in the churchyard. He was very interested and then because we had talked so much and he was in need of refreshment, he offered me to partake of refreshment at..." Sylvia paused, hesitant to utter the final words, "At the Peacock Inn and...."

Her father interrupted, "You entered that hostelry unchaperoned? Oh, Sylvia, what have I told you about the ways of men and the temptations of the flesh? I pray you were circumspect and stayed in full view of old Tom the landlord at all times?"

"Of course I did, Papa, and Master Cavendish is such a gentleman – why, in fact he made it known of his intention to visit you on his next passage along this way." And with that their discussion of the matter ended but leaving the Reverend Charles Leach with his private thoughts as to what the stranger really wanted...

***

True to his word, Henry stopped at the church on midsummer quarter day. As before, he left his rapier at the door, and as before, he saw Sylvia industriously occupied dusting the pews. Henry observed that she looked more radiant than ever; it seemed she had taken especial care with her hair for it shone like a field of corn on a sun kissed morn.

After the formal pleasantries were exchanged, Hal enquired, "Have you ever been into Derby?"

"What, all that way? It must be all of sixteen miles; I went once when father had to visit the Dean. We stayed for two whole days, and the buildings... so big, so many people, but I was fair pleased to come home. I prefer the quieter life here in Limbury."

"Methinks I shall speak to your father. Our family has good associations with All Saints in Derby, and I may, with your father's permission, of course, take you on my next visit to the church. Can you ride?" he asked.

"A little, sir; I ride father's mare occasionally, although I use a side-saddle as it would be improper to ride as a man."

Henry thought for a moment then declared, "You would be chaperoned, of course, but a visit to the big city would enhance and broaden your outlook. Fair mistress, I shall speak with your father forthwith, that is, if I have your permission?"

Sylvia seemed speechless; here was a gentleman of means wishing to take an interest in a lowly vicar's daughter, albeit a pretty one.

"Forsooth, sir, I would very much like that, if it pleases you."

"That's settled then, I am today on family business into Derby but on my return journey I shall speak with your father to enquire if he is willing to allow me to make suitable arrangements. Farewell, dear mistress, until next week."

It was dusk as Henry rode into Derby. Still mounted, he threaded his way on horseback down the lanes to enter through the old friars' gate. He rode in the centre, avoiding the sides of the rat-infested roads and streets that were strewn with rushes and made his way into Iron Gate Lane, drawing Dudley to a halt in front of the Dolphin coaching inn. Dismounting, Henry grasped the reins and coaxed, "Come along, old fellow, water and food for you now."

He led Dudley through an arch into a cobbled courtyard. Tossing a coin to a young stable lad who was a chewing on a piece of straw, he said, "Make sure he's fed and watered, and rubbed down, then stable him for the night."

"Aye, sir, I will indeed," the lad replied, and began whistling slowly as he led Dudley away for a bag of oats.

Henry stayed in Derby a few days longer than he would have wished due to the fact that the work for his mother's memorial stonework in All Saints Church was taking longer than planned. Then on the last day of June, before noon, Henry paid his hostelry charges, mounted Dudley and cantered off to his unfinished business in Limbury.

Henry arrived at the village as supper time approached. Dismounting at the parsonage, he walked casually up the path. His quick eye noticed the new fashion of a chimney buttress that had been added to the building. He paused on the threshold, his heart quickening; he did not know whether it was in anticipation of seeing Sylvia again or in trepidation at the possibility of rejection by her father. Taking a deep breath Henry knocked on the door.

He heard a chair move inside the cottage and then the door opened slightly to reveal a balding middle-aged man dressed in breeches and a coarse linen shirt.

"May I introduce myself, good, sir, my name is Henry Cavendish and I had the fortune to speak to your daughter Mistress Sylvia when I was hereabouts last week. She and I talked about the local history of the village and she seemed so well informed. I said I would call on you, sir, unannounced if that is agreeable."

The door opened wider and Charles Leach smiled as he quickly evaluated the gentleman caller, "You are welcome, sir, although I was taken aback at your temerity in inviting my daughter, without chaperone, to an ale house, and if it was not for my belief in the good character of old Tom at the Peacock I would be most displeased. However, no harm done, do enter our humble abode. Have you travelled far?"

"Only from Derby, a mere sixteen miles, but with a good horse and in this dry weather it took only three hours, but thank the Lord I encountered no ruffians, although I always travel prepared and well armed."

The reverend nodded, "Praise the Lord indeed," he said, "These pack tracks can be dangerous places at times. Why, only three months ago a gentleman such as you was travelling towards Clay Cross and he was set upon by two robbers. They wielded an old blunderbuss, ordered him off his mount, beat him senseless, took his money bag, stole his horse and left him for dead. Luckily for him a small troop of cavalry from Bolsover Castle happened on him and took him to a nearby church where he was cared for until he could travel. They apprehended the two villains and they were tried and hanged. I'm told their rotting corpses still hang in chains from the gibbet at Bolsover. But enough of that, can I offer you a tankard of wine to wash the dust from your palate?" Henry accepted graciously and the pair took seat at the vicar's table. Henry looked round the room, pleasantly surprised at what he saw; along one wall stood a sideboard displaying pewter plates and tygs. The walls of the room were panelled in the Elizabethan fashion of the gentry.

"Are you travelling on tonight or staying at the Peacock?" enquired Charles.

"I think I shall stable my horse at the inn and bed down there, for I must be on my way by early morn."

At that moment the door opened and Sylvia entered, "Good day, sir," she said, "We expected you nigh three days ago. Are you well?"

Henry rose, greeted Sylvia and then took his place back at table, "Supper will not be long father. I bought a pair of leverets from big Abraham; methinks he's been snaring over at Manor Woods again, but no matter so long as the queen's forester doesn't

8

catch him." Sylvia took her leave and went into the kitchen to begin preparing the supper.

As Charles refilled his tankard, Henry said, "You have a dutiful daughter in Mistress Sylvia. I have spoken with her on a couple of passing visits to your parish church and I would like to increase her knowledge of worldly matters by escorting her, chaperoned of course, on my next visit into Derby."

Charles remained silent for a few moments then he arose and summoned Sylvia from the kitchen.

"We have matters to discuss, Sylvia; will our supper victuals serve an extra person?"

"Yes father, I can cook extra cauliflower and potatoes to eke out."

Henry overheard the conversation and said, "Do not trouble so for me, for I can eat at the Peacock."

Charles returned to the table, "It is no trouble. We bid you partake of our board tonight and you may rest here until the morrow, for we have a spare room that is hardly ever used."

"Then I must care for my horse, he needs water and a feed," Henry said, "I suppose for one night Dudley can graze in your back pasture."

Henry and Charles rose from the table to tend to Dudley's needs. Later that evening, over supper, the three talked by candlelight and Henry outlined his proposal to bring one of his mother's maids together with a pair of docile mares equipped with side saddles. After the three had eaten and Sylvia had cleared the table, Charles yawned and proclaimed that he thought it time for them all to withdraw to their bed chambers, "Come, Sylvia, give your father a goodnight kiss. Sleep well, Henry, till the morrow and may God protect you in your slumbers."

Sleep did not come easy to Henry as he lay still, his thoughts of Sylvia. At the far end of the parsonage, Sylvia also lay awake. At first she thought of her forthcoming excursion into Derby but then as the warmth of the covers overcame her, she began to think of the handsome gentleman who had come into her life. Occasionally in the past she had experienced what she called palpitations and a queer sensation in her abdomen, but now as she lay still she felt the desire to place a hand between her thighs and she was shocked to find herself quite wet, not as her monthly made her wet but more a lubricating wetness that increased and grew more intense as she touched herself. Her breathing deepened as she experienced a whole new world of feelings. In a burst of light the feelings subsided. Stunned by the experience Sylvia lay still as gradually her breathing returned to normal, then as she drifted into sleep she was became blissfully aware that she had entered a new phase in her life.

Derbyshire Days

John's forefathers had given Hardwick farm its name and although John Hardwick was simply a gentleman farmer, upright and locally respected with no pretensions to greatness, he could, nevertheless trace his ancestral roots back to Edward I and Queen Eleanor of Castile. The family farmhouse had been developed over two centuries until in 1527 the old farm had become such a focal point in the community that it was now known as Hardwick Manor Hall. From a packers' lane that ran adjacent to the family home, the skyline was broken by the myriad of chimneyed buildings, which stood prominently on a slight rocky hill top pointing like fingers to the sky, almost proclaiming that this is the beginning of the house of Cavendish.

The old half-timbered manor hall with its multitude of chimneyed buildings embraced barnyards, stables and a cobbled dovecot yard. It was here that Bess of Hardwick was born. It was in that same family manor house that Henry had been born in 1550 and it was from the family home, at a very early hour on Sunday the twenty-seventh of September 1598, two days before the Michaelmas quarter day, when Henry rode forth. Tethered behind Dudley was a spare mount and accompanying him and mounted side saddle was Marianne; one of his mother's maids, her role to act as chaperone to Mistress Leach; the vicars daughter.

In the early dawn autumn mist, the couple rode at a brisk pace. The weak sun was not yet strong enough to keep at bay the morning chill. The leaves on the trees glowed with a russet hue.

Just after ten, the couple reigned in at the Peacock Inn; in the distance Henry heard the church bells calling the protestant faithful to morning service. The pair dismounted, "We can partake of refreshments I think Mistress Marianne." Henry helped her dismount then he hitched the bridles to a post before entering to take some sustenance. Shortly after twelve, feeling revived, Henry paid and they left the hostelry. Leading the horses they walked the short distance to the vicarage. Before Henry could knock, the door was opened by an excited Sylvia who had clearly anticipated their arrival.

"Father is visiting a sick lady at Squire End farm. He went after morning service but I came home. But do come in, I am sure father will not be too long."

Henry and Marianne entered the vicarage and were sat comfortably at the table whilst Sylvia excused herself and adjourned to the scullery to prepare her father's evening meal. Within minutes the vicarage door opened and Charles stood silhouetted in the afternoon sun.

"Greetings, my son, and welcome to our humble abode."

Henry rose to the greeting and Charles gave him a quick embrace, then as he turned towards Marianne, Henry pre-empted the question and introduced her.

"This is Mistress Marianne, my mother's maid and will chaperone your daughter, if that is acceptable to you?"

Sylvia returned to the room finding the conversation was becoming very friendly between Charles and Henry. Sylvia took Marianne out into the garden for a walk, and then as the evening sun began to lose some of its warmth she turned to Marianne and suggested, they should adjourn inside and rejoin the men, "No doubt they will be wanting some supper."

The evening passed with casual conversation about country life and gossip from the London season. After supper, the four gathered by the log fire, again making polite conversation interspersed with periods of silence and as the group meditated, they watched the flames lick the brickwork seemingly mesmerized by the smoke drawn up the chimney like long lazy curling flumes.

Next morning, after rising early, they ate breakfast, "We must make ready to depart." Henry commented as he rose from the table. Joined by Charles, the pair gathered Dudley and the two mares from the pasture. Charles disappeared inside and returned carrying a linen bag containing a few extra items for Sylvia's journey. Securing the bag to the pommel of Sylvia's saddle, he stood back and watched Henry attaching his and Marianne's bags to their saddles.

"All ready now," called Charles.

Sylvia accompanied by Marianne left the confines of the vicarage, "I have written a letter of introduction to the Dean, it's in the linen bag, keep it safe and he will watch over you during your stay."

Sylvia thanked him, kissed her father on the cheek, and as he helped her onto her side-saddle she reassured him that she would be careful in the city, stay close to Marianne at all times and return before the next Sabbath.

If at that moment Henry could have read Sylvia's mind, he would have realized that he was escorting a young woman on the verge of escaping from the rigid confines of her home for a few days of freedom and adventure. Then with final salutations, the three rode off at a measured pace which Henry hoped would get them to their destination before dusk.

About four of the clock, after a couple of halts for a rest and for Sylvia and Marianne to discreetly answer calls of nature behind trees and shrubs, the three riders crested the brow of a hill and in the distance they saw the smoky haze from the wood of the hearth fires of Derby. Henry quickened the pace, now passing through a small wood; the dappled sunlight on the trees giving an appearance of tranquillity, then as the afternoon shadows began to lengthen the three travellers entered the city.

Henry guided them along the road through the old friar's gate, "Keep to the centre," he advised Sylvia and Marianne, "We are almost at the finest inn in Derbyshire. Soon we can wash and refresh ourselves."

A wooden sign on a post proclaimed they were entering Iron Gate Lane, and then rounding a bend in the lane Henry reined in at the Dolphin. Dismounting, he gathered the bridles from the mares and led the three horses through into the cobbled courtyard. A stable boy ran over with a mounting stool and Henry assisted Sylvia and Marianne to dismount.

"Make sure the horses are fed, watered and rubbed down then stable them for the night." He handing a coin to the boy, adding, "Oh and bring the baggage into the inn."

"Aye, sir, I will indeed." The lad began whistling softly as he led Dudley and the mares away.

"That lad never stops whistling." commented Henry to Sylvia.

Leading his two female companions into the inn, he instructed the innkeeper, "My usual room, landlord, and for the ladies, the extra room I booked on my last visit. Have clean water brought up, please."

Henry led Sylvia and Marianne across the flagged floor and up the stairway to a balustraded minstrel gallery from which several oak doors led to rooms. Opening the first door on the right, Henry escorted Sylvia and Marianne into a medium-sized room with two cots, both screened with curtained fabric for privacy.

"This will be your room, fair ladies, your personal effects will come in a few moments and I will leave you now so you can perform your ablutions."

With a gesture of the hand, Henry took his leave backing out into the corridor. Turning, he walked with a spring in his step to the end door and entered his double bedded room. Slowly he unbuckled his belt and rapier, threw them onto a wooden chest in the corner, pulled off his riding boots, lay on the bed and considered his next move…

The Chaperone

Over a supper of fine ground manchet bread and cheese, accompanied by a full-bodied red wine, Sylvia and the maid felt a bond of friendship developing as they talked of lace fashions and ribbons worn at court by Marianne's mistress. Henry feigned some interest but then he entered into conversation with a group of drovers and cattlemen while leaving Sylvia and Marianne engrossed in ladies' talk. The male-dominated group soon became raucous in the confines of the communal eating room and at the first opportunity Henry bade his goodnights. Taking two candle lamps from the landlord, he escorted his two charges to their rooms.

"Marianne, take this lamp for your room and sleep well, ladies. Tomorrow you can visit the shops and the market whilst I conduct my business. I have an early start so shall breakfast at seven, but you two ladies may linger and breakfast when you wish. Oh, by the way," he added, "when you have taken in enough of the sights, present yourselves at the Dean's office in the cathedral for I shall be meeting with him most of the forenoon. I will await you about midday." Henry bowed, taking Sylvia's small hand, he kissed it, then bowed his head to Marianne and carrying his candle lamp he took his leave.

***

In the confines of their room, Sylvia and Marianne undressed, then Marianne snuffed the candle and each climbed into her own bed.

After a few moments of silence, Sylvia muttered, "Marianne,

I'm not sleepy, tell me about the big house that you live in. Does your mistress keep up with the fashions? Tell me the court news from London."

"Occasionally we do overhear stories about the person who has the 'queen's ear' and who is out of favour. I hear that, only last winter, the Earl of Essex was in serious trouble because he had had secret communication with the Scottish King James. When Her Majesty called him to account, he publicly insulted her and turned his back on her, which isn't the best of policies when dealing with a Tudor. But she soon forgave him, though that's not surprising. He has been the queen's favourite for many years. It seems his family is highly favoured, his step-father was Dudley the first Earl of Leicester and he was also a favourite."

"I've heard about him," interrupted Sylvia, "Wasn't he the queen's cousin?" Without pausing for an answer, Sylvia went on, "It was country gossip that Dudley took the queen's maidenhead when he was imprisoned in the Tower with her; but I suppose that is only idle banter, they were probably too well guarded for that to have happened."

"My mistress says that Essex is so handsome in appearance. He's charming and witty and it is said that ladies swoon in his bedchamber at his comely manner."

"Go on, tell me more, Marianne, is it true that he too has had the queen's favours?"

"Well, I have heard it said that he cometh not to his own lodging till birds sing in the morning, but as he is very discreet with whom he has laid. Nothing can be said with assurance."

"Nevertheless, as you know he is very brave. Father's told me that only last year our fleet and the Dutch fleet attacked Cadiz and the Earl of Essex was on board the *Repulse*. He led a detachment of men to land on the mainland. Father said that he drove all before him until he reached the market place at Cadiz. Apparently after 'eighty-seven, when Drake sailed into Cadiz harbour with his fire ships to *'singe the King of Spain's beard'*, as they say, the Spanish are so terrified of English sailors that the town surrendered in great order and all England thinks him a hero."

The girls talked into the small hours; then as Sylvia grew sleepy she commented, "I think Henry could be my hero; he's so handsome, and I feel my heart race when I am near to him. Have you a beau, Marian?"

"I do have a young man, Sylvia, he is a footman named John at my mistress's manor. We haven't set a day yet but I think we shall wed when we can afford it. My mistress Bess is very generous with her staff and always gives sums of money to help newlyweds on her estates. My John is so ambitious and he wants to provide well for me, he says soon he may be promoted to assistant butler, but I feel that will be some time away."

"Can you wait, Marian? Um…have you ever…" Sylvia hesitated, "…made him happy, you know… has John made you a woman yet?"

"Of course not, he wants to and sometimes I also feel I must surrender my virtue, but I hope we shall wait. Are you still a virgin, Sylvia?"

"Indeed I am. Father says I must not let feelings of the flesh overcome me, so I will wait but I do get strange feelings."

"Me too," admitted Marianne, "Well, goodnight, Sylvia, God bless and keep you."

"God bless you, Mistress Marianne."

Both girls sank beneath their quilts as sleep overcame them.

The Seduction

Henry had eaten and already departed when the two ladies appeared. After breakfasting, they ventured out of the inn into the narrow, cobbled, and slippery street. With the houses crammed together, very little daylight penetrated to street level. Sylvia was apprehensive as she took Marianne's arm for comfort and support.

"What a stench," Sylvia muttered, holding a handkerchief to her nostrils as they walked with care to avoid piles of rubbish that had been thrown from upper windows and was now piled in decaying slimy heaps. Every few yards they passed even darker furtive alleys reeking of rotting flotsam mixed with human waste. Amongst the waste, kites scavenged on dead rats, rotting cats, decomposing dogs digesting anything with a greedy enthusiasm.

"My mistress says kites are a miracle sent by God to rid our cities of some of the rubbish. In London, she says that it's a miracle that they have come into the towns to build their nests in the forks of trees from scraps of rags and bits of discarded rubbish," said Marianne.

"They seem such graceful birds. It seems odd they can be such scavengers, but praise be to God he has provided them," replied Sylvia.

The pair walked slowly until on a corner they saw a millinery and haberdashery shop. The girls entered and Sylvia purchased some pink and green ribbons for her Sunday dress.

"Are you not buying some ribbons to please a bonnet for your John?" Sylvia asked but Marianne was content just to browse and

18

save her pennies for her wedding.

Later that morning the pair adjourned to the cathedral and Henry introduced Sylvia to the Dean, "I have a correspondence from my father," she said, handing the Dean the letter.

The Dean withdrew a pace, broke the seal on the letter and read the letter. He rejoined the group and responded warmly, "Your father Charles was my friend at our pastoral college. Do give him my fondest felicitations when you return home for I remember him well, we spent many hours debating the Good Book. Your dear father requests that I should care for you whilst you are visiting us and if there be any service that I can provide during your stay please know that I will do my best to fulfil it."

Sylvia, Henry and Marianne took their leave and returned to the Dolphin for dinner. It was only toward the end of their meal that Sylvia noticed Marianne seemed to be tired, her eyes drooped and there were longer bouts of silence in her conversation. Henry had also noticed Marianne's incapacity.

"That's what comes from talking into the small hours," he commented to Sylvia, "Methinks our chaperone will need to slumber this afternoon. Shall we help her to your room?"

Henry and Sylvia rose from the table. Sylvia gave Marianne her arm for support as the pair began to make their way towards the staircase.

"Can you manage her, Sylvia?" Henry asked politely, "I will finish my flagon and then I too may seek the arms of Morpheus."

Sylvia half turned, "You surprise me sir, your education is extensive. My father being a theologian studied Greek and he taught me about Morpheus who was the Greek god of dreams. But you make reference in conversation."

Henry bent a knee in mock servitude, "It is surprising what knowledge a gentleman picks up on his grand tour and in life."

"Then sir I leave you with a quote from young Will Shakespeare, 'Sleep, perchance to dream'."

With that parting remark, the girls climbed the stairs to their room, leaving Henry deep in thought of the remarkable woman who had entered his life. Henry finished his wine and climbed the stair to his room. As he passed Sylvia's room he halted, then hesitantly he gave a gentle tap on the door. Henry waited, hoping he wasn't being too forward. He heard a footfall from inside. The door slowly opened just enough for Henry to see Sylvia's angelic face peering through the gap. Coyly she put a finger to her lips, "Marianne is sleeping; methinks she drank her wine rather quickly."

"I wondered..." countered Henry hesitantly, "I have an alquerque game board in my room. Do you play?" His words tumbled forth in a nervous manner, "I thought maybe we could relieve the afternoon with a few games."

Sylvia looked nervously back into the room then opened the door a little wider. "I don't know," she murmured. Her eyelids fluttered, "It would be most improper to visit a gentleman's room unchaperoned, but kind, sir, I do admit I am somewhat bored without some conversation and Marianne will not be rising for an hour or so."

Sylvia made up her mind. "One moment, Henry, I will gather my cloak to ward off any chill in the rooms."

Taking a final look at Marianne to ensure she was sleeping soundly, she noticed the woman's mouth slightly open and faint snores emitting from her mouth. Giggling, Sylvia tiptoed from the room and quietly closed the door behind her, "I fear Marianne is also in the arms of Morpheus. It is likely she is dreaming of her beau." Then with a quickening heart beat, she followed Henry down the passageway to his room.

Once inside, Henry took her cloak and laid it on the chest on the corner of his room, then he opened his travel bag and produced a well worn alquerque board and the pieces. "Take a stool, Sylvia, and make yourself comfortable."

He pulled up a stool for himself and set the board up for the first game.

Being gallant, Henry planned to let Sylvia win the first game or two but he soon found to his cost that she was an adept player, "You play like a queen," he commented.

"Well, sir, I have had plenty of practice; my father and I spend many an evening playing. Come on, Henry, set up another game and we will see if I can better you for a fourth time."

Henry stood, retrieved a piece that had fallen to the rush covered floor; he carefully set the pieces in place.

Noticing a slight shiver run down her body, he asked, "Are

you warm enough, Sylvia?"

"A little chilly, perhaps," she admitted, "The afternoons are cooling now that autumn is on us. I fear we may be having another cold winter."

Henry went over to the chest and retrieved Sylvia's cloak. Unfurling it with a flourish, he placed it over her shoulders and as he drew the cord under her chin, his hand brushed her cheek. Henry noticed a slight tremble course through Sylvia's body and her cheeks flushed slightly. From past experience of mistresses, Henry knew the signs that Sylvia was inwardly shivering in delight.

During the next hour they chatted and continued to play the game but Sylvia's mind was not concentrating and she lost.

"Shall I get us some mulled wine from the landlord?" asked Henry.

"Um, that would be nice but methinks you may chance to get me a little merry, and I fear for my virtue."

He stood up, and walked round to where she was seated. He stood behind her and proceeded to gently massage her neck and shoulders.

They both fell silent and at first Sylvia tensed then he felt her shoulders relax as she enjoyed his attentions. Henry, a master of seduction with years of practice, didn't rush. When Sylvia was completely relaxed and with her eyes half closed Henry moved one hand to caress the nape of her neck whilst he slowly lowered his head until he could smell her body. He gently kissed her ear and neck whilst maintaining a gentle caressing with his fingers.

Sylvia uttered a low moan and submitted to his touch. So slowly, ever so slowly, he took her arm and raised her to her feet. Turning her towards him, he continued to caress her shoulders and nibble her ear. She was now completely under his spell and he slowly walked her towards the bed, all the time whispering adulations of love into her ear. With one hand he lifted her chin and placed his lips on hers; she slowly responded and he felt her lips part and the tip of her tongue probed his lips. Her arms were round his neck as she kissed him, their tongues searching each other. Henry's hand went to her breast and he felt its nipple hard and erect.

Sylvia arched her back and they fell onto the bed. For a moment Sylvia pulled away, hesitant, gasping yet breathless at the situation that was escalating out of her control. At that moment Henry raised the hem of her dress with his free hand and sought her.

She groaned and he was surprised she was so wet. Sylvia had her arms around Henry's neck, grasping at his hair. All her protests had vanished. He slid off his breeches, his manhood roused; he parted her legs with one hand and then gently entered her. Sylvia gave a little moan and then a little gasp of pain.

"Oh my Lord," she whispered, "This is so wonderful, it's beautiful, so beautiful, don't stop, go on, Henry, I'm not afraid." And so they made love. It lasted only a few minutes before Henry climaxed but she had him locked in, with her legs entwined with his; she gave a shudder, followed by a meowing noise that seemed to emit from her soul. Drained they lay in each others arms.

"Methinks Henry that you have made a woman of me," whispered Sylvia, "You will care for me, won't you?"

"Of course I will," he murmured. He knew in his heart that although Sylvia pleased him, she was just another passing fancy that had fallen for his aristocratic but charming manner, "Of course I will look after you."

"Will you speak to father when we go home?"

"We must bide our time, Sylvia, but all will be well, I promise that." Sylvia pressed her body even closer to her protector and lay with her head on his chest. They made love again, this time more slowly and with a tenderness that surprised even the experienced Henry.

Then he drifted off into sleep. Sylvia lay in his arms for a while longer then slowly she eased herself away, slipping from his bed. She dressed and straightened her attire. Looking down on him she saw a man she thought she loved. He lay in the crumpled covers. The only evidence of their love was a small bloodstain and a damp patch on the cover, witness' of her lost maidenhood and their passion. Sylvia silently tiptoed from the room along the corridor and opened her door. Marianne was still asleep; unaware she had failed in her duty to protect Sylvia's honour.

The Cavendish Story

That evening as the three companions partook of supper, Marianne was apologetic for what she termed her "indisposition". "I am so sorry, Sylvia, for neglecting you. The exhaustion of the journey and the wine made me so very tired. I hope you were not too lonely."

A glance passed between Henry and Sylvia as she responded, "Do not fret, Marianne, Henry kept me good company and in good spirit."

The supper passed jovially with Sylvia bewitched by Henry's charm. "You seem very happy tonight, Sylvia, your eyes are sparkling."

She responded to their shared secret, "Indeed I am, sir, I feel like the sparkles come from stars within my head."

"Methinks you have the vapours," Marianne commented dryly, but Sylvia continued as if she had not heard Marianne's jibe.

"And what are you doing in the cathedral on these visits, Henry? It must be an important project to take up so much of your time."

"As I recall, Mistress Sylvia I told you that my mother is Bess of Hardwick. She is in her eightieth year and now in failing health, but she has always been a benefactor to the poor and aged. Why, only last year she commissioned the building of almshouses on Full Street here in Derby. The almshouses will accommodate a dozen aged and deserving persons. I have had the notary prepare the deeds, which were completed on my last visit, and Mother has endowed them to the city in perpetuity. Mother has also bequeathed that all residents will receive an annual stipend of thirty-three shillings and four pence and they will never be in rags for she has also bequeathed a suit of clothes to every resident."

"What a generous kind lady Bess must be, I shall look forward to meeting her."

Warning bells rang in Henry's brain, bells that told him he might have a problem with Sylvia's attachment to him, but he continued, "I fear Bess will soon shuffle off this mortal coil and she has requested that I also do the preparation work to leave a lasting memorial to her. You may not realize it but Bess is not popular with some members of the establishment. She feels that a memorial will have to be commissioned before her demise or she fears it will not be done after her death."

"And what type of memorial are you proposing, Henry?"

Mother and I propose a free-standing mausoleum constructed from the finest local marble enclosing an interment sarcophagus. It is to be designed by Robert Smythson, who is the finest architect and master mason in all of England. It is going to be regal as befits a person with royal connections."

"How wonderful that your mother has entrusted you with such a task. But let us pray that it is many years before she is taken from us." Henry noticed Sylvia's use of the word 'us' and silently he prayed she was speaking objectively and not adjectively.

"Oh, Hal…" Sylvia used Henry's nickname which he had used when he first introduced himself. It seemed like an age since that fateful introduction in her father's church. "I know so little about you or your family, do keep us entertained with your heritage."

"Well," he paused, "let me see. It's a long story but first let us avail ourselves of another flagon of the landlord's wine."

The wine was brought to the table by the landlord's daughter, a comely wench of marriageable age. "Is that all, sir?" she asked.

"My thanks, fair maiden, that will be all for now. So where do I start?" Henry thought for a moment then continued. "Bess my mother will be seventy-three on the fourth of October; it's just three years after our family moved into our new home at Hardwick Hall on Mother's seventieth. The hall wasn't completed until last year but Bess wanted to celebrate her birthday with style. She is a very shrewd business lady. Do you know, she has been married four times, by which I do not mean to imply she married for money but maybe, if we are honest, she married for status?"

"I believe my father did a sermon once on the 'widow's mite' and Bess's four marriages did get mentioned in a conversation at that time. Father says that it seems to be God's will Lady Cavendish will always be widowed. What is it like living in such a large house, Marianne?"

Sylvia realized her remark had been less than diplomatic and in an effort to divert the conversation away from Henry she turned to Marianne to involve her in the conversation.

"It's a beautiful house. It is so light inside with all its glass windows that the colourful tapestries on the walls can be seen and admired even on the dullest day. I believe your mother purchased the tapestries herself; am I correct, sir?" Marianne maintained her respectful mode of address to the son of her employer.

"Quite correct, Marianne. Well, to continue, Mother has had four husbands. She first married at the age of fifteen to Robert Barlow, who was himself a mere child and very sickly. Mother says that they were both too young, and he too sick to consummate their marriage before he died. But as Robert's widow she was entitled to a pension of one third of the income from the Barlow estate. Over the years that has led to legislation and many courts of appeal. When she was widowed, Mother needed stability in her young life. Because she came from a farming family that had good connections, she took a position in the household of Henry Grey and Frances Brandon who were the Duke and Duchess of Suffolk. Bess spent the next five years with their daughters Lady Mary and Lady Jane Grey. It was whilst in service at the Greys' that, at the age of twenty she met and married my father William Cavendish. She says she was still a maiden when she married my father. He was a knight of the realm and mother thus became Lady Cavendish. Sadly, Father died back in 'fifty-seven, leaving me as the eldest son with a couple of brothers, William and Charles, plus two sisters, Elizabeth and Mary. I had another three siblings, Frances, Temperance and Lucres but they all died in infancy."

"Oh, how sad," Sylvia exclaimed.

"No matter, it is life; but to continue, when old King Hal died back in 'forty-seven Bess, and my father had just married and

Mother was pregnant with Frances, her firstborn. Frances died at birth and the following year Temperance died. The distress of them both dying meant the family were away from the court during those three turbulent years. I was born in 1550 and was only three when King Hal's son young Edward VI died. As you remember, poor Lady Jane Grey was proclaimed Queen but her reign was only nine days before Bloody Mary seized the throne for herself. That was the same Jane Grey with whom mother had been in service. It didn't take long for Bloody Mary to have Lady Jane, plus her husband and Jane's father all executed for treason. Praise be to God that Mary didn't reign for long, for in those five terrible years of her reign it meant a return to Catholicism with thousands of Protestants burnt as heretics. Then good Queen Bess came to the throne and Mother became a lady-in-waiting to the Queen."

Marianne had been listening intently and at that point she interjected, "You know of course that Queen Elizabeth and my employer have become firm friends over the years."

"That's correct. When I was born, the Queen honoured our family when she consented to be my godmother."

Sylvia seemed mesmerized at the talk of court intrigue and gossip.

Henry noticed Sylvia's look of fascination, the look of a woman in love, "You will have some fine stories to relay to your father when you return home."

Mention of a return to home jolted Sylvia from her mesmerized state.

Henry continued. "Of course, heretics are still burnt today. I suppose you heard of the martyrdom of two Catholic priests and a convert, only two years ago, here in Derby?"

"We did hear of the barbaric act and their suffering. Father was rather upset at the time as he thought the days of intolerance were gone. He told me that in the year of Drake's defeat of the Armada, three Catholic priests were charged here in Derby with 'trying to seduce Her Majesty's people to Catholicism'. Father said they were found guilty on the twenty-fourth of July and sentenced to be hanged, drawn and quartered."

"You're so well informed, Sylvia, but do let me recount more of my family's history and then you can relate our family to those

26

awful events of that time. As I said, William, my father, was Mother's second husband; consequently, when he died in 'fifty-seven, Mother was heartbroken. My parents had a loving marriage and after a year of mourning, she returned to court. It was whilst at court that she became acquainted and subsequently married a gentleman and captain of the Queens guard named William St. Loe who was also a knight of the realm."

"Your mistress certainly intends to remain a Lady," whispered Sylvia to Marianne.

Henry pretended he hadn't heard the remark and continued, "When Sir William St. Loe died in 'sixty-four after five years of wedlock, he disinherited his kinsfolk and left Mother all his estate. But that isn't all; we now come to Mother's last husband."

Turning to Sylvia he said, "I overheard your whisper, Sylvia, and this time Mother wasn't content with being just a Lady, now she set her sights on becoming a Countess. To that end she chose an Earl for her husband. He was George Talbot, the sixth Earl of Shrewsbury. They married within a year of old Captain Loe's demise, and I fear it was a case of 'marry in haste and repent at leisure'. My own personal knowledge of their marriage was that after the brief time of physically enjoying each other, they were in fact incompatible. He was much too cautious with his money whereas Mother does like to spend and acquire assets for the estate. Consequently there was a lot of friction in the household. I was told by confidants that he often referred to my mother as a sharp bitter shrew; but methinks he got that fashionable jibe from Master Shakespeare's *Taming of the Shrew*. In reality, the taming of Mother was something George Talbot was not capable of doing considering her forceful personality. She has quite a strong but kind disposition once you understand her. Anyway, Sylvia, that is enough of my opinions of Mother. I think the other main problem in their marriage was that the Earl spent so much time on affairs of state about the Queen's business. It's a fact that two years after mother married the Earl, he was made the guardian of Mary, Queen of the Scots, a position which proclaimed at court that ours was a favoured family in the realm. I presume that you are aware that Elizabeth's cousin, Queen Mary, was under arrest for years before her execution in 'eighty-six. The Earl used our properties of Wingfield and Sheffield Manors and Sheffield Castle plus

Mother's home at Chatsworth to imprison Mary. Well, it was a situation that lasted for fifteen years from 'sixty-nine until 'eighty-four. For security reasons the Earl kept moving Queen Mary to foil any plot for escape and it was during 1580 that Mother had a terrible falling out with the Earl and they separated. She left her home at Chatsworth. Mother said it was because she didn't wish to be under the same roof as the Earl but if we are honest, Mother was short of cash due to the miserly Earl. She moved all our family back to her birthplace at Hardwick Hall which for the past ten years is now the old hall as compared to our new one. Our fortunes changed when the Earl died back in 1590. Mother then inherited all his money and she has built us our new home."

A look a sadness overcame Henry, it was almost as if he was remembering his childhood days at the old Hall, "It's sad, I fear Old Hardwick Hall is now becoming neglected," then his countenance brightened,

"Well, to get back to my family history, when mother and the Earl separated, that year was a very bad time for our family. Mother happened to see the Earl and a serving wench, Elenor Britton, in an act of intimacy in her own quarters. Bess rightly or wrongly sought revenge and I am embarrassed to say that I became involved in her scheme for retribution. Mother began to spread rumours that the Earl and Queen Mary had conducted an adulterous liaison for some time and that Queen Mary bore him two children through the adultery. Mother's scurrilous rumour reached the ears of Queen Elizabeth and naturally the Earl and Queen Mary were very angry." Henry paused, then in a humbler voice he said, "I would not be telling you ladies this story except that I have repented for my slanderous and unfounded rumours and I always feel contrite as I unburden my soul to anyone who will listen."

Marianne remained silent whilst Sylvia, influenced no doubt by her father's Protestant vocation, murmured, "God will no doubt forgive a penitent, but a priest cannot."

Henry ignored the jibe at his own family's leanings towards Catholicism. "Mother and I were ordered to appear before Elizabeth to retract the accusations and sign a declaration that Mary Queen of Scots had not had a child since being in England."

"Queen Elizabeth was very forgiving to your mother and

your family. You were very lucky," Sylvia added.

Henry agreed. "Yes, the signing of the declaration saw an end to the matter. Seven years later, as you know, Mary was executed at Fotheringay and Mother and the Earl were reconciled for a short time at Wingfield Manor, but it didn't last long because he couldn't stand Mother's vitriolic comments about his whore Elenor Britton. Eventually he moved away to be with mistress Britton and to live at Handsworth Manor in Sheffield. That's when we became in debt as a family, but since Mother has been widowed these last ten years our finances are sound."

"What events your family have witnessed," said Sylvia. "But we were talking about local martyrs, how did we drift into talk about the Earl of Shrewsbury and your mother?"

"I'm just coming to that," said Henry. "Two years before my stepfather, the Earl of Shrewsbury, died, he made a raid on the village of Padley on the Hathersage estate to arrest Sir Thomas Fitzherbert, a childless widower, and his brother John, both of whom were staunch Catholics. The news of the arrests reached our home at Hardwick that the Earl had made a huge haul that day. Included in the arrests of Sir Thomas and his brother John were his daughters, Jane and Mary. But the big catch was discovered when the arresting officers entered the family home and found two priests named Nicholas Garlick and Robert Ludlam hiding in a chimney of the house.

"Jane and Mary were taken away and placed in the custody of the Protestant rectors at Aston and Weston upon Trent whilst Sir Thomas was sent to the Tower; I believe Sir Thomas died of neglect in the Tower about nine years ago. John and the priests were taken to the county gaol here in Derby to await trial, but John's family bribed the court with ten thousand pounds and John served two years in Derby prison and then he too was sent to London to die in Fleet prison a year before Sir Thomas. Meanwhile, the two priests who had been imprisoned in Derby gaol had encountered a Richard Sympson, a local lay preacher who had converted to Catholicism. Richard Sympson was on the verge of giving up his beliefs to avoid execution but the three bonded together and made a brave decision to remain true Catholics no matter what the punishment."

"How brave and devout," said Marianne. "I could not be so

resolute."

"Me neither," said Henry. "Anyway, to shorten this overlong tale, twelve years ago, back in 'eighty-eight, all three were found guilty. They were sentenced to be hanged, drawn and quartered for treason. Tied to frames they were dragged by horses in an upside-down and backwards manner through these very streets to Saint Mary's Gate. The priest Garlick took a final opportunity to preach the Catholic faith. It's on record that all three were then hanged until they became unconscious and their bodies were then cut open and their entrails and organs removed and burnt. I heard, though cannot vouchsafe the truth, that Garlick regained consciousness when his insides were removed."

"How barbaric, and I do believe that crowds turned out to watch. I remember the news of the executions reaching our village, we all felt disgust at such brutality," whispered Sylvia.

"That's not the end though, all three were then beheaded and their arms and legs removed to be shown around the city. Their heads were placed on spikes on St Mary's Bridge and all done to warn those entering Derby that heretics were not tolerated."

Henry took a sip of his wine. "I believe the two priests would not have been taken, and neither would John Fitzherbert have died in prison, had it not been for a spy and fiendish scoundrel named Richard Topcliffe who was in the pay of my stepfather the Earl. I hear that Topcliffe was entrusted by Queen Elizabeth herself."

"We are intrigued," Marianne and Sylvia chorused. "Do go on, Henry."

"Well, apparently this unscrupulous and scheming spy, who was appointed by the Privy Council, ingratiated himself with the Fitzherberts, and partook of their hospitality before he betrayed them, but all that is as nothing compared to what he had done previously at Uxenden Hall in London.

"Uxenden Hall is the Bellamy family home and back in 'eight-six when Sir Francis Walsingham uncovered the Babington plot to assassinate Queen Elizabeth and place the Queen of the Scots on the throne, it appears that Jerome Bellamy was involved and he and Babington were executed on Tower Hill. Consequently all the Bellamy family were under suspicion and constantly watched until, in 'ninety-two, the entire Bellamy family were arrested and charged with being recusants. On the specific orders of Walter Copeland, who was Bishop of London, the gentle, well-bred young lady Anne Bellamy, daughter of the household, was incarcerated in the Westminster gatehouse. I believe that later that year Topcliffe had her moved to Helborn gatehouse prison were he personally undertook her torture. On the promise of leniency for her family, Richard seduced Anne and got her with child. The fiendish villain then arranged for her to be married to Nicholas Jones, an under-keeper of the gatehouse prison. It's now about six years since the bastard child of Topcliffe was born and Topcliffe then had the audacity to ask Anne's father for a marriage dowry that included the Preston manor house as a residence for Anne and husband. The outcome of Topcliff's interrogation of Anne was that he thoroughly traumatized the young woman into betraying her family. She confessed to Topcliffe of the procedures used in the Bellamy household to secretly hear Mass and receive instruction. He even extracted the location of the priest holes in the Bellamy home and with that information he provided more Catholic martyrs for the executioner."

"The times have definitely become harsher in the Queen's old age," said Marianne. "I hear that when she came to the throne back in 'fifty-eight, she was tolerant to Catholics but the failed invasion by Spain and attempts for a restoration of a Catholic monarchy have hardened Elizabeth's attitude. Now it seems that Catholics are burnt as often as the Protestants were during the reign of Bloody Mary."

"Well, it's almost time for our slumbers," said Henry, "We have a tiring day tomorrow when we must travel home."

Henry thought he saw a hint of dejection on Sylvia's face and inwardly he wondered if she would dare to visit his room that night for a final rendezvous...

Henry rose from the table, "So now you know some of our family history and why mother has tried to avoid involvement with either the Catholic or Protestant camps. During her early pregnancies she was always away from court during the Catholic purges and then she distanced herself from the Protestant excesses of the Earl of Shrewsbury."

The three rose from their table, took candle lamps from the inn keeper and climbed the stairs. At the doorway to Sylvia's room Henry took Marianne's hand and kissed it, "Goodnight, fair Marianne," Marianne flushed and bade her goodnights before entering her room.

Sylvia lingered a second. Henry took her hand, placed his lips to it and whispered, "Come to me if you can, fair Sylvia, I shall await you. If not, sleep well till morn, lovely lady." Henry turned and walked to his room.

Sylvia's eyes followed the disappearing form with a longing that made her heart beat a trifle faster. She turned, closed the door behind her and noticed that Marianne was already disrobed and under her covers.

Sylvia undressed and then taking a cloth and water from a bowl, she carefully washed the dust and odours of the day from her body. She pulled her nightshift over her head, snuffed out Marianne's candle, and leaving hers flickering in the night air, she climbed into bed.

"Goodnight, Marianne," not expecting a response, she was not disappointed when none came; she was happy; silence reigned, the sound of deep breathing interspersed with a slight snore coming from the direction of Marianne's bed.

Sylvia lay still, desperately fighting off drowsiness with only the faint light from her candle lamp casting soft shadows onto the whitewashed wall of her room. She must have lain like that for nearly an hour, then satisfied that Marianne was deep in sleep, she drew back her covers, placing her bare feet onto the rush covered floor. Taking her candle lamp, she tiptoed to the door; opening it slowly, fearful a squeaking hinge would awaken her chaperone; then carefully she closed the door and with a beating heart she made her way to Hal's room…

Love Fulfilled

Hal lay on his bed, having almost given up hope that she would come. Then he heard the click of the latch and the tiny almost inaudible squeak of a hinge. For a brief moment Sylvia was silhouetted in the doorway, and then she quietly closed the door behind her. The glow from her candle put a warm glow around her body as she approached Hal's bed. She placed the candle lamp on the chest and was about to snuff out the flame when Hal whispered, "Leave it, Sylvia, come closer, let me look at your beauty." Sylvia shivered, then slipped her night shift from her shoulders and let it drop to the floor. She placed her hands to cover her modesty. Henry saw the silhouette of her pert breasts in the candle glow as she walked towards him. He reached out a hand, and taking one of hers he gently guided her beneath his bed cover.

As she lay next to him, he felt the warmth of her body. For a while they caressed, kissing fondly before they gently made love, the only sound permeating the stillness of the rooms was their heavy breathing and Sylvia's whimpers of *'beautiful, oh beautiful'* coupled with her catlike meowing as she climaxed.

They both lay quite for some time in each other's arms before Sylvia took the initiative and she made ecstatic love to her man. The candle had flickered and gone out when Henry awoke.

Outside, it was still dark and after a while a church clock chimed the hour of three. He gently awoke her.

"I do not want to compromise your virtue and good name in the eyes of your companion; do you want to return to your room before Marianne awakes, maybe when she attends a call of nature?"

Sylvia snuggled closer and in a dreamy whisper implored Hal to lay quiet and talk to her, "Marianne does not use the slop bucket too frequently and I trust she will sleep till five. Now tell me more about yourself, Hal."

"There's not a great deal that would interest you, Sylvia. I did the grand tour when I was in my teens. Later I fought alongside William of Orange in the Netherlands but war and fighting are not for me. I am… how shall I put it… a man of the arts. I am enthusiastic over music except when my wife…" He had been about to add that he enjoyed music except when Grace played her virginal, but now the moment had passed, and he stopped in mid sentence, feeling Sylvia's body stiffen.

"You're married, Hal? Oh, how could you take advantage of a simple country maid?" She gave a slight sob, "I was a virgin, you took that from me and now I hear you are wed. Oh, Hal, how could you, what is to become of me?"

"I notice you are not leaving my bed, Sylvia."

"What is the point, sir? I have given you my maidenhead, my love and now I am helpless. My being is in your hands, Hal. What if I have conceived? What if I am pregnant?" A tone of hysteria entered her voice, "I will bear a bastard and be the talk of our village – and me, the daughter of a respected vicar, my father will be so displeased; I fear he may cast me out of his home."

"Don't fret, Sylvia, you are not the first and definitely not the last, but in the unlikely event that you are with child, I have several illegitimate sons and daughters in the county and I have provided well for them all."

Sylvia quietened her sobs as Hal spoke softly to her. He compared her to one of his young horses. She was like a frightened young filly that had just been broken in to a bridle and saddle, but she relaxed as Hal stroked her forehead and gently ran his fingers through her locks.

"Oh, Hal, you're such a gentleman, I fear I shall always love you. Tell me; is your wife beautiful? Do you love her? Were you in love when you married?"

"The answer to your questions is nay, we had an arranged marriage, we were mere children. She is named Grace but I fear she is without any. Her stature is small, with a girth almost as tall as she. All of which makes her a most unattractive bed partner. Consequently we have no children, nor are we ever likely to have any. I avoid the matrimonial bed at all times. I think that she has her desires satisfied with self-abuse and the odd servant who will bed her. I have no proof but I have called her a harlot in public. She cares not that I seek and find pleasures elsewhere. This day I have found my deepest desire and pleasure in you, Sylvia. But enough of Grace, I have a family secret," Henry paused a moment before continuing, "Not so much a secret, it is a private family matter of which I could not speak in front of Marianne."

Sylvia sighed, happy in the mistaken belief that she was to be included in the Cavendish family confidences, whilst in reality Hal was trying to allay Sylvia's misgivings.

He knew that what he was about to tell Sylvia was probably common gossip in court circles and in the Cavendish household staff of which Marianne was a part, but the family could not admit or speak openly in case they were accused of conspiracy.

"Back in 'seventy-four, before mother separated from the Earl, my sister Elizabeth became acquainted with Charles Stuart, the Earl of Lennox, who was the brother of Lord Darnley, a most spoilt and, I believe, petulant man."

Sylvia interrupted, "I hope none of those traits have come through to you, Henry."

"I should hope not; but to continue, Darnley was a second cousin and the second husband of Mary Queen of Scots who got his deserts back in 'sixty-seven when he was murdered just outside the city walls of Edinburgh. That murder and her third marriage to the Earl of Bothwell, who was the alleged murderer, led Queen Mary to flee to England in 'sixty-eight to seek the protection of our Queen Bess. Well, the rest you know because my step-father the Earl of Shrewsbury was her gaoler and guardian for most of the nineteen years until her execution for treason."

Henry gave Sylvia an affectionate kiss and then he continued, "Darnley had a brother, named Charles Stuart. My sister Elizabeth married Darnley's brother, and because he had both Tudor and Stuart blood in his veins, my niece, who was born from the liaison between Charles Stuart and my sister, has a legitimate claim to the English throne when good Queen Bess eventually passes away."

35

Henry paused in his narrative; a pregnant silence pervaded the room. Sylvia looked up, inwardly Henry was concerned his lover may be filled with trepidation at being involved with royal intrigues and court scandals then the silence was broken.

"Do go on, Hal. I am thrilled to be your confident."

"So, back in 'seventy-five, when my sister Elizabeth gave birth to the result of that liaison which happened to be a girl, she was christened Arbella Stuart. Sadly consumption took Charles Stuart when Arbella was only one year old. For financial reasons, my sister and baby Arbella came home to Chatsworth to live with Bess. Five years later at the age of six, Arbella was left an orphan when my sister died suddenly during the Twelfth Night celebrations at Sheffield Castle. She complained of feeling unwell, and collapsed and died that night. There is no proof of course, but Elizabeth may well have been poisoned."

Henry shuffled into a more comfortable position and as he did so, he noticed that Sylvia; who appeared to be listening intently, had raised herself onto one side and was cupping her chin in the palm of one hand.

"What beautiful brown eyes you have Henry. Oh I'm sorry for interrupting." She paused then, "How sad for your niece to be orphaned at the age of six... She must be about twenty-three by now, so what happened to her?"

"Sylvia, behave, you're the first woman ever to comment on the colour of my eyes."

Inwardly he was rather flattered, "She actually is twenty-five. When she was about eight, mother arranged a betrothal for her to Lord Denbigh, the two-year-old son of the Earl of Leicester. What a furore that raised at court. Needless to say the Queen was furious, but it was of little consequence, for the infant Lord Denbigh died the following year. But mother was again in trouble with the Queen."

Sylvia repositioned her hand that supported her propped-up position then whispered, "Hal, I am captivated by your stories, the memory of this day will be forever in my heart." And she leaned over him and kissed his cheek.

"Oh, gentle Mistress Sylvia, how my heart pounds in my breast for your companionship, for that is all it ever can be, but my family shall look after you as a favourite." He kissed her, nibbling at her lips while whispering terms of endearment.

They broke apart as he continued, "Oh, sweet Sylvia, it distresses me that I am not the young man I was. Tonight, I fear, I cannot make another coupling, but I do want you by my side, so do you wish to hear more?"

Sylvia nodded confirmation.

Henry made himself more comfortable on the bolster then, cradling Sylvia, he continued, "Bess has always hoped that when the Queen had hinted at making Arbella her heir, the queen would honour that hint, so you see, the Cavendish family can always boast that we have had one foot on the throne of England. In our household, Marianne can confirm that Arbella is treated as royalty by the servants, albeit I think it is in mockery when they address my precocious niece as 'Your Highness'. Of late though, I fear that Bess and Arbella are not as grandmother and granddaughter should be. Arbella has confided in me that she feels a prisoner in our house, but I think Bess is just trying to protect her from the wiles and schemes of the court. Then it all changed in 'eighty-seven after the execution of Queen Mary. Arbella was invited to court and was made very happy as she was firmly entrenched as niece of the dead traitor Mary Queen of Scots. But I suspect she was at court to be kept under the watchful eye of her cousin the Queen. All did not turn out for the best, however. When Arbella was seventeen, the Queen and Bess discussed a possible marriage for her to the son of the Duke of Parma, but fate intervened and was unkind to my niece. The Duke died during the negotiations."

"She does seem as though death stalks her," Sylvia commented.

"We fear that Arbella may do something drastic as she is a very self-willed child, so we shall wait and see if fortune continues to shine or wane on the Cavendish house. Now I fear we must part for the hour is late. Take care, my Sylvia, not to wake Marianne."

With that parting comment, Hal kissed his mistress goodnight. Sylvia reluctantly rose from her lover's bed and quietly stole back to her room, warmed by the ardour and the memory and odour of their love making and with the innocent confidence he would never desert her.

Homeward Bound

The journey back to Oakenthorpe was uneventful. Marianne and Sylvia chatted while Henry attempted to keep the party cheerful with anecdotes of court life and his travelling experiences but as the group neared the vicarage, Henry noticed that Sylvia grew silent. In his heart he knew she must be feeling the hurt at being parted from her love. Even Marianne's idle chatter could not lift her spirits.

Finally reining their mounts at the vicarage gate, Sylvia took Henry's hand as helped her dismount; she saw the front door of her home swing open and Charles, his countenance beaming, came hurrying down the garden path.

"Welcome home. These last few days I have been beside myself with worry in case some mishap had befallen you." Then without pause he continued, "Do come in, all of you, and rest awhile. Will you stay the night, Henry? You and the serving girl are most welcome."

A glance passed between Sylvia and Henry and he saw an almost imperceptible nod. "That will be most gracious, Charles. I did not look forward to travelling any further and I am sure Marianne is weary. And another night in an inn would see me undone."

"That's settled then, I'm afraid we only have cold fare. Whilst my Sylvia has been absent I have been neglecting my culinary needs. You all go to your rooms and I will look after the horses."

Henry washed the dust from his hands and faces and sat on a stool contemplating what he should do next to extricate himself from a family home were he had seduced the vicar's daughter.

In the next room the girls chatted as they completed their ablutions; then they rejoined Charles. As Henry had not yet appeared, Sylvia took the opportunity to acquaint her father with news from the city.

"...And the mausoleum he has commissioned for Lady Cavendish is going to be so beautiful, it is all marble and very regal."

Sylvia prattled on as Charles listened for a little longer before addressing Marianne, "Well, mistress Marianne, did you chaperone my daughter in a diligent manner?"

"Of course she did," interrupted Sylvia, but Charles couldn't help noticing a small flush of embarrassment that came to her features and he thought that maybe she had interjected rather nervously. At that moment Henry appeared and Sylvia and Marianne adjourned to the kitchen to prepare a cold supper of bread, cheeses and some cooked meats.

Next morning after breakfast Henry and Marianne said their goodbyes to Charles and Sylvia.

"When will you be passing this way again? I suppose it will be spring before you can travel as it will be mid-winter on the next quarter day?"

"That's correct, Charles, I hope to conclude my business in Derby next March on quarter day and if convenient I shall call in passing."

Henry shook Charles by the hand then he took Sylvia's hand and placed a firm kiss on it.

Sylvia's eyes were damp as she held back tears. "Do take care, dear Hal, and dearest Marianne, it will be a long winter 'fore we meet again."

Henry helped Marianne to mount then quickly placing his boot into the stirrup sprang into his saddle, tugged the reins to turn Dudley's head and the pair trotted side by side down the potholed lane.

Sylvia watched them until they were out of sight, and then she took Charles by the arm. "Come on in father, I have so much to tell you. Do you know........."

***

Autumn drifted into early winter. It was a favourite time of

39

the year for Sylvia; usually she loved the cold dry mornings, when hoar frost decked the fields in a white crisp blanket from which a million facets of light sparked as the sun crept over the hills, but this year she was not enchanted.

She was three weeks late and in her heart she knew she was in trouble. Should she, could she, tell her father? She lay awake at night, worried, unable to sleep, but when sleep did come it was a troubled sleep and she usually awoke in a cold sweat feeling disheartened. She was alone and she knew it – well, not completely alone: she always had her father's charity, or had she…?

Eventually she could no longer keep her shame or fear from Charles.

"Oh Sylvia, how could you bring this on our home? I trusted you, and what of your chaperone? She failed in her duty. Duty is important in God's eyes…" And so the Reverend Leach ranted and raved.

After a few days of recriminations during which Sylvia was cast into even deeper depths of despair, Charles relaxed and took her in his arms to give her a fatherly hug. "We have two options, Sylvia," he commented over supper on the third day. "We can send you away to your Aunt Amelia in Eckington; she will care for you until the baby is born. Or you can stay here in our village and face the scorn of our parishioners. There is a third option. You can visit Hardwick Hall and throw yourself on the mercy of that scoundrel Henry, but alas, I fear that will be of no use as I hear the man has cast his seeds in more houses than mine. What do you wish, Sylvia, what do you want to do?"

She remained silent, deep in thought, and then at last she came to a decision. "I am going to combine two options father; first we can compose a letter to Henry informing him of my situation, then, if there is no response by Christmas, I will be starting to show my condition and I won't be able to hide it any longer from our parish folk so I shall slip away to Aunt Amelia's home. Once I am at Aunt Amelia's, and depending on circumstances, I shall decide on my," she paused and corrected herself, "Our future."

***

The weeks sped by without any word or response from Henry. "As I feared, the man is without honour," was all Charles would say. The festive season approached and went without any mishaps. Charles let it be known to the congregation that his daughter was sick with the flux and she may have to go away to take the waters in Buxton or Matlock. Twelfth Night fell on the Sabbath in 1601, so early next morning Sylvia packed her belongings and with the Reverend Leach driving a borrowed horse and wagon, the couple set forth, not to Buxton or Matlock as had been suggested to the congregation but secretly for the day's drive to Eckington.

Charles' sister Amelia was waiting to greet them at the door of her cottage. He had previously written informing her of Sylvia's condition and she had responded with a willingness to look after the poor child during her confinement.

With his daughter settled with Amelia, Charles drove back to an empty home. The vicarage was quiet without his daughter's laughter. In his heart he knew the parishioners guessed the reason for her departure but out of respect to Charles and his position as their pastoral leader nobody in the village had voiced disapproval.

***

During March 1601, Henry again passed through Limbury and with some trepidation he called at the vicarage.

Henry was surprised to see that Charles had aged considerably during the winter months. Charles let Henry into his home. This time there were neither Christian embraces nor handshakes as he took a stool and beckoned Henry to do the same. The pair sat at the kitchen table, and Charles with some semblance of his Christian duty to travellers, offered Henry a flagon of ale to refresh his thirst.

After drinking deeply, Henry wiped a trace of foam from his lips. "I know that in your heart you cannot forgive my unchivalrous treatment of Sylvia," he said, "and I do regret the trouble I have caused to you both. How is she, by the way?"

"She is staying with my sister in Eckington and she is in good health for one in her condition. So why this visit, Henry? Have you come to flaunt yourself because your manhood is something that your breeding has omitted from your character?"

"I know you are bitter, Charles, and I deserve the lashings from your tongue, but hear me out. I am neither without respon-

41

sibility nor compassion and in fact wish to offer some restitution. I am here to propose that I set in place a trust so that you can dispense monies to support orphaned and illegitimate children in the care of your parish. This means that after Sylvia's child is born," Charles interrupted, "You should clarify that sir, you mean after your child is born..."

"All right." Henry conceded, "After our child is born." Henry paused, "Sylvia, of whom I am very fond, nay, of whom I love intensely, but and this you must understand; due to my social and marital status, I cannot wed, can return to your home without any blight to her character. Then, with my offer of a trust, your sister could travel here with 'our child' and present it as an orphan from Eckington for your care. That way you will have funds for my child's education and Sylvia can live with respectability with you. One final stipulation to my proposal is that the child should be registered in your baptism records as an orphan from deceased parentage of the name Cavendish."

Charles seemed to brighten as he realized that soon he would have his beloved Sylvia back in the family home, but he would also have a grandchild, albeit a surreptitious one. He rose and grasped Henry's hand. "Sir, you have made a good decision and the arrangements are both logical and satisfactory to me and I am sure Sylvia will acquiesce to them. Take a seat a little longer, Henry, we are short of news in this village. What of Lord Essex? I believe he was arrested in January for an act of treason."

Henry sat down and sighed. "It is bad news, your knowledge is out of date, Charles. The Queen signed Essex's death warrant on Shrove Tuesday and he went to the block on Ash Wednesday the twenty-fifth of February."

Charles was visibly shaken at the news, "Oh dear, it's awful that one of the Queen's favourites should end like that."

Henry continued, "It all started as a demand from the Queen as to why Essex had not taken decisive action in Ireland against the rebel Tyrone. Apparently when Essex was sent for, he burst into the Queen's bedchamber just as a lady in waiting was dressing her for the day. The Queen was livid and placed him under house arrest. What followed next was a downward series of events that led to his execution. Mind you, Charles, I hear on good authority that the wily manipulator Robert Cecil helped him along the way with a plot to discredit Essex even further. It seems that whilst Essex was under house arrest in London, Cecil started a rumour that the Queen was about to send Essex to the Tower. Essex; always an egoist, was persuaded that he was so popular with the people that with a hundred horsemen, he could rally the citizens of London to stage a revolt against the Queen. It was a stupid act of treason for which Essex paid the penalty."

Charles rose and took the arm of Henry as the pair made for the door. "You are always welcome within this house, Henry, and I trust from time to time you will call to enquire how our 'orphan' and my daughter are progressing."

Charles watched as Henry mounted Dudley, turned his head towards Derby and cantered off down the lane, Charles returned to his fireside a happier and more contented soul.

***

It was during the Easter celebrations of 1601 that a letter from a Derbyshire notary arrived at the vicarage. Charles broke the seal and read,

> I Henry Cavendish of Hardwick Hall in the Shire of Derby do set forth on this Lady Quarter Day of the twenty-fifth of March sixteen hundred and one, a sum of One hundred pounds per annum to be given in Trust until the Lady Quarter Day in the year of our Lord 1651. I also state that the sum shall be set aside, free of all taxes whether they be church or state and that the aforesaid sum shall be given freely to the Church of All Saints in the parish of Limbury for the care, education and needs of orphaned and or bastard children as shall be in the care of the parish or born of the poor women of the parish. The Trustees for the monies shall be Charles Leach the vicar of the aforementioned church and his subsequent replacements.
>
> Signed on this day 25th March 1601

The letter was duly signed and witnessed.

During that Easter day service, Charles gave the details of the trust to the congregation and later prayers were offered in thanks for the kind and charitable name of the Cavendish family.

***

The flowering of the May blossom heralded the spring followed by a warm June. Sylvia went into labour in Aunt Amelia's

43

small rear bedroom and after a lengthy confinement she was de-livered of a son on the twelfth of June 1601 whom she named him Robert.

In the care of her aunt, Sylvia quickly regained her strength and two weeks later Charles arrived by horse and wagon; again conveniently borrowed from a farming parishioner. He quickly conveyed the news of Henry's proposals for the care and later ed-ucation of his son and after a time for consideration Sylvia agreed that it was the best solution to her predicament and agreed to return home. The baby would travel a few weeks later under the pretext that Aunt Amelia had made it known in Eckington that she would find a suitable home for the *'orphaned'* Robert.

And so a sense of tranquillity settled on the Leach household, Sylvia took up her duties to housekeep for her father and to tidy and clean the church whilst the local parishioners welcomed her return after her *'long illness'* and wished for her a swift return to full health. A month later Aunt Amelia arrived bearing *'orphan'* Robert whom she placed in the care of Limbury church, beseech-ing her brother to take in and succour the infant.

During that summer and winter they saw nothing of Henry and it was into the summer of 1602 when one late afternoon Charles was in the garden playing with young Robert when a horseman rode along the packhorse lane. It was Henry; as he ap-proached the front of the vicarage he dismounted, tethered his mount to the gate post and unobtrusively approached the pair.

Charles made a pretence that he had not heard or seen the visitor until young Robert tugged at his coat and pointed to the approaching Henry.

Charles turned and feigned surprise. "Good day, Henry, and to what do we owe this pleasure? It is a full fifteen or sixteen months since I last saw you."

Henry shook the proffered hand, "And who is this little fel-low? He's a sturdy chap. What is his name?"

"It is young master Robert, an orphan from Eckington. My sister asked us to bring him up when both his parents were taken by an outbreak of the fever. We have baptised him Robert Cav-endish to honour your family's name and the trust that you have generously donated to our church."

Henry stooped down and ruffled Robert's hair with the palm

44

of his hand. "It pleases me so much to see such a fine fellow."

"Will you enter our home, Henry, and partake of some refreshment? Sylvia is not here at the moment, she has taken charitable donations of food to an ailing widow who, I fear, is not to be with us much longer, but she will return within the hour, I am sure."

Charles and Henry took young Robert by the hand and retired into the vicarage. "So, Henry, how keeps you and your family? I believe your young brother Charles had a lucky escape when he was set upon and wounded in an affray? Is he now recovered and in good health?"

"Oh, that affair, yes, it's almost two years back. He's fully recovered now although both he and the leader of the affray have been charged by the Queen's sheriff to be of good behaviour."

"So what happened to cause such behaviour?"

"Well, it seems that it was early morn when Sir Charles, accompanied by a groom and a page, was travelling from his home in Sherwood Forest over to a brickworks. They had ridden but a few hundred yards when Charles espied a group of about twenty horsemen heading towards them. Charles says he thought they were out hunting but then he realized that it was an attack on his person. The horsemen charged towards Charles and his two companions, the three fled towards the sanctuary of the brickworks where some of the workers ran to help but unfortunately Charles was unseated from his mount. Getting to his feet, he and his two servants gave a good account of themselves. Armed with only rapiers and a dagger, they unhorsed six of the attackers, two of whom were killed and a third died later in the forest but Charles suffered pistol shot wounds to his thigh and buttocks. For over a year my brother suffered from his wounds to such an extent that eventually the Queen herself took concern and sent her own physician to try to probe the wound to remove the bullet from his thigh. Since the Queen's intervention, now praise be to God he is fully recovered."

Sylvia's voice came from the direction of the front door. "Good Queen Bess certainly favours your family." Charles and Henry both turned, "Good day, Sylvia, it is good to see you again," said Henry.

Hesitantly she took a few paces toward him; paused and cast

a doubtful glance towards her father. Charles looked on with a smile on his face remembering his youth when he had loved Sylvia's mother; imperceptibly he nodded, turned and left the room, leaving the lovers alone.

Henry was the first to speak, "How I have missed you, my love. It has hurt me so much not to be able to visit you more frequently, but alas pressing family matters keep me busy to the point of exhaustion."

Sylvia raised her lips and Hal gave a gentle kiss. Taking his hand she led him to the table and when the pair where seated, he picked up Robert and sat him on his knee. "Now," he said, "I want to hear all about this little fellow. I want to hear all the details about him, all that I have missed."

At that moment Charles brought a jug of wine and three goblets to the table and rejoined them.

Henry took a sip of wine then eager for news of his son, he said, "When did he take his first step and what was his first words?"

Henry listened with all the intent and passion of a returning father. For over an hour Sylvia and Charles talked about the child and the happiness that was in their lives.

Finally as the initial excitement waned, and Robert grew restless, Sylvia rose and laid him in his cradle for a sleep. When she returned, she implored Henry to tell them all his news since they had last parted. "I overheard you saying how the Queen was to send her physician to the aid of your brother's wounds."

"That is correct, she is usually of a generous and caring nature but of late she is cross with mother and my sister Arbella. I don't know if you have heard but some time ago Arbella was sent from court and came back to live with Bess at Hardwick Hall. Understandably, Arbella feels she is living the life of a prisoner with a domineering grandmother." Henry coughed to clear his throat before continuing, "Arbella has always been hot-headed and now we discover that she has foolishly been plotting to escape from mother's dominance by secretly arranging her own wedding to Edward Seymour, who happens to be the eldest grandson of the Earl of Hertford and Catherine Grey. We fear that the Queen may hear of the plot for Arbella to wed, which is in contravention of the Royal Marriage Act and we are now living in daily trepidation as to what the Queen will do."

Sylvia gasped. "You're not in danger, are you, Hal? I couldn't bear it if you were put in prison." And so the afternoon slipped past with Henry entertaining Sylvia and Charles with court gossip.

As evening drew near, Sylvia rose to prepare supper but it had been a long day and soon the three retired to separate rooms. Sylvia did not stray to Henry's room that night; she had learned her lesson and was content. She had her son Robert as the living witness of her loving relationship with Henry Cavendish.

***

Henry visited Sylvia and Charles again in the late autumn and this time he was the conveyer of bad news regarding Arbella. "The Queen is furious with mother for allowing Arbella to make plans for a wedding. Elizabeth has ordered Arbella to be escorted from Hardwick Hall and for her to be placed in custody with the Earl of Kent. Mother has now lost all control over Arbella and the Cavendish family is very near to ruin."

Sylvia tried to comfort him and that night she did consent to Henry sharing her bed. In his room, Charles was too weak to notice the nocturnal activities of his daughter. Sylvia did try to suppress her cries as Henry withdrew just as she climaxed.

After the Christmas festivities at Chatsworth House, Henry retired to Hardwick Hall and on the first opportunity and a break in the winter weather; he mounted Dudley and set off alone to visit Limbury but it was a distressing visit as Henry was saddened to see Charles in failing health.

"What will I do when father dies?" asked Sylvia. "The stipend will go and a new vicar will be appointed. I feel I shall be thrown onto the parish as homeless, and what will become of Robert?"

Sylvia fought to hold back the tears as she clutched at Henry's arm.

"Don't worry, Sylvia my love, the trust provides ample funds for Robert and I will find a solution to provide a suitable home for both of you."

The Passing

On the twenty-fifth of March 1603 Charles passed away in his sleep. Later that day, messages were received that beacons had been lit the previous night to tell of the passing away of the Queen. It was the heralding of a new age.

James VI of Scotland was proclaimed James I of England. Henry stayed in Limbury for a few days and attended the interment of his friend the Reverend Charles Leach by a minister from Alfreton.

Later Henry retired to the Peacock Inn in order to protect the virtuous name of Sylvia.

The following morning after a few words and gestures of comfort to Sylvia, he informed her of his plans to purchase the nearby Ufton Manor as an investment property and he offered Sylvia the position of governess to Robert. "If you accept the position, it means that you and Robert will always have a roof over your heads. You can bring up Robert in the manner that is your wish, and I shall have the comfort and peace of mind to know that you and my son are safe. So what say you, Mistress Sylvia?"

Sylvia, always a spirited person and with a sense of humour that Henry found enchanting, bent a knee and said, "Me thinks, sir, that you would spoil me, you have already taken my virtue and now I am to be your servant, but I accept your kind offer and," she fluttered her eyes, "I shall always love you."

Three months later, in the autumn of 1603, Henry Cavendish received ownership of Ufton Manor, whereupon he visited Sylvia and amidst much gossiping from her late father's parishioners she took up her new position as *governess* to Henry's illegitimate son.

Henry was overjoyed with his property investment and even managed to persuade Bess to allow Marianne to take up employment as a maidservant at his newly acquired Ufton Manor. Before she took up her new employment, she and John the footman married, with Bess giving a sum of money as a wedding gift. John also came to work as butler for Henry at Ufton Manor and ten months later, Marianne and John became proud parents of a daughter that they named Elizabeth.

And so life at Ufton developed into a happy household but Henry's joy was tempered by the news that Arbella was now seen as a real threat to the security of King James and had been banished from court.

The next three years sped by with Henry visiting his social peers on a regular basis and on such occasions, using the opportunity to womanise and sometimes partake in heavy gambling. On these excursions when Henry visited his other mistresses that were scattered around the county, he always found time to visit Ufton Manor, the residence of Sylvia, who remained his favourite lover.

But it could not continue. Henry's irresponsible life style earned him the displeasure of his mother who was becoming old and frail with arthritis. Bess also began to think of the Cavendish dynasty and after much thought she summoned Henry into the library and issued him with an ultimatum.

"Henry, I've decided that your income is to be cut. You are a philanderer and waster; because of your gambling debts you are ruining the family fortunes. Furthermore it has come to my attention that you continue to be irresponsible with the fathering of bastards all over the county."

"But, mother, do not be so harsh on me, I was…." Henry was halted in mid sentence.

"Silence." Bess lambasted him with more of her anger. Now her voice was raised an octave, "You can father bastards, but you won't give me a grandchild. I need a legitimate heir to our family fortune."

Henry went to his rooms and there he remained for some weeks in a state of deep depression.

***

It was early in the February of 1608 when Bess of Hardwick, at the age of eighty, finally took to her bed, and at five o'clock in the evening of the thirteenth of February 1608, Henry's mother breathed her last.

A period of mourning descended on the household but later that year the family's hopes were lifted when Arbella was welcomed back at court and she and King James were reconciled. Henry was pleased; he secretly knew in his heart that his late mother would have been happy at achieving her ambition of having Arbella at court; a serious contender to any future claim to the throne of England. That joy was short lived, for two years later in 1610, the headstrong, self-willed Arbella entered into a secret marriage at Greenwich with William Seymour, the younger brother of Edward Seymour, the man she had tried to marry back in 1602. That previous attempt had brought down the wrath of the late Queen with the result that Arbella had been banished to live with the Earl of Kent.

But that was history: now nine years on, Henry was visiting his mistress Sylvia. The lovers were relaxed after a pleasant day riding the lanes and the pastures and now after a hearty supper they sat talking round the fire. Eight-year-old Robert came to kiss his "governess" good night and to shake the hand of his "benefactor" before going off to bed.

"Will you ever tell him the truth?" Henry asked.

"Maybe one day," Sylvia said, "when he is old enough to keep secrets. But for now, Robert is happy to be a privileged young man, albeit an orphan, who is growing up in a loving household."

The conversation then became focused on the latest court gossip with Henry recalling that with the realm now well into the Stuart reign of James I, Arbella's marriage had caused some panic at court.

"Mother certainly harboured a pit of serpents when she took my niece Arbella into the family home and groomed her as a 'Royal'. With the news of Arbella's marriage to William Seymour, I perceive that there is a real danger to our family. That silly child Arbella poses a real threat to the whole Stuart dynasty and the reign of James. Do you realize, my dearest love, that both of the newly weds are direct descendants in the Tudor line? They are both related to the sisters of old King Hal. I fear they are both in serious danger. This time there won't be just banishment from court, this time I hear Arbella and William have been separated to avoid an embarrassing and a troublesome pregnancy. Only this last week our family has been informed that Arbella has been imprisoned in Lambeth at the house of a Sir Thomas Perry whilst William languishes in the Tower."

The talk of intrigue and gossip went on until the glow from the fire embers began to diminish and the warmth from the fire coupled with the after-effects of the wine put the pair in a mellow mood. They rose and made their way to bed. That night their love making was tender, a stark comparison to the wild passionate couplings of their younger days. Now all that had given way to a gentle pleasure that came from years of affection for each other.

And so another summer and winter passed with Henry visiting Sylvia and Robert as often as possible. Then during a mid-summer weekend in June 1611, after a breakfast at Ufton Manor, Henry had adjourned to the courtyard to saddle Dudley for a late-morning canter over to Wingfield Manor when he heard the sound of hooves. He stopped adjusting the saddle straps and gazed towards the entrance to the courtyard. A horseman came into view.

Reining in, the dusty rider dismounted and gasped, "Sir Henry, I bear news from London."

Henry put his arm around the messenger's shoulder so their heads were drawn closer together to prevent any eavesdropping. "Now slowly, what is this news? Is it bad?"

"I fear so, my Lord, it is Arbella, she has escaped from Lambeth disguised in men's clothing. From all accounts, her husband has also escaped from the Tower disguised as a carter's boy. Fellow conspirators have been arrested and confessed that the couple were supposed to join each other at Lee in Kent." The messenger went on to say that Arbella had been recaptured in Calais and was now imprisoned in the Tower, but William was still free and last seen in Ostend.

Henry learned later that William had in fact been delayed on his way to the boat and the escaping couple had sailed to France in separate ships.

"Thank you for the news, now go to the kitchens and have cook serve you hot nourishment and refreshments before you convey the word to Chatsworth."

The messenger handed the reins of his mount over to a groom and Henry followed him inside, leaving the groom to unsaddle Dudley.

Henry found Sylvia with Robert and he explained the situation.

"I shall have to take my leave of you both. My presence may be needed if there are to be any family repercussions. I will get news to you when I can." Henry gave Robert an embrace then taking Sylvia's hand he led her out of earshot.

"Take care of him, dearest Sylvia. These are dangerous times and I hope with God's will we shall meet again."

***

Retributions on the Cavendish household were not undertaken and the next three years passed uneventfully. Henry and Sylvia continued to meet as often as his family commitments allowed but Henry was now feeling the onset of his ageing years. At one of their weekend encounters Sylvia heard the news that Arbella had attempted to escape from the Tower. She failed and the family were saddened to hear that Arbella was gradually losing her mind and all reasoning. The end came on the twenty-seventh of September 1615 when Arbella Stuart died peacefully in the Tower.

She had starved herself to death. The following day she was interred privately at Westminster Abbey to lie alongside Mary Queen of the Scots, who was her aunt.

For sixteen years Henry and Sylvia had been in a loving relationship. During that time Sylvia had not conceived further bastards and in 1616, Henry died within a year of Arbella. He bequeathed the manor to Robert to do with as he pleased, but he stipulated that Sylvia should have the right to live in Ufton Manor for the remainder of her days. Sylvia lived on in the manor for a further thirty-four years and died in her sleep on the twenty-seventh of September 1654, fifty-two years after she had fallen in love with the handsome adventurer Henry Cavendish.

In life they had been together as much as possible. Sadly but inevitably, in death they were separated.

Henry was interred in the vault on the Cavendish family estate whilst Sylvia was laid to rest in a grave in the church were her father Charles had once been the vicar.

London 1660

When Henry died in 1616, Sylvia retained Marianne and John as faithful servants. Now, in the spring of 1660, Marianne, Sylvia's maid and friend and the last survivor of the Derby week of 1601, passed away. Robert Cavendish, the illegitimate son of Henry and inheritor of Ufton Manor, had married Elizabeth, the daughter of John and Marianne.

The couple had been married for seven years and lost three children in infancy before a son that they named Henry in memory of his grand father was born in 1637. Now at the age of twenty-three, and with nothing more than a small inheritance and some letters of introduction to personages in the city, young Henry was about to seek his fortune in London. It was a joyous time to be going up to the capital.

The harsh puritan lifestyle of the Cromwell years and the commonwealth were over. After a nine-year exile in France; Charles II at the age of thirty, had returned to England on the twenty-fifth of May 1660. The country once more had a Stuart monarchy. The land was again considered to be Merry England.

***

Robert and Elizabeth stood in the courtyard of Ufton Manor as Henry saddled his horse; Elizabeth had packed spare clothes into a saddlebag. Two years previously on Henry's twenty-first birthday, Robert had given him a pair of flintlock pistols and these were now primed and holstered to the saddle. Although not an accomplished swordsman, he had a rapier at his side.

Henry assured his father he had his letters of introduction, amongst which was one to Robert's cousin Sir William Cavendish, who was Bess of Hardwick's grandson.

"Contacts, my boy, maintain contacts," Robert said. "Your grand father Henry always said you must maintain your contacts; and remember, friends you make whilst young and at social functions, they become your key to maintaining a proper social status. Oh, and watch out for tricksters and gamblers. Avoid them, they were your grand father's undoing at the end."

"Oh, stop harassing the boy, Robert! He is of an age to take care for himself," Elizabeth scolded her husband.

"But…" Robert was about to interrupt when Henry took the opportunity, gave his mother a farewell kiss, bade Robert to be of good cheer, and placing one foot in the stirrup, he mounted. Turning the horse's head, he cantered out of the courtyard onto the old packhorse lane and headed south. Three days later Henry rode through Moorfields and entered London through Bishopsgate.

Henry rode his mount in the centre of the lanes to avoid slops that were thrown from upper-storey windows. Slowly he made his way to Holborn, where he found accommodation at the Saracen's Head in Snow Hill, within a mile of Whitehall. His room overlooked a central courtyard and although his sleep was frequently disturbed, he soon adjusted to the noise of city life produced by its twin factions of aristocratic and vibrant business communities, the two of which never openly socialized. Henry as a Cavendish, albeit a minor player in the framework of that family, had a toehold in both camp factions. He had his father's letters to some merchant traders and also letters of introduction to distant family contacts within the court circle.

A few days after Henry arrived in the city he learned something that was to change his life and make his fortune.

It was now towards the end of July, when by chance he called into a coffee house and discovered that to meet personages and men of merit; he should spend more time in the popular coffee houses in the proximity of Whitehall; consequently having breakfasted, next day he took a sedan chair from his rooms to the corner of Bow Street and Great Russell Street.

The two porters halted the sedan at the front door of Wills the most fashionable coffee house. Henry paid them off and entered to be welcomed by the landlord, a man named William Urwin, who prompted Henry to take a seat near the window so he could observe the passing public.

Henry looked about him and noticed an elderly gentleman sitting at a table by the fireplace, an inkpot to his fore and in his hand a quill pen.

The landlord saw the glance, and giving an almost imperceptible nod commented,

"That's John Dryden, our most celebrated writer and poet. I believe he's working on a new play for the theatre. We always keep that seat by the fireplace reserved for him. Now, sir, what can I serve you? A pot of my best coffee or possibly a cup of chocolate served hot and sweet?"

"Coffee, please." Henry looked around the room. Dryden continued to write industriously by the fireplace, it was mid summer and the grate was unlit, but logs lay in a corner niche ready for any inclement weather. Henry's coffee arrived. Being alone, he continued to observe other customers. His thoughts and observations were interrupted by a middle-aged man who was about to join him at his table.

"Good day sir; it is lighter here in the window, are you expecting company or may I join you?"

A startled Henry regained his composure "Certainly, sir, please join me for I lack company, having just arrived in the city from my family home in the Shire of Derby."

Henry offered his hand and continued, "My name, for I fear we cannot be introduced by others, is Henry Cavendish."

"I am pleased to be of your acquaintance, Mister Cavendish. My name is Samuel, Samuel Pepys." Samuel seated himself. "So what brings you to London? Is it business or social? Or maybe you are partaking pleasures from the fleshpots of the town? If so, I can readily direct you towards some very fine establishments, which are by nature of their clientele, very discreet."

"No, Mister Pepys, it is very kind of you to offer but I am seeking a patron who would introduce and 'open doors' to providing business opportunities or employment. Meanwhile I am taking temporary accommodation at the Saracen's Head. The letters of introduction are to a few of my father's friends and to some distant contacts from his grand father, Sir Henry Cavendish."

Mister Pepys listened as Henry continued, "I have a letter to Sir William Cavendish who is my father's cousin and who, I understand, commanded his Whitecoats and fought valiantly at Marston Moor alongside Prince Rupert. I also have a letter to Edward Montague, who, I believe, is involved in naval matters."

Pepys chuckled. "Involved? Involved? Why, indeed he is, and very highly too, I may say. Your letters are indeed to notable personages. So how do you come to have a letter of introduction to Edward Montague?"

Henry paused, wondering if he had said more than he should have done, then he decided he was not committing any indiscretions so continued. "One day, father was telling me of my ancestral history and he remarked that his grand father, my great-great-grand father, was old Sir William Cavendish and he had a brother named Sir Thomas Cavendish who was apparently a privateer. In 1586 he sailed with Sir Richard Grenville. Father told me that he believes some of the family fortunes came from prize money seized in 'eighty-eight from some Spanish galleon named… I think father said," Henry hesitated, "the *Santa Ana*."

Samuel Pepys listened while making some mental notes as Henry continued, "So with a letter describing my family's naval connections, I thought I may be able to obtain some form of employment from this gentleman named Edward Montague, or if I am really fortunate, then perhaps Prince Rupert may become my patron, that is assuming that I can persuade Sir William to speak for me."

Samuel gave a nod. "I believe, sir, that this day you are most fortunate for I am employed by Edward Montague, but I should make you aware that since fifty-six, Edward Montague has been the General-at-Sea to our English fleet. He has served our gracious Majesty well and was made Admiral Commander of the fleet when he escorted King Charles back from exile in 1660. But that is not the end of Edward's rise to power. Why, only last week, the king made him Baron Montague of St Neots, Viscount Hinchinbroke, and the Earl of Sandwich. So you must realize you have a letter of introduction to one of the most influential men in the king's service."

Henry was aghast, but before he could respond, Samuel went on, "And I, Samuel Pepys, sir, am at your service, for in the foreseeable future, I expect to be appointed as the earl's administrator in naval matters. I doubt if you will find the earl easily available to receive your letter or yourself, he is a very busy man. At the moment he is not at sea; a fact to which I can vouchsafe, as I will be meeting with him on the morrow. I will if you so wish inform the admiral of your presence in town and maybe, and I say only maybe, I may be able to get an appointment for you to meet with my Lord."

Henry was overwhelmed. "Indeed, sir, this is more than I could ever have hoped. Your coffee is cold, Mister Pepys, can I take the pleasure of purchasing us both a fresh pot?"

"That is very generous of you, Henry, I may call you Henry?"

The fresh coffee pots had just been served when a tall moustached gentleman of military bearing and sporting a Van Dyke beard entered the coffee house. He had dark hair falling in waves onto his shoulders. Around his waste, a sash and belt supported a rapier at his side.

The man gave an almost imperceptible nod towards John Dryden then turning he approached Samuel's table, "Good day, Samuel, thought I might find you here. We have been summoned to the Navy Office. I called in at Grays Inn and I was informed you may be partaking of coffee at Wills. "

Samuel rose to his feet "And a very good day to you, Sir William, do take a seat while I finish my beverage. May I offer you a cup?"

William declined the offer. Samuel gestured towards Henry then spoke again to Sir William. "May I introduce you to Mister Henry Cavendish."

Henry rose and offered his hand to Sir William who shook it. "Are you related to the Cavendishes of Chatsworth?" William enquired.

"I am, Sir, but with distant connections from my grand father's side and I am honoured to make your acquaintance, Sir William."

Addressing Henry, Pepys interrupted, "Sir William served on the *Naseby* when it brought Charles back from the continent."

"I thought the *Naseby* had been renamed the *Royal Charles* in honour of the restoration."

Henry's correction of Samuel's error brought the hint of a smile to Sir William's facial expressions.

"Quite right, Henry, it was remiss of me. You seem very well acquainted with naval facts; perhaps we should find some employment for you. I shall speak for you tomorrow as promised. But for now, Henry, Sir William and I must bid our leave. We have business to attend and I will be in touch. The Saracen's Head, I believe you said, was your accommodation."

Samuel and William departed to walk towards Westminster and take a barge down river to the Tower from were it was only a short stroll to the Navy Office in Seething Lane.

Meanwhile, Henry finished his coffee, settled his account and as the hour of noon approached; he exited Wills and again took a sedan chair, not directly back to the Saracen's Head but through the Holbein Gateway to the Palace of Whitehall.

On Henry's signal, the porters stopped, he disembarked and paid the porters outside the Banqueting House designed by Inigo Jones where on that cold January day in 1649, Charles I had been led out onto the scaffold. Henry then spent the rest of the day strolling Whitehall. He strolled the embankment along the river, then on the hour of four, thoroughly satisfied with a successful day, he returned to his rooms at the Saracen's Head.

***

To occupy his time Henry took daily exercise riding his horse in the fields of Holborn with an occasional jaunt through St James's Park. Some days he even ventured further afield by riding his mount over London Bridge and into the countryside on the south bank. The days passed slowly, Henry a stranger in a big city was lonely as the days turned to a couple of weeks. He had heard nothing from Mister Pepys and a mood of despondency began to settle on him; in his mind he began to doubt the sincerity of the man he had met, a man who had promised so much and delivered nothing.

It was at the end of the first week in August when Henry again visited Wills, and again John Dryden was sitting at the reserved table by the fireside. Sitting next to the poet-writer was Pepys, whom Henry had not seen since that first meeting in July.

"Good day to you, Henry, pardon me for not calling on you at the Saracen's but I have been out of town for some time. I had

59

cause to ride to Cambridge on family business and although all was satisfactory, I fear I ate and drank a little too well and although I have been back for a full day, I fear I need some strong coffee to clear my head. But I am negligent in my manners in not introducing you to Mister Dryden." Samuel made the appropriate introductions.

"Are you related by chance to Sir William Cavendish?" Dryden enquired.

"Indeed I am, sir, he is a family cousin. Why do you ask?

"It is of no importance but I seem to remember Sir William in your company at this establishment a few weeks ago. By coincidence he is coming to meet with me this very afternoon. He is attempting to translate a play by Molière, but it is too much for him, and his translation, I have to say, is rather poor and consequently he is seeking my assistance. I fear I may eventually have to write the whole work myself."

The writer summoned the landlord and ordered three pots of coffee.

"So, Samuel, I hear that Lord General Monk is very ill. I hope that he can soon return to his duties. The Coldstream Guards will surely miss his leadership if he should die."

"Indeed the country would miss such support that he has given to the king."

At that moment, Sir William entered and with one hand on the hilt of his sword, he gave a brief nod to Henry and to Samuel and addressed John Dryden. "Good afternoon, sir, I see you are in company, I trust I may join you?"

Dryden rose to welcome Sir William. "I think you know Samuel Pepys, and this gentleman here is a somewhat distant relation to you. May I introduce Mister Henry Cavendish."

Sir William nodded to Samuel then turning to Henry he offered his hand. "We were introduced briefly a few weeks ago. So, Mister Cavendish, to which part of our family are you related?"

"My grand father Sir Henry was, I understand, your cousin, his wife was named Grace but it is common knowledge that there was no legitimate issue."

William interrupted, "Um, yes, I do recall that he had one or two fair mistresses in the county."

William was about to address further conversation to John

60

when Henry spoke, "If it pleases you, Sir William, I have a letter of introduction from your cousin's wife; Lady Christian Bruce."

Henry handed the letter to William who broke the seal and read…

Dearest Sir William,

May I be so bold as to offer this letter of introduction of one, namely Mister Henry Cavendish who is to my knowledge a trustworthy and honourable grandson of your dear departed uncle Sir Henry Cavendish who passed from us in the year of our Lord 1616. Mister Cavendish is seeking a patron to promote his worldly status and I therefore prey you may find him worthy of your care and patronage.

I trust this letter finds you and Lady Margaret in good health and that she continues with her writing.

I remain, sir, your cousin by marriage

Christian Bruce   *dated 22nd May 1660.*

Henry looked on. Samuel and John remained silent as William read. Then, folding the letter and putting in his pocket, William broke the silence. "Well, my boy, it seems we are related even if it is from the wrong side of the sheets. You may call on me next week; Tuesday at two will be fine."

William offered Henry his card. The four companions then ordered coffees and settled down to spend the rest of the afternoon discussing the theatre and the actors.

Seeing that Henry was lost in the strange subject of the theatre and was unable to contribute much to the conversation regarding the London social scene, John Dryden addressed his conversations directly to Henry. "We play writers are favoured at the moment. The king has given patents to re-establish the Kings Men as an acting company in Drury Lane. The leading player is Charles Hart, an excellent actor, although it is rumoured he doth lie with some of the actresses. I hear his latest mistress is named Eleanor Gwynne. He calls her his Nell, she was an orange seller outside the theatre and Hart was so taken with her wit that he has given her a minor part in the next production."

Before Henry could comment, Samuel cut in, "One cannot place blame on him, and some of the actresses are comely wenches. Why, only last Wednesday, after dining at the Wardrobe with Captain Ferrers, we went to the opera. We saw *The Witts* again; there is a wench in that play that I would bed myself and the production was exceedingly good and most humorous. You will have to come to the theatre with us one night, Henry, it will broaden your intellect and you will meet people on a social level."

Henry smiled. "That would be very pleasant, I shall await an invite."

"I was also at the opera last Wednesday," John remarked, "and I noticed quite a few personages from court were present. I glimpsed Elizabeth the Queen of Bohemia and cousin to King Charles; she is quite elderly, isn't she? I believe she is about sixty-four. She was escorted by Lord Craven."

"Lord Craven, Yes I noticed him escorting her, it was a very enjoyable evening," Samuel said. "The captain and I finished it off with a few drinks at the Devil tavern."

It was getting towards five when the four friends departed, with Samuel assuring Henry that he would speak to Montague about a possible position.

The following Tuesday, Henry took a sedan to Sir William's house in Whitehall. With a beating heart he knocked at the large door that was presently opened by a well-groomed liveried foot-man. After presenting his card onto a silver tray, he was admit-ted to a drawing room. Shortly Sir William joined him and each taking a seat, William summoned a house servant and requested a pot of tea, which was now the fashionable beverage in the aris-tocratic London houses.

"Now, Henry, I do not know what you expect of me or what your ambitions are; so let us be honest with each other, how are you funded? Have you any capital?"

Henry was rather taken aback at such a direct manner; hesi-tantly at first, Henry explained that he had a small inheritance and he wished to establish himself in the city as a business man.

"I have a small annual allowance of two hundred a year from my father who was left a small inheritance plus our family home at Ufton Manor from his father Sir Henry Cavendish. The estate is farming land and father has managed it well so we are comfort-ably provided."

"The reason I ask is that an old trading company set up by

merchant adventurers in Elizabeth's reign, may soon be expanding by royal charter and maybe an investment in the East Indies would suit you. It would bring some substantial return in the next few years, but for now there is profit to be made from tobacco from the New World."

Sir William paused for a moment to sip his tea. "I remember our ancestor Sir Thomas, who sailed with Grenville to Virginia in 1585, made a discovery to sweeten the tobacco leaves with sugar. Now is probably the time to invest in Virginian tobacco. You may not know this, Henry, but last year in an effort to create government wealth, the king formed a new committee of the Privy Council, which he named the Lords of Trade and Plantations; they were charged with making a policy to tax our colonies in the New World."

"Will the colonials accept those taxes when they are not represented in parliament?" Unwittingly Henry was prophesising events would become reality when rebellion did erupt with the Boston Tea party in 1773.

"The colonists will do what is good for England," Sir William answered arrogantly, "Consequently, Parliament has passed the Navigations Act, which in effect bans certain goods such as sugar, indigo and tobacco from being transported to or from any English or colonial port unless it is carried on an English ship. Now, with the help of your friend Samuel Pepys at the Navy Office and my contacts at court, I think we can put together a small group of investors to take advantage of the situation. So what think you, Henry, are you willing to invest a small sum to establish your business?"

Henry did not need to think, he grasped the opportunity and in the autumn of 1661 Henry Cavendish contributed the first investment in making 'Out-Roads' towards the family fortunes when he became a minor investor with the sum of twenty pounds into a consortium of businessmen who called themselves the Virginian Merchants.

Several prominent persons took shares on an investment in total of two hundred pounds to purchase a fifty-ton ketch that was already four years old. The ship was lightly armed with four cannon and had a crew of ten. The ketch, named the *Prince*, was captained by a Joshua Woodman. In February 1662, the *Prince*, with her main and mizzen masts both rigged with three jibs, set sail from Deptford bound for Virginia. In her hold she carried mixed merchandise of farm implements, tools and woollen goods and after a voyage lasting one hundred and eighteen days, she made landfall in Chesapeake Bay and sailed up the James River to berth at Jamestown on Saturday the tenth of June 1662.

Two days later, as morning dawned, Joshua Woodman was standing on the poop deck overseeing the unloading of the *Prince.*

"Hawkins, put your back into it lad." A box of farm tools began to falter as the rope from the hoist began to snag. Slowly the cargo was lifted and swung onto the wharf to be loaded onto carts.

Jim Hawkins the young sailor cursed under his breath and vowed if he got safely back to England this would be his last voyage. He would not end his days, an old sea dog, he would try to make a new life. From other sailors, he had heard that Bristol was a thriving port and offered opportunities for anyone willing to work.

"Hawkins, damn you lad, heave on that rope." The berating by the captain jolted Jim back into reality and he quickly returned to the job in hand; applying himself to the rope, he strained and another load emerged from the hold. All day in the heat the crew toiled as slowly the hold was emptied and the goods transported to the market place were they were sold to the colonists. With holds empty, the captain and first mate took a few days to begin purchasing hogsheads of tobacco that had been harvested the previous autumn and cured in the warehouses during the winter months. The captain purchased one hundred and eighty hogsheads of cured tobacco.

It took another week to load provisions and water but finally with the ketch fully laden, she set sail for London with her cargo of prime Virginian tobacco for sale on the London market.

The profits from that single voyage were slightly lower than expectations, due to an overproduction in the colonies, but even with a reduced price, the eighty tons of tobacco still gave the investors a handsome profit. Each investor redeemed his initial stake and the net profit was used to purchase a second ketch, which they named the *Cavendish,* in honour of the youngest investor in their company. In the spring of '63 the *Prince* and the *Cavendish* both set sail for Virginia.

Parliamentary events of that year made that voyage especially profitable due to new legislation passed by Parliament. The new law stated that all goods from the colonies not only had to be on English ships but all goods from Europe that were destined to or from the colonies also had to be by English merchants. The initial investors of the Virginian Merchants were on now on a financial roll, with the new legislation giving them an additional bonus. They were now the middlemen who could inflate prices of the foreign goods for additional profit. By the late summer all the tobacco harvest for 'sixty-four had been transported from Virginia to London. The Virginian Merchants had acquired four more ships for the following season.

England was beginning to prosper from its colonies.

Invitation to Supper

Life for Henry was good. At the age of twenty-five he was now a modestly rich businessman who was making a small fortune from the import of tobacco. It was a time of change for Henry; in the summer of '64 he vacated his lodgings and purchased a house in the fashionable rural village of Newington Green, located only a short coach journey from Westminster. Henry's choice of village abode had been easy. A number of notable personages were already investing and building country houses in the area, which they considered to be located far away from the pestilences that occasionally ravaged the metropolis yet near enough for coach travel to indulge in the social fleshpots within the city.

On the north-east corner of Newington village green stood a large house in its own acreage. The house was owned by the Earl of Northumberland whose ancestor had been given it by Henry VIII. The villagers called it The Palace.

Henry's house was located on the west side of the green and stood regally in the centre of a row of town houses that had been constructed two years before the restoration of the monarchy. On completion of his purchase Henry promptly employed a stone mason to inscribe, **CAVENDISH HOUSE** on the stone portal above his front door.

One summer morning in early August of 1664, Henry was on a visit to the Navy Office to speak to Samuel. He had summoned a hackney cab and they were passing through the village of Shoreditch when the cab threw a wheel. The driver pulled rein and Henry was forced to dismount. The cab lay disabled in a lane that formed one side of a square. A sign on a wall proclaimed it to be Hoxton Square.

From were Henry stood at the nearside of the square he saw a row of newly built stone houses. He had heard that the area had become fashionable with the more prosperous merchants and Huguenot silk weavers were now purchasing homes nearer the city.

As the coachman, William Usburn, helped Henry to climb down safely from the disabled cab he said, "Afraid we cannot precede further, sir, until this wheel's back on. If I can get a couple of strong lads to help, it should be fixed in an hour."

William escorted Henry to one of the houses, and in response to a firm rap, the door was opened by a middle-aged woman. Observing that she was particularly well dressed, Henry raised his hat and made a slight bow.

"I do beg your indulgence on this liberty, but as you can see, my coach driver has had a mishap and cast a wheel from his coach. I wonder if I may rest awhile until a repair is done."

The door was opened wider. "You are very welcome, sir." Henry noticed that the woman spoke in a quiet, educated voice that had a foreign inclination. She turned to address William, who was standing dutifully behind Henry with his cap in his hand. "Your passenger will be quite safe with me. I think you will find a smithy about a half mile along this lane. He will no doubt attend to your repairs."

William turned to Henry. "Now don't you worry, Mr Cavendish, I will get the coach fixed within the hour."

William replaced his cap, turned and walked off down the lane.

"Do step into my drawing room and take a seat. I will get my daughter to fetch us some refreshment, would you prefer wine or beer?"

"That is most kind; a tyg of wine would be most suitable."

The woman left the room and returned a few minutes later to take a seat on the settle facing Henry. "Have you travelled far, Mr Cavendish – that is your name, is it not?"

"It is, madam. We have travelled little distance, in fact only from Newington Green."

"Why, we are almost neighbours," the lady responded. "My name is Madam Chouart an unusual name, you may think, for I was born in England but as a governess I lived in Paris where I met my husband a Frenchman named Médard Chouart. I returned to England when I was widowed."

"What a fascinating life you must have led," said Henry, but before he could continue, the drawing room door opened and an attractive young woman entered the room carrying a tray with a tyg of red wine. Henry rose to his feet as the girl entered.

"Mr Cavendish, this is my daughter Jane, a great help and comfort to me."

Henry took the offered wine. "Thank you, Miss Chouart, your mother has been most kind in giving shelter to a traveller and keeping me entertained with accounts of her life in Paris. Thank you for the wine."

The young lady smiled. "You are welcome, sir. It is a most pleasant diversion to have some company to add a little excitement in our day." Jane fluttered her eyelashes then lowered her face to present a demure look that Henry found attractive.

Madam Chouart patted the padded seat and invited Jane to sit beside her as Henry resumed his seat.

"If it is not to bold, madam, may I suggest that you kind ladies call me Henry?"

"And you may call me Constance." Madam Chouart responded, "From your speech, Henry, may I assume that you are not from London?"

"You are correct, madam, and I must comment that you have a good ear for dialects; I am in fact from Derbyshire."

For some considerable time Henry talked enthusiastically giving his reasons why, as a single man, he had left his family home to seek his fortune in the city. He spoke of how he had been lucky to meet a gentleman named Samuel Pepys in a coffee house and how he had invested in a venture to bring tobacco from Virginia in the New World.

Henry enthused about how he was determined to make his fortune in London. He spoke with all the fervour of a young man. Jane was mesmerized by the handsome visitor.

Time sped past, as is the case when engrossed in pleasant conversation, and all too soon, a knock at the front door announced

William's return for Henry to continue on his journey.

Jane looked crestfallen at his imminent departure and Constance quickly noticing this said, "Henry, would you honour us with your presence for supper next Thursday?"

Henry was taken by surprise at the Parisian-style approach of Jane's mother. "I would be honoured to accept," he replied.

During the next few days the hands of time seemed to stand still for Henry. He tried to busy himself with minor shipping details for another voyage but he couldn't concentrate, his thoughts kept returning to the charming young lady who had come into her life.

The following Thursday Henry presented himself at Madam Chouart's home, and after a brief exchange of greetings, Constance and Jane led him into a small dining room. An oak dining table sat majestically in the centre, and on it where three place settings of knives and spoons plus forks, an item of cutlery now fashionable in the wealthier homes. Three pewter plates where accompanied by three pewter tygs for the wine. A fire burnt in the hearth, and from its glowing embers wraiths of smoke rose to spiral lazily up into the chimney.

Henry noticed that nobody was placed with their back to the fire.

"Do be seated, Henry, and you too, Jane. I have baked an eel and oyster pie. But first may I pour us all some white Bordeaux wine? I found that this wine is most agreeable with fish and I was introduced to it when I was living in Paris."

Constance filled their tygs and proposed a toast to a long and happy friendship then she left the young couple alone while she went to her kitchen fetch the supper.

"The pie is one of mother's speciality dishes," Jane said proudly. "I do hope you like it."

"I am sure it will be delicious. Maybe it will put a sparkle into my eye to match yours," said Henry.

Jane blushed and for a moment she seemed lost for words, but with Constance away from the table Henry continued to make his flirtatious remarks, hoping that Madam Chouart had not heard. A few moments later Constance returned, placing the eel and oyster pie in the centre of the table and proceeded to serve her guest.

As they ate Henry was already planning how to make more

visits to the Chouart household for he was becoming enchanted with the young woman that had entered his life. Little did he know of the life changing events that would unfold because of the carriage casting its wheel and that invitation to supper.

The Wedding

Henry and Jane had a whirlwind romance. It was obvious to all that the couple were totally besotted and in love. Within three weeks, Henry asked Constance for her daughter's hand in marriage. Constance immediately gave her consent and visited the local parish church of St. Leonard's to arrange the wedding and the happy couple were married a few months later in September 1664.

After the ceremony and a festive village meal at which Samuel and his wife were guest of honour, Henry escorted his bride to a flower-decked coach and the bride and groom were driven back to Cavendish House in Newington Green. With a show of elegance, the coach driver lowered the steps for Henry to assist his Jane to be helped down.

The coachman bade the happy pair a long and happy life and drove off leaving Henry to escort Jane into her new home.

Once inside and the front door firmly closed, Henry took Jane in his arms and gave her a long lingering kiss. He felt her body trembling like a frightened foal's. "Shall we sit in the lounge for a while or retire?" he said.

Jane looked at him with doe-like eyes that said it all, silently the couple ascended the stairs to their bedroom in which Constance had made sure that they had clean linen and new bed covers. Jane stood inside the bedroom looking hesitantly at the large four-poster bed. Henry stood behind her and putting his hands around her waist pulled her back into his arms, nuzzling her neck with warm soft kisses. The couple slowly became aware that they were alone at last.

Shyly, Jane removed some of her clothing, then pausing she let Henry remove the remainder. At seventeen, Jane had the body of a mature young woman. Her breasts were small and pert with rose-coloured nipples, each encircled in a brown halo. Henry's eyes wandered to the dark curly hair that covered her intimate parts.

Jane stepped away and pulling back the bed covers slipped into bed. "Do not be too long joining me," she said, "for I fear it is chilly in this large bed and I need you to warm me."

Henry quickly removed his clothing and climbed in beside her. Taking her in his arms, he kissed her and they caressed each other with gentleness. Jane, trembling like a frightened rabbit, gave a small cry of pain as he entered her, then he was thrusting deeper as if to reach her very soul. Henry moved faster and faster. Jane began to breath heavily and then, all too soon it was over. As he regained his breath, he lay by her side with a contented look on his face and whispered, "That was beautiful, I am told that women sometimes experience feelings of excitement; did you feel anything, Jane?"

"A very nice feeling began to rise within me, my love, but then it disappeared as you finished. Maybe next time it will last longer and be better for me, but I am so happy just to be here with you."

Henry dozed for a short time, and when he awoke, his hand sought her and she gave a small tremble. "That's nice, touch me just there again, that makes me tingle with love for you."

Henry stroked her gently and she began to gasp, then he entered her again. Her breathing became heavy as she began to cry in ecstasy.

"Love me, my love, love me slowly so I can enjoy this moment for ever," she whispered, her legs entwined around his, and after a few minutes her back arched and she gasped, "Oh Henry, Henry, I love you, I love you, love you…" Her whispers faded as they slumped back, trying to regain their breath.

Dawn was breaking when they finally fell asleep.

The Christmas festivities were especially happy that year as Constance informed Henry that she was pregnant. Henry and Jane passed the glad tidings on to Constance who exclaimed,

"I am too young to be a grandmother." Then immediately she started crying with joy.

Later alone with Constance, Jane admitted, "I think I conceived on our wedding night. I had no showing at the end of September so it's possible our baby will be born late May or very early in June."

The winter drifted by with the newlyweds enjoying each other's bodies and learning to live as a couple. Soon it was spring with new life in the fields in the form of spring lambs, daffodils raised their golden heads and the bluebells bloomed in their thousands and Jane began to show a slight swelling of her stomach.

Down on the Thames, Henry and Samuel watched as the six ships of the Virginian Merchants set sail to collect the summer crop of tobacco.

Two weeks later, Jane gave birth to a son, whom the happy couple named James but the fortunes of Henry Cavendish were to take a plunge; for in June, with James just four weeks old, the plague was to visit London.

The Plague

The plague came to London when two Frenchmen who lodged in a family house at the top of Drury Lane, in St Giles in the Fields, were reported to be sick. St Giles was a heavily populated poor area to the west of the walled city. Those two victims were only the beginning and by the end of May, eleven more cases were reported. Alarm began to beset the residents of London.

On the fifth of June the Lord Mayor and Aldermen of the City of London closed the Theatre Royal, along with all other places of entertainment.

Henry ceased going into the city; he had not met with Samuel since Christmas but then on the Monday evening he received a foot runner with a message suggesting that if convenient, Henry should call on Samuel at seven the following evening for a supper party. Henry immediately requested the runner to wait while he penned a response. Henry quickly wrote an acceptance sealed the envelope and wrote Samuel's address on the letter. Then, paying the man sixpence, he requested him to also make a call at the Angel in Islington and ask William Usburn the licensed hackney coachman to present himself with his coach at Henry's home the following evening.

After a tranquil day in which Henry and Jane did very little except talk about the pestilence and what steps they would take if it came nearer, the couple retired to bed praying that their family would be spared.

On the hour of six, Jane was nursing their son James when

the coach arrived. Henry donned his cloak and kissed Jane good-night, "Do not wait up for me, Jane. I may be late as I have business to discuss with Samuel." Henry closed the front door, William the coachman opened the coach door and Henry took his seat, "Mr Pepys' house in Seething Lane."

William flicked his whip, the horse took the strain and the coach moved along the rutted lane. A few minutes before seven, Henry knocked on Samuel's door for it to be opened by Wayneman.

Samuel's trusted servant recognized Henry from his many visits and immediately took his cape to reveal Henry's red doublet over a cream linen shirt. "Mr Pepys, sir, is waiting for you in the library, sir."

The servant knocked on the library door and opened it to announce, "Mr Henry Cavendish, sir."

Samuel rose to his feet. "Good evening, Henry, I am pleased you are early, my other guests will be here in thirty minutes and you and I need to discuss a few details for furthering our interests. Take a seat. May I offer you a glass of Madeira?"

Henry sat and took the glass.

"As you are aware, Henry, the American colonies have been over-productive of tobacco this last three or four years and I am given to understand that Maryland has banned planting for a year to stop over-production."

"That will certainly mean a fall in tobacco supply and a rise in prices next season," Henry conceded, "I think that after this season, when our ships return in the autumn we should talk to our fellow investors and propose to look for new markets."

Samuel agreed. "At the Navy Office I have learnt that New France and the Hudson River in particular is a land rich in resources and well worth investment. Rumours are circulating that Prince Rupert himself may be interested in a naval expedition so I feel we must meet later this year to discuss the possibilities. What I am doing, Henry, is sounding you out as to any thoughts and proposals you have to offer."

Henry took a sip of his Madeira. "I am willing to be guided by your advice, Samuel. I could approach Sir William, who has some connections at the French court as well as here in Whitehall."

"Very good idea, I shall leave that to you. By the way, Henry, you may wonder why you have been invited to my dinner party tonight. As I may have previously told you, in the March of 'fifty-eight, I underwent the awful procedure of an operation to remove a stone-like object from my bladder at the home of Mrs Turner."

"You have told me, Samuel, but do proceed, I can listen once more."

"Well, my boy, I was lucky to survive the surgeon's knife. The operation was done by Thomas Holier and his brilliant assistant Doctor Joyliffe. They were wonderful. The reason for repeating myself, and for that I do humbly apologize, is that each year on March the twenty-sixth I hold a celebratory stone-feast and I always invite Mrs Turner. This year March the twenty-sixth fell on Easter Sunday and Mrs Turner preferred not to attend so I postponed the feast until tonight. Now let us proceed to my drawing room so that Elizabeth and I can welcome our other guests."

Henry followed Samuel into the drawing room. "Henry, you know Elizabeth my wife."

Henry greeted Elizabeth and kissed her hand. A knock at the front door interrupted their polite conversation. "Look too that will you," Samuel called to Wayneman.

Voices could be heard in the hall then a small group of guests entered the room.

Ordering a maid to take care of their cloaks and capes, Samuel introduced the arrivals to Henry, "Mr. Honiwood and Mrs. Wilde, and finally my cousin Roger Pepys who is a barrister." Samuel continued, "We only await Mrs Turner and Joyce and then we can be seated at table."

Wayneman served drinks as Roger now spoke to address the general company, "I had cause to go into Drury Lane yesterday and, Lord have mercy upon us for I saw three houses marked as plague houses, they had a red cross daubed on their doors and the poor occupants were locked in. To my recollection I have never seen plague houses so close. I was so concerned that I purchased some tobacco to ward off the plague air."

"I hope it was Cavendish tobacco," Henry jested. "Why, I heard that a boy at Eton was flogged last week when it was discovered he was not smoking. It is astonishing that youths of today can be so inconsiderate as not to smoke to ward off the plague."

"And no doubt to bolster your profits," Roger added.

"I fear we shall not be safe even out here near the Tower of London," Elizabeth said. "Why, only yesterday morning I rose at two and took mother and four servants on a ship to Gravesend so that we could refresh ourselves away from the foul plague air."

With an attempt at humour Samuel changed the subject, "Enough of this talk of your mother Elizabeth, and of the plague. I hear that off shore from Lowestoft, there has been a great victory last week"

"That is good news," a jubilant Henry commented, "At last our merchant fleets can now sail with a little more safety."

"Ah, Henry, I think you speak with some vested interest," Roger jibed. "Do continue, Samuel."

"Well, the news at the Navy Office is that on the third of June our fleet of one hundred and nine ships commanded by James, Duke of York engaged one hundred and three ships of the Dutch fleet. A battle took place out near Dogger Bank off the Suffolk coast and it is said the battle guns could be heard like thunder in the town itself. Our intelligence informs us that this latest conflict has…" Samuel paused, worried that he was being indiscreet. He thought for a moment, then continued, "I can tell you this for by now it is common knowledge. A couple of weeks ago, the Dutch fleet was marauding near the Dogger Bank when they captured a convoy of twenty English merchant ships."

Henry interrupted, "None of the Virginian Merchantmen, I pray?"

"No, we are assured of that. However, the Duke of York, in his flagship the *Royal Charles*, weighed anchor from Gunfleet sands. The Duke had two of our generals-at-sea as commanders of the squadrons. One commander was Prince Rupert and the other was Edward Montague, a relative of yours, Henry."

The others turned to see Henry nod confirmation as Samuel continued, "The report says that after maneuvering for position the two fleets joined in battle at dawn with each fleet passing in line astern on opposite tacks. Each ship of the line engaged the enemy as the guns came within range. Of course this all led to the battle degenerating into a grand melee with each ship fighting for survival. In the centre of the melee were the opposing flagships, the eighty-gun *Royal Charles* and the seventy-six-gun Dutch *Eendracht*. Apparently it was bitter fighting and at one moment the valiant crew of the enemy nearly boarded the *Royal Charles*. About noon after eight hours of battle, the two flagships were at close quarters, when one chain shot from the enemy took off the heads of the Earl of Falmouth, Lord Musgrave, who some of you know as Muskerry, and Mister Richard Boyle, who was the Earl of Burlington's youngest son. The account is quite gruesome but Sir William Penn the Duke's flag captain chronicled us that with that one shot their blood and brains flew in the Duke's face, and the head of Mister Boyle actually struck the Duke."

Mrs Wilde, one of the guests, fanned her face. "Such brave men, I feel quite flushed from the telling of that."

Samuel continued, "My dear, all ended well, not for those unfortunates, may I add, but as the ships drew apart, the *Een-dracht* received a shot in her powder room and she exploded with such devastating force that we believe only five survived from her complement of hundreds. Our glorious fleet gradually gained the upper hand and the Dutch began to give way as the great war-ships of both fleets fouled each other and some caught fire. It is said that the Dutch lost at least seven ships that way. It is a tribute to the excellent seamanship of the enemy that they managed to make a strategic withdrawal towards the Dutch coast which they reached safely in the late evening after a battle that had raged for eighteen hours."

"What an account, Samuel, and what were our losses, do you have any details?" Roger asked.

"Actually we came off very well; we only lost one ship, the *Charity*, which was captured very early in the battle. Our total loss of life was two hundred and eighty-three killed and four hundred and forty wounded, whilst the enemy lost thirty-two ships. Un-fortunately, we took only nine of those as prizes, but the Dutch casualties – and this is only a provisional figure – amounted to about four thousand killed. We ended up taking two thousand prisoners." Samuel smiled. "And to celebrate our victory, I pur-chased a new silk suit. Elizabeth has chastised me for spending so freely, complaining that I bought one only a month ago, but I felt so excited and it made me feel good."

"Now, Samuel, you know you spend far too much on finery," Elizabeth scolded.

For another half hour the social talk continued, until finally

Mrs Turner and her daughter Joyce arrived by coach.

Samuel and Henry stood alone whilst Elizabeth made sure the seating arrangements were all correct before they adjourned for supper.

"The suit, Henry, was not my only extravagance to celebrate the naval victory," Samuel confided. "I also visited a pretty seamstress that I know. She gives me great pleasure. As an excuse I purchased some stockings from her husband and while he was searching the stockroom I managed a quick fumble." As he spoke, Samuel nudged Henry in the ribs with his elbow and gave him a wink.

Elizabeth, now satisfied with the arrangements, took Samuel's arm and led her guests to the table where they all dined well on venison pasty and several bottles of fine burgundy. Some drank more than others and it was rather late when a merry group finally left the "stone feast" to venture home. It was a very warm summer evening as Samuel escorted his guests to the Exchange, where they all took hackneys. It was a warm balmy June night as Samuel strolled back home; the guests and friends would not meet again for over a year, by then it would be in a London that would be transformed forever.

***

The plague hit Islington in July 1665. A well dressed escapee from a plaque house in Aldersgate Street tried in vain to gain admission at the Angel and the White Horse, in Islington. He then approached the Pied Horse where he claimed he was a traveller on his way to Lincolnshire and entirely free from infection. The man said he only required lodgings for one night, and, as it happened, that was all he needed.

The landlord, expecting cattle drovers the next day on the way to Smithfield market, said he had an empty bed in the garret for one night and a serving girl showed the infected man to the room. With a sigh the "traveller" sat on the bed and said to the girl, "I have seldom lain in such a poor lodging, my girl, but will make do as it is only for one night, and we live in such a dreadful time. Will you bring me a pint of warm ale, please?"

The serving girl closed the garret door, climbed down the stairs and promptly forgot the order.

Next morning when the owner asked what had become of

the gentleman, the maid appeared startled. "Bless me, sir, he requested warm ale, but I forgot it."

Joseph the labourer went up to the garret and opened the door, and found the traveller lying on the bed in a most frightful posture. His eyes were glazed, his jaw had fallen open and his clothes were pulled off as if in a fit. The cover of the bed was clasped hard in one hand. The plague had arrived. Fourteen died that week in Islington.

Meanwhile, Samuel had heard the news of the spread of the plague and decided that the city was too dangerous. He closed his home after sending Elizabeth over the river to the safer hamlet of Woolwich. Samuel took his work to Greenwich for the remainder of the summer.

July slipped into August and with it the heat increased, bringing the plague to epidemic proportions with three thousand two hundred and sixteen deaths in St Giles alone. Things were so bad even the brothels near the Drury Lane theatre closed through lack of customers.

Henry decided that he must also protect his family and so on Tuesday the 23rd of July, with the plague virtually on his doorstep, he hastily sent a messenger to the Black Swan in Holborn requesting two seats be reserved to Newark on the York coach that left at five every Thursday morning.

With Samuel out of town, Henry penned a letter stating his intention to leave London until the plague was over and if Samuel needed to contact him on business, he could be contacted by post at Ufton Manor. Henry then wrote a second letter to his father and dispatched it by a courier.

Suppertime at Ufton Manor two days later saw Robert in his library when he was disturbed by the sound of horse's hooves. Looking up, he gazed towards the entrance to the courtyard, where a horseman dismounted. Robert hurried to the front entrance, the man gasping for breath spoke, "Sir, I have an urgent letter from London, addressed for deliverance to Robert Cavendish." Robert took the letter, broke the seal and read…

Dearest Father,

First some good news for you and mother: you are now grandparents to James who is aged five months and quite a strong baby. My wife Jane is well and, God willing, we shall travel to visit you this week. You may be aware that this has been a long hot summer and a serious epidemic of the plague is in the city. The bad air that is its cause is coming nearer to our home. Yesterday there were new cases reported only two miles away so I have decided to leave London with my wife Jane and James on Thursday the 25th day of July and travel north on the York-bound coach. God willing, we shall disembark from the coach on Saturday 27th and stay at the Saracen's Head where I believe the Twentyman family keep a good house. I believe our majesty's father once slept there. If it pleases you, could you arrange for some transports to collect us on Monday the 29th to convey us from the Saracen's Head to Ufton Manor where our family can be united until this pestilence leaves our city. Until we meet, may I send felicitations to mother. I remain, sir,

Your obedient son
Henry.

Robert thanked the rider, gave him two shillings and dispatched him to the kitchens for refreshments and a night's rest.

Meanwhile in Newington Green, Henry arranged for two trunks to be packed, and then he sent a runner to William Usburn the hackney coach owner with a request to present himself with his coach at three o'clock on Thursday.

At dawn on the day, the coach arrived on time and William loaded the trunks while his passengers took their seats. An hour and a half later, during which baby James slept in Jane's arms, the coach pulled into the yard at the Black Swan. William helped his customers alight, then went to find the driver for the York staging coach and together they stored Henry's trunks onto that coach.

Just as the York driver was about to leave, William reached under the seat of his coach and said, "I have 'ere a package of cloth that is bound for Derbyshire. I 'ave been paid to deliver it to the driver of the York stage for carriage back to Derbyshire. It has to go to a tailor in Eyam, wherever that be, but I believe that the passengers I have just brought to you are bound for Newark and that they are travelling into Derbyshire, so maybe they will carry the parcel into that shire for you."

William handed the parcel of cloth to the driver who put it into the box under his seat and thanked William.

"I'll be leaving you now. That will be one shilling, sir. I hope the journey is not too hard for the little one."

Henry paid William, then turning to Jane, said, "Shall we take our seats?"

They had three men and two women as companions on the arduous journey and Henry hoped that the conversation would not be too boring. Prompt on the hour of five the staging coach left Holborn. It would take three days to reach Newark, and as they headed out on the road towards Cambridgeshire, the driver made three stops that first day, at Enfield, Ware and Buntingford, to change the horses. Finally, after a twenty-two-hour journey, they arrived at the George Inn in Huntingdon at a quarter before four in the morning. Wearily Henry tipped the driver and guard each a shilling before helping Jane and son James from the coach. Although it was such an early hour they adjourned into the inn for breakfast whilst the guard, the coachman and the horses were again changed. After an hour's rest and a brief wash to remove some of the travel dust, the weary passengers embarked to set off on the exhausting journey up to Stilton in Leicestershire.

It was about midday on the Friday that the coach pulled into the courtyard of the Bell Inn. Henry and Jane, wishing to observe the church tradition of a meatless day, shared a quarter of stilton cheese with wine and bread with the two other passengers before boarding the coach for the final leg of their journey. After passing through Grantham, they finally arrived in Newark at the Saracen's Head just after nine in the evening.

Henry helped a travel weary and dishevelled Jane from the coach. She had managed to pacify James who withstood the rigours of the journey surprisingly well as he had slept for most of the time.

The driver, an amiable man with ruddy cheeks, unloaded Henry's two trunks and deposited them on the cobbled yard and accepted Henry's tip. Then with an afterthought, he said, "I believe that you will be travelling on to the shire of Derby?"

"That's correct."

"Would you know of the village of Eyam? You see sir we have

a parcel on board to be delivered to that place. I don't know of it sir, but it's somewhere in Derbyshire and I thought would be near to your destination, otherwise, sir, we shall have to take it up to Sheffield and it can be delivered from there. It would be quicker if you could take it, sir, and maybe you could pass it on locally. That's actually what I mean, sir."

Henry smiled. "Yes, give me the parcel; I'm sure I can get it dispatched to the correct place."

"Its addressed to a Mr George Vicars, 'Tailor', Eyam, Derbyshire, I'm afraid it's a little damp from being under my seat for three days."

The driver handed Henry the wrapped parcel. Henry escorted Jane up to their room and promptly threw the parcel into a cold dark corner of the room then after having a wash he lay down on the bed while Jane gave James an evening feed. Making sure James was asleep the pair went down into the inn for a late supper of eels, a fat goose and mushrooms.

The weekend passed with the couple resting after their arduous journey. It was late on Monday morning when the sound of wheels heralded the arrival of a coach into the courtyard of the Saracen's Head. The driver reined in the horses and Robert sprang from the coach almost before it had stopped. "Look to the horses, Tom. Make sure they are watered and rubbed down, and get the landlord to accommodate you in the stables. I think we shall delay our return until the morrow."

Robert turned and embraced Henry. "Good to see you, my boy, you're putting on weight." Robert gave Henry a fatherly jab in the stomach. "Now let's look to your wife and this grandson of mine. How is he? It's no journey on which to bring a baby but I suppose the devil must ride when he calls the tune, eh, my boy?" Henry hadn't had chance to utter a word as Robert put his arm around his shoulder and side by side they went into the inn.

During the course of that day Robert got to know his daughter-in-law and expressed to Henry that in his opinion he had chosen well and that Jane seemed a delightful, intelligent and lovely young lady and with regards to James, Robert was thrilled to be a grand father. After dinner and while the three enjoyed a wine, Robert posed the question, "And who are the godparents to James?"

83

Before Henry could answer, Jane said, "We have good friends in London, a family named Pepys, so we asked them to do us the honour."

Henry volunteered more information: "Samuel Pepys is a business associate of mine. He is very well placed at the Navy Office and has friends at court, so we thought as a couple they would be our best choice for godparents. Even though Elizabeth his wife is sometimes sickly, she has a good nature."

"Very suitable, I'm sure," commented Robert. "And what of your family, Jane? With a name such as Chouart, you must be of French origin?"

"Papa is French. He is, I believe, a titled aristocrat in his own country. His title is Médard Chouart, Sieur Des Groseilliers, which I believe is the equivalent of an English knight. My mother is English and named Constance. Mother met father in Paris when she was an English tutor to a French family. They became lovers, unfortunately she became pregnant. He told her he wouldn't marry her as he had too much taste for adventure in his blood, so he could never settle down and become a dutiful husband. Mother loved him and accepted the fact he was an adventurer and she could never hold the father of her child."

Robert listened in silence as Jane took a sip of wine before continuing, "I was born in Paris in sixteen forty-six and mother came home to London. For propriety, mother claimed that she was a widow; whilst father, always a free spirit, sailed with his brother-in-law Pierre-Esprit Radisson to the New World."

"What an interesting story," said Robert. "Your father must have been a very adventurous but callous man."

"Oh there are lots more stories to tell you. Mother has told me that apparently two years after I was born, Papa wrote his first letter to her; it was to say that he had arrived in the French colony known as New France. He wrote that it was a particularly bad time. The letter mentioned a war with the natives that they call Indians. The letters from Papa continued to arrive once a year and in one later letter he wrote that while some tribes of Indians are friendly, one savage tribe called the Iroquois waged war for about five years. Apparently the valley where Papa lived was near a place called Quebec and was not a safe place for white men. Papa wrote that the Iroquois warriors used to lurk near the settlements and no hunter, wood gatherer or trapper was safe. But it's safe now, Papa writes to say those bad days are long gone and although mother and I have not seen him for some years, he sends correspondence and financial support for our home in London."

"How amazing," Robert declared. "My son Henry certainly seems to have chosen a bride from a family with character and free spirit."

"One letter, written in September 'fifty-six, said that Papa had taken friendly Indians in canoes and explored somewhere called Lake Superior. The exploration took two years to complete and when he returned he was escorting fifty canoes carrying a fortune in beaver furs."

"So your father is making a fortune in fur trade."

"I suppose that's correct, but we only received a small allowance. Mother had a letter from him last year with news that was already four years old. It seems that in sixteen fifty-nine, Papa and Pierre made another exploration on to Lake Superior; when they sailed back to the trading post the following year, they had another fortune in furs but then disaster struck."

Jane paused to reflect in her mind's eye the events that had befallen her father before continuing, "Papa's letter went on to say that he was put in gaol and his furs were confiscated by the French Governor for illegal trading with the Indians without a licence. When Papa was finally released, he wrote to say that because of his bad treatment by his own countrymen he went down to offer his services to the English at somewhere called Port Royal in Nova Scotia. The letter we received last year was already two years old and written in sixteen hundred and sixty two; Papa and his brother-in-law, Pierre-Esprit Radisson, were then in Boston trying to get support from the English traders for another trading expedition back into this place called Hudson Bay."

"You speak of places that we country folk have never heard of and can scarcely understand. I find it so interesting. I suppose that is why they call it the New World," said Robert.

And so the conversation continued with the day passing as the family got to know each other and Henry caught up on news and gossip.

Next morning, Robert determined to make an early start, had the coach ready and he was settling the bills. The group where entering the coach as Tom secured their baggage when Henry paused, turned and shouted to Tom, "Wait a moment, I have forgotten something."

Henry raced back inside, climbed the stairs two at a time and flung open the bedroom door; in the dark corner lay the corded parcel, Henry gathered it, and with a quick glance around to make sure nothing else was left, he closed the door and hurried back to the coach.

He strolled quickly over to Tom who was holding the coach door for him. "Tom, this parcel is to go to a tailor in Eyam; I believe that's about twenty-five miles from Limbury, so perhaps some local rider can deliver it? Can you put it in the box under your seat?"

"Certainly, Master Henry"

Henry smiled. Tom never could get used to addressing him as Mister Henry.

Henry climbed into his seat. Tom closed the door, threw the parcel under his seat then picking up the reins headed the coach on the road to Alfreton then up to Limbury. It was late afternoon as Tom drove into the courtyard at Ufton Manor.

Elizabeth was sitting in the drawing room when she heard the coach approaching down the lane; getting to her feet, she got to the front door and was in the yard, shuffling from one foot to the other to relieve a little of the arthritic pain that was troubling her in her middle years when the coach finally halted and Henry leapt down. She opened her arms and threw them around his neck before finally giving him a kiss on the cheek.

"Mother, you are making a fuss in front of the servants," he said, but let her embrace him for a few moments longer. Then as she pulled away he said, "Let me introduce my wife Jane."

Jane nervously eyed her mother-in-law and held out a hand, which Elizabeth took gently, then she parted the baby's shawl and exclaimed, "So this is our little James Cavendish? When we get inside I want to hold my grandson and you can tell me all about what my son has been up to these past months. Do you know there's hardly been a letter from him these last two years? I admit, he did write to say he got married and that he was investing in the tobacco trade, but I want to hear everything."

86

Elizabeth took Jane by the arm and led her and the family into the house, leaving Tom to arrange for the trunks to be brought inside. In the excitement, the parcel lay forgotten, damp and neglected under the coach seat.

Next morning, Tom had risen at five and was cleaning the coach when he found the parcel. Putting it aside, he completed the cleaning then he went over to the manor house and managed to speak with Henry just as he was going in to breakfast. "That package, Master Henry, do you want me to take one of the horses and ride over to Eyam with it? It will take me all day there and back. If I leave in the next hour, as it's only seven, I should be back by nightfall providing I have fair weather. I don't believe Mister Robert has any special task for me today."

Henry thought for a moment than gave Tom his permission.

Tom saddled up Brutus, an old quarter horse, and taking the parcel, which was still damp, he placed it in a saddle bag and cantered off towards Chesterfield and then on to Eyam.

Unwittingly, he was about to deliver a potential time bomb to the village of Eyam.

The Parcel

It was past noon when Tom, riding at a leisurely pace, entered the outskirts of Eyam and immediately saw the church. Reining in at the lichgate, Tom noticed a gravedigger trimming the grass round a Saxon cross carved with pagan and Christian symbols.

Tom hailed him. "Good day, my good fellow, I have a package for a George Vicars, could you be telling me were I can find a person of that name?"

The gravedigger straightened his back, "Aye, and a good day to you, sir." The man paused, scratching his head in thought. "I think the fellow you want be a journeyman to our tailor at Mary Cooper's cottage, or I should say Mary Hadfield as she is now named. You see, she's got herself a new husband. A tailor named Alexander Hadfield. She lives with him and her own two sons. I believe the journeyman is this George Vicars you want, he works for Mister Hadfield. Anyway enough of this gossip, that's the Cooper cottage, the middle one of the three." The man pointed with his soiled hand. "Past this church, on the right."

Tom thanked him. "One more question, is there a tavern nearby were I can take an ale or two before I depart?"

"Aye, sir, if you ride back down the lane to the square and take yon lane by the bull ring on the left, up there be the King's Head. It lies up behind this church. It's the only ale house we have, it were built back in the thirties before we had trouble with that Cromwell fellow. My father said he remembers it being built for the lads when they'd done a day's work and came down from the lead mines."

Tom thanked the man again and rode off. He tethered Brutus outside the Derbyshire stone cottage and then knocked on the door. After a few moments' delay, the door was opened by a small woman dressed in the style of a black puritan dress with a white collar.

"Good day, mam, is this the Cooper cottage? I have here a parcel from London for a George Vicars, does he live here?"

At that moment the door opened wider and a tall young man came into view.

"I am George Vicars. We have been expecting that parcel of cloth." The man took the parcel and said, "Thank you very much."

"It's a little damp, I'm afraid," Tom apologised.

"No matter, we can dry it in front of the fire."

The woman had remained silent but now she spoke up. "Come in and rest awhile and have some refreshment."

"No thank you, mam, I am expected back in Limbury this evening. I shall retire to the Kings Head and partake of a flagon of ale and a short rest."

Tom knuckled his forehead in a farewell gesture and walked Brutus through the village, letting him drink at one of the stone troughs.

As he walked the lane Tom took deep breaths of the fresh country air, admiring the view of the hillside rising majestically behind the village, finally tethering Brutus outside the ale house.

Entering a low beamed room, he addressed the inn keeper. "Good day, sir, I'm travel weary and in need of a flagon of ale and a platter of bread and cheese if you would be so kind."

An hour later, a refreshed Tom mounted Brutus and headed back home, unaware of the time bomb he had just delivered on Tuesday the first of September 1665. It was the day the plague came to Eyam.

***

Inside the Cooper home George opened the parcel, unrolled the bundle of cloth and laid it before the fire to dry.

"This will soon dry out, Mary; I can start cutting your new dress tomorrow." George resumed his seat and continued to work to finish off other garments. For three hours he worked.

Mary sat quietly in the corner of the room, her two sons, Edward and Jonathon, were playing in the garden at the rear. Alexander, her new husband, was the village tailor. She considered she was fortunate to have remarried a tradesman when her first husband had died leaving her a widow with two children. Her husband was away today visiting a nearby village and a few farms, delivering dresses for the ladies and some working clothes for the men folk.

Mary's thoughts were interrupted as Edward came in from the garden. Mary sat for a few more moments as George's diligent fingers sewed with the speed of a craftsman then she rose from her seat. "I'll be getting supper ready," she said. "Alexander will be home soon."

Her husband came home later than expected. "Supper's on the table, I suppose you stopped off at the Kings Head for a wet or two," Mary grumbled. "Come sit thee down, George, and leave that sewing for now."

George rose, scratching his leg; it felt like a flea bite on his calf. Next morning, he laid the new cloth out to start cutting. He worked all day and by evening the dress was almost complete. Mary slipped it over her head and George made some adjustments.

That evening, the family sat at the supper table, but George picked at his food.

"You don' look too good, George," Alexander commented, "and yer not eating much of Ma's broth."

"I don't feel good and that's the truth, I feel hot and yet a little shivery and so thirsty."

"'Ere, George, have a swill of ale."

George took the jug from Alexander and drank deeply, and then wiping his lips with the back of his hand, he gave the flagon back.

"What's wrong, George?" Jonathon asked. "You look all pink and sweaty."

Next morning George was worse, he had a temperature and stayed in his bed refusing food and just sipping at wine to relieve his thirst. By the Friday, George was delirious with bouts of diarrhoea and vomiting and his neck was swollen. Mary was desperate for help and sent word to the vicar that her lodger was seriously ill.

William Mompesson, the vicar, called late on Saturday evening. By that time George was haemorrhaging from his mouth and nose and he had a swelling in his groin. William stepped back in horror, realizing what he was witnessing.

Hurriedly he made his way into the main room of the cottage.

"I fear that your lodger will not last the night, Mary. I believe that we have a case of the plague and neither you nor any of your family can leave the cottage. I will arrange for food and liquids to be left at your door but until this pestilence is passed you must stay inside. I will inform your neighbours at service on the morrow." William made a fast exit from the cottage.

On the Sunday, William Mompesson stood in the Jacobean pulpit to the north side of the chancel; to his left and right rose the majestic Norman columns, gaunt reminders of the historical past of this fine church.

"In the name of our Father, and the Son and the Holy Ghost, pleased be seated." William's voice reverberated through the church. "Before we begin our devotions today, I have a serious announcement to make." William paused as he struggled to find the correct words. "Some here may have heard the rumours; I fear that we have plague in our community."

There was a gasp of horror in the congregation coupled with some cries of anguish.

William continued, "Now we must all maintain our Christian values in this time of sickness. I shall meet after the service today with Thomas Stanley who served you well as your previous minister in the church. Thomas and I shall find a way to meet this tribulation but for now I suggest that no one leaves the village. You must all go to your homes and try to avoid contact with other families. Talk to each other from distances apart. We have time on our side, for it is now in the month of September, the hot summer is behind us and the foul air that carries this pestilence will be cooling with the approach of winter. Now with God's help and blessing, we shall pass through these times. I have to announce that all church services until further notice will be held in the valley at Cucklett Delf. And now after the blessing I think we should all go to our homes and pray."

William gave a brief prayer and blessed the community. The congregation rose; mothers protectively gathered their children and hurriedly they left the church. That Sunday, there was no dallying or waiting to speak to neighbours, everyone was avoiding contact, in the community of Eyam, fear reigned supreme on that Sabbath.

Forever known as Black Monday in Eyam, the seventh of September sixteen hundred and sixty five was the day the Eyam plague claimed its first victim, the day George Vicars died.

Fifteen days later, the fleas again sent out the Grim Reaper to claim their second victim; it was Edward, Mary's youngest son.

By the end of October, another twenty-seven villagers were dead. Panic took hold as some of the wealthier families began to leave the village.

Although it was late autumn and the onset of winter would see a decline in the deaths, William Mompesson and Thomas Stanley thought it necessary to call a meeting in the valley at Cucklett Delf.

William began with a prayer, then speaking with an authoritative voice he informed the villagers that the Lord had called on them for acts of self-sacrifice to avoid the spread of the pestilence to other villages. The villagers listened in silence as he spoke of the consequences of the plaque scourging the countryside if it escaped from Eyam.

With a final shout and raising his arms toward the heavens, William cried, "Eyam must be quarantined. We must all act with courage and self-discipline and not go beyond the village boundary stones."

The villagers took in his words, and then in twos and threes they nodded in agreement. William gave his blessing and the congregation dispersed quietly to their homes.

Eyam was a mere fifteen miles away from Chatsworth House. The Earl of Devonshire was in residence when news of the Eyam plaque and the brave decision of the villagers reached him. He knew the plight of the villagers was desperate and immediately arranged for donations of food and medical supplies to be delivered and arranged for them to be left at a safe distance at the boundary stones to the village. Neighbouring villages now realized the selfless action that the Eyam residents had taken and also rallied to donate essential items.

***

The weeks slipped by and the Grim Reaper continued to claim his toll. One Sunday afternoon during a service in the valley, Emmott Sydall, a girl from Eyam, saw a glimpse of her lover from a neighbouring village; his name was Rowland Torre. For safety, he was standing amongst the rocks away from the worshippers. The lovers blew kisses to each other and by signs arranged to meet later.

In order to respect the quarantine the couple refrained from physical contact but called to each other across the rocks, planning their life together when the good times returned.

Some evenings as they lay in the shelter of the rocks they pretended they were in each other's arms... So winter drifted into the spring.

***

Tom had long since returned to Limbury unaware of the lethal consequences of his delivery.

The Black Death

Life at Ufton Manor returned to normal with Robert and Elizabeth enjoying their newly acquired family while Henry and Jane settled down to the relaxed country life. September drifted into October, and word reached Limbury and Wingfield that the plague, or Black Death as it came to be known, had struck in Eyam. No association was made at that stage to the delivery of the parcel of cloth, although in future years Tom often told of the time when he'd been in Eyam just seven days before the plague struck.

One Sunday after church, Henry confided in Jane, "Father tells me that my grand parents first met in this church. She was called Sylvia, the daughter of the vicar of the parish."

Jane listened then added, "It would be fitting if we had James baptized again here, although I know we had a baptism ceremony in London with Samuel and Elizabeth as godparents. Perhaps we could speak with the vicar to enquire if we can have some form of ceremony in this old church with its family connections and this time Robert and Elizabeth can be present."

Although not initially condoned by the bishop; after a suitable donation had been made to his diocese, Henry and Robert managed to convince him that it was in James' interest to have a further baptismal ceremony in the church of his heritage at Limbury.

***

There was not much of a festive season for the residents in Eyam in 1665; the death rate continued, although at a reduced

94

pace, with two victims on Christmas Eve and nine more during the first month into the New Year.

However with the advent of spring there was freshness in the air, the daisies and buttercups were giving a floral crown in the meadow and the spirits of the villagers began to rise. Maybe the worst was over.

Emmott made her way to Cucklett Delf to speak with Rowland. "I love you, Rowland. When this pestilence leaves us, and if God spares us, we will marry, will we not?"

"Most certainly, my dear sweet Emmott, for I love you and so miss our times when we were lovers and could hold each other and touch."

The couple continued to talk across the rocks and spoke of how they would make love to each other forever when the plague was over. Emmott shouted her farewells and turned to leave her lover. Rowland watched as she walked away back towards Eyam. He never saw her again. Five days later, the Grim Reaper claimed her.

Through that summer the plague caused the deaths of another five members of Emmott Sydall's family.

The self-imposed quarantine held well with only one violation. A woman from Eyam broke the rules to go to market day in the nearby village of Tideswell. She was identified and had to flee for her life under a hail of stones.

It was into August when the epidemic peaked.

On the outskirts of the village lay Riley's Farm, managed by Elizabeth Hancock and her husband who farmed the land. The farm was isolated and the Hancock family assumed they were reasonably safe from the pestilence. Then, early one morning, Elizabeth got a cry for help from a neighbour's wife. She had lost all her family and her husband had just died. Elizabeth couldn't refuse a neighbour in distress so she went to help bury the woman's husband.

Sadly Elizabeth carried the plague back into her home. Although not infected herself, within a week Elizabeth had to personally bury her husband and six of her children, all lost to the pestilence.

On the twenty-fifth of August tragedy struck at the rectory itself. The vicar, who had been the advocate for quarantine, lost his wife Katherine Mompesson. William's wife died in his arms; she was aged twenty-eight and the two hundred and eighth victim.

***

During the troubles, news from the outside world was sparse and mainly conveyed to the survivors in Eyam by shouting it from the boundary stones; so when William Mompesson received a September copy of the *London Gazette* from the Earl of Devonshire it was to contain news that was to shock the village.

On Sunday the twenty-third of September William Mompesson, who was still in state of grief for his wife, announced from his makeshift pulpit, "Before we begin our devotions here today in Cucklett Delf, a valley that is decked in the beautiful autumn colours that remind us that we are in God's countryside, I have to inform you that I received today a copy of the *London Gazette* with news of the events of the third to the tenth of September. I am sorry to have to inform you that God has laid his mighty hand and devastated the city of London."

The congregation remained silent, some gazing with fear in their eyes at the thought of hearing of more terrible news of a new pestilence.

"The terrible news I bear is that a great fire; believed to have started in the King's bakery in Pudding Lane on the second day of this month, has raged for almost five days and destroyed most of London. Praise to God, their majesties are safe but there are thousands of homeless people. I ask that in our prayers today, we ask for a deliverance from our suffering from the plague, but let us also pray for the poor and homeless in London."

With that announcement William led the congregation in their devotions.

***

At the time the news of the London fires reached Chatsworth, the *London Gazette* news sheet also reached Ufton Manor.

"This is a disaster," Robert exclaimed as he read the paper. "Is not your house near to Islington? It says in the paper that with so many homeless in London, thousands are fleeing the city for safety. The *Gazette* says that there are thousands watching the city burn as they camp on the high ground at Moorefield, Parliament Hill and Islington."

Henry had already absorbed the news and was gazing out of the window, deep in thought. He turned towards Robert. "You are correct father; we should be getting back to our house. During the last year while we have been living here, I have maintained my business contacts by letters, but now the plague is over, well, there will be a lot of work to do."

"And money to be made," added Robert. "I have been thinking, Henry. It's a long time since I was in London and after this latest catastrophe, their will be a need for a lot of rebuilding and there will be opportunities to invest." Robert paused. "If you agree, I can travel to London with you all. I suggest we use my coach. Old Tom can drive and bring the coach back or if you can find stabling for the coach and horses, Tom can bring me back home in a few weeks."

Arrangements were completed, Elizabeth was to remain in Ufton and on Monday the fourth of October 1666 the travellers set forth from Ufton Manor leaving a tearful Elizabeth languishing at being parted from her grandson and family.

***

The onset of autumn witnessed the countryside flushed with multi-shades of amber as October drifted into November. The plague in Eyam ran its course and claimed its last victim. Two hundred and sixty villagers had died out of a total of three hundred and fifty inhabitants.

Tom never realized his lucky escape from the plague. He had left Limbury; he was on his way to London.

London Rebuilt

The journey to London was uneventful, but on the afternoon of the third day, as the coach mounted the hill at Southgate, the travellers got their first sight of the destruction to the great city caused by the fire. Tom pulled rein and halted the coach, and the occupants dismounted to get a better view and absorb the magnitude of the disaster. The blackened area of what had been London was spread before them. What had been a vast city area was now an area of black acrid-smelling, twisted, half-charred timbers pointing like black chagrined fingers towards the sky. Here and there an odd movement could be seen as scavengers and looters sifted through the remains to salvage anything of value; over the scene of destruction there hung a veil of silence.

The travellers took their seats once more and the coach moved off at a walking pace. Inside, Robert, Henry and Jane remained silent, stunned at what they had seen.

It was dusk as Tom finally drew rein in Newington Green. After safely carrying their trunks into the house, Tom accompanied Henry as they walked the coach and horses across to the northeast corner of the green to Miller's farm.

Joan Miller, the woman who stood in the doorway of the farmhouse to greet them was middle aged and had the appearance of a hard-working country woman, her hands were slightly deformed with signs of early arthritis, her face showed signs of ageing and when she spoke, it could be seen that one incisor was missing with the rest showing varying signs of decay.

"Good evening, Master Henry. What can I do for you? We

thought you'd left for good, it must be a year or more since we set eyes on you."

Henry nodded, "It has indeed, but first may I introduce Tom my father's coachman?"

Tom stepped forward, cap in hand. "Pleased to meet you, mam."

Joan smiled and gave a brief welcome as Henry continued, "Well, as you know, Mistress Miller, we left to flee from the pestilence, we were lucky. I took my family up to Derbyshire, where we have been living with my parents, but now we are back and never expected the sights we have just seen. The fire, it must have been frightening for you and the crowds fleeing the fire. Did you not get robbed or molested living here all alone?"

"Why, no, sir, most of the people stayed up on the common at Islington; not many ventured down here. But the sights, oh Lord, the heavens were lit as if it were day, and the smell. You could smell the smoke, for weeks. Even now, it's still in the air. I've heard the king nearly lost Whitehall and the Tower to the fire. It's said that the guards at the Tower used gunpowder to blow up some houses to stop the fire reaching it. We heard the explosions up here. People hereabouts say its God's vengeance for all the loose morals of the day." Joan shook her head sadly, "Anyway Master Henry, enough of this gossip, it is just nice to have you back all safe and well and that's a fact. How are Mistress Jane and the baby?"

Eventually, when all the news was exchanged, Henry got to the purpose of his visit, "I have a request, Mistress Miller. My father and Old Tom here are staying for a few weeks and our house has no stabling facilities. Could we pay to graze the horses in your pasture and keep the coach on your land? Tom will come over and groom them of course."

With agreements made and money paid, Henry left Tom to walk the horses over into the field.

During the course of the next week, Henry soon discovered that most of the business and social establishments including the coffee meeting houses had been destroyed in the fire, although a few nearer to Whitehall had survived. Consequently it took him some time to re-establish his business connections before he began to put his affairs in some semblance of order. He called at

Samuel's house in Seething Lane only to find it locked and unin-
habited. Further enquiries with Henry's business associates also
came to nothing. Nobody had seen or heard of Samuel for some
time. There was no knowledge as to whether he had survived the
plague or the fire.

Henry was at a loss. In the evenings Jane and Robert spent
time with him in the drawing room sitting round the fire and talking about the day's events and trying to offer some support and
hope for his depressed mind after what they had all seen of the
devastation and the attempts to start the rebuilding of the city.

One evening as the conversation lapsed; Robert drew Jane
into conversing about her adventurous father.

"I hear from Henry that at the moment your father is living in
London. Is he staying with your mother?"

"To both your questions; the answer is yes, mother said he
could stay and have a room while in London. It was a great surprise to us when he arrived after all the years of separation. The
explanation for his visit is that he made an expedition back to the
Hudson Bay from Boston but it was aborted. The Boston traders
in New England then persuaded father to bring a report with his
proposals to London. That is why he came home to mother just
before the Great Fire. At the moment Papa is trying to gather support for a new expedition back to Hudson Bay."

"So you see your father regularly?"

"Of course, and now I have you, Robert, it seems I have two
Papas."

Jane fluttered her eyelashes and Robert beamed with pleasure.

A week later, Henry and Robert paid a visit to the Theatre
Royal in Bridges Street. The theatre had been closed for eighteen
months during the plague; it had then survived the fire. When
Henry and Robert entered the theatre just before three, Henry
noticed that since his last visit with Samuel Pepys back in 'sixty-
four it had undergone renovation.

He guided Robert to one of the green baize benches in the
pit.

"I hope that you will not be too uncomfortable father, these
benches have no rear supports and they play havoc with the back
but these are the only seats available as it is rumoured that the

King may visit the theatre today."

"Don't worry, Henry, these seats in the pit are fine, the floor slopes, so we shall be able to view the actors and see the stage perfectly."

Robert noticed a serving wench approaching. The young girl was wearing a full skirt and low-cut blouse that displayed her firm breasts to their best advantage. On her arm she carried a basket of lemons and oranges. "Buy an orange, sir, six pennies each?"

Henry took out his purse and selected two sixpences.

"Thank you kindly, sir. Enjoy the play," said the girl, and with a flick of her head she turned to serve another customer.

"A very comely wench," remarked Robert.

"Behave father, most of the orange girls sell their charms as well as oranges. The King's new mistress Nell Gwynne was an orange seller here. It is said her charms caught the King's eye, but after he had bedded her, he discovered that she also had a ready wit so he used his influence to have her promoted to some leading roles, and now Mistress Nell is the talk of the court."

At that moment the theatre audience rose to its feet as a group of personages entered a prominent box on the first gallery. The party was led by the king escorted by his favourite mistress Barbara Villiers, Countess of Castlemaine and his chief minister Edward Hyde, the first Earl of Clarendon. The audience applauded. Charles, making a slight bow to acknowledge the adulation of his subjects, took his seat and the audience resumed theirs. The play *The Humorous Lieutenant* commenced.

As the first act drew to its conclusion, Henry and Robert rose to exercise their cramped limbs when in the far aisle Henry saw Samuel accompanied by his wife Elizabeth.

"Father, I have seen Mister Pepys, my good friend and colleague. I would like you to meet him. Mister Pepys works in the Navy Office and is highly thought of by the Lords of the Admiralty."

Henry guided Robert across the theatre towards Samuel. "Good day, Samuel. It is nice to see you again after all this time. May I introduce my father, Mister Robert Cavendish."

Robert shook Samuel's hand and then made the politest of bows to accept Elizabeth's offered hand.

101

"And what do you make of our city, Mister Cavendish, after the fire?"

"It will need a lot of planning, Mister Pepys, a lot of planning," said Robert, "But it will be a chance to design a new city with wide open parks and a magnificent new Saint Paul's Cathedral."

"I hear the king is commissioning the architect Christopher Wren to submit plans, but I fear it's going to take years to rebuild." Then turning to Henry Samuel added, "There is talk of a new business venture that may benefit us both, Henry. It may come to nought but we need some investment and we need to arrange a meeting to discuss matters." Turning to Robert he said, "Maybe you have some available funds to invest, Mister Cavendish? It's doing no good locked up in Derbyshire."

Robert was taken aback but regained his composure. "I suppose I could look at any proposal whilst I am in town. I intend to travel back home before the festive season in December."

"Good fellow." Pepys slapped his hand on Robert's shoulder. "Then I shall leave it with Henry to arrange a meeting."

With cheerful farewells, they bade good day and returned to their seats for the completion of the play.

New Investments

Jane was tending to James's needs on the Monday morning as Henry was sitting down to breakfast with Robert; their meal was interrupted by the delivery of a note. Henry broke the seal and read the contents. "Do you recall when we were at the theatre and I introduced you to Mister Pepys?"

Robert nodded.

"Well, he is requesting for us to meet him at eleven tomorrow at Will's Coffee House. I know the establishment very well for it is a favourite coffee house for Samuel due to its proximity to the Admiralty."

After breakfast Henry stepped out onto the green, he found a runner and requested him to find a hackney coach to convey Robert and himself into the city. An hour later a coach arrived and on the way, Henry explained to Robert that he had brought his father away from the house so they could have a quiet day together to discuss the possibilities for expanding Henry's investments and how Robert could become involved. Eventually the coach pulled up in White Hall.

"So this is the place were the Parliamentarians executed the old king," Robert said as he stood outside the high-fronted stone building. "It seemed a drastic action to get rid of the king but then I suppose the man was a tyrant and caused a civil war."

The pair continued to engage in conversation as they took a short stroll down to the river. "It's such a pleasant autumn day Robert, let's take a barge down the Thames to the Tower."

All that day they discussed their finances and finally each

agreed the amount they could safely afford to invest if Samuel's proposals were acceptable.

Rising early, Henry was in the hall and about to take advantage of the quiet of the early morning to take a stroll around the green before breakfast when he was joined by Robert. The pair stepped outside and immediately their breath was transformed into willow wraiths on the freezing morning air.

"It's a damn cold morning, Robert; I fear we shall be in for a hard winter again."

As they strolled, Robert reminisced of his young days but finally Henry interrupted, "I suppose those were turbulent times, eh, father?"

"Indeed they were, son. Mother used to say she never knew if there was a warrant issued to arrest your grand father and the family. Thankfully those days are now long gone."

Henry and Robert strolled back to the house and an hour later Tom went to Miller's farm to prepare the carriage. The cold morning air had stiffened the harness and it was some time before Tom's arthritic fingers managed to harness the horses and the carriage finally drew up at Henry's door.

Henry had been watching from the window and opened the front door as Tom applied the brake, climbed down and unfolded the steps for Henry and Robert to take their seats for the short journey to White Hall.

The pair sat side by side with woollen blankets around their legs for warmth; Robert gave a shiver and Henry grew concerned. "Father, I realize Derbyshire woollen blankets are good to ward off the chill in the home but during these cold winters, which seem to be becoming more frequent, well, to put it politely you're not a young man, you are almost sixty and need to take care of your health. You need to purchase some animal furs for your carriage journeys. Furs are more expensive but you must take care of yourself and mother. Maybe this cold morning is an omen to tell us to invest in Samuel's scheme in the fur trade."

Robert remained silent.

***

Tom drove the carriage carefully, letting the horses navigate around any rotten or burnt timbers still lying in the lanes. One fortuitous spin-off from the great fire was that there was a lack of rotting rubbish or sewage in the roads. All that bore witness to were houses had stood were the charcoaled black outlines marking the foundations. Some residents had returned and erected wooden stakes and woven latticework over their old foundations and daubed the latticework with a mixture of mud and straw to provide temporary shelter and wind breaks from the elements. Everywhere poor homeless people were wandering, each trying to come to terms with the disaster and wondering how or when the city would come to life again.

As the coach manoeuvred the lanes, the burnt areas finally gave way to stone buildings of the city centre and Whitehall came in sight, Tom reined in the horses at Will's Coffee House, jumped down and lowered the step for Robert and Henry to step onto the road.

"It's nearly eleven, Tom; we shall be here for about two hours. Find some rest place for yourself and the horses and return at one o'clock."

"Very good, Master Robert sir," Tom said. He climbed back onto the driving seat and drove the coach to a grassed area where other coachmen were waiting for their masters.

Meanwhile Henry and Robert entered the coffee house; Robert was immediately impressed at the height and length of the room, and as he looked around, his eyes were drawn to the far end corner where logs were burning and crackling in the fireplace. The aroma of roasted coffee beans filled the air. Robert could see several people preparing the beverages for the serving girls.

Finding a vacant table in the window, the pair took a seat, and almost immediately a serving girl approached their table. "Two pots of your best coffee," Henry ordered. The girl nodded and returned a few moments later with two steaming pots of coffee "That will be three pence, sir."

"And a penny for you, my girl," Henry said as he pulled out his purse.

"That seems a strange habit to be paying for someone to bring a drink to your table," commented Robert.

"It's a habit that has taken hold in the ale houses and coffee houses in London in the last two years.

"Very strange habits these Londoners have," Robert muttered.

"Father, you are becoming a disgruntled old man."

At that moment Henry saw Samuel entering the room and summoning the serving girl, Henry ordered another coffee.

Removing his coat and his high-crowned hat Samuel hung them on one of the wooden pegs, and sporting the splendour of his French wig he made his way to Henry's table.

After handshakes and an exchange of pleasantries, the three quietly drank their coffee while, careful not to be overheard; Samuel expounded his plans for new investments.

"I have heard that there is a French Aristocrat and adventurer named Médard Chouart, Sieur Des Groseilliers in London. Apparently he is on a mission to try to gain royal support for an English expedition to a place named Hudson Bay in the New World,"

Samuel paused as Robert looked askance at Henry who felt his own heart rate increase a beat or two before he imparted the news to Samuel, "I think you should know, this French adventurer that you mention is my wife's father. He has been in the New World for some years but I know that the French have treated him very badly; in fact the French Governor in Quebec practically robbed Médard Chouart of his profits from his last expedition."

Henry then proceeded to tell Samuel the full story as it had been told to Robert on that first family evening before the Eyam plague.

Samuel listened in silence; when Henry had finished, he leaned forward in his chair. "This could be good news for us," he said. "I hear Prince Rupert, the king's nephew, is extremely interested in the New World. I think you should arrange for me to meet with Jane's father, possibly at your house, Henry."

Samuel pulled a few sheets of paper from his jacket to consult his diary. "Today is the twenty-fourth of October and later I have to go to Whitehall to meet Mister Hayes, who is Prince Rupert's secretary. He is a very ingenious man, and one, I think, who will be fit to contract in friendship; although I cannot appear to be too involved in monetary ventures. Meanwhile, if you can arrange a meeting in the privacy of your home for next week with your father-in-law, this Médard Chouart, then the four of us can discuss his ideas and his plans. I will leave that to you, Henry, but let us remain circumspect. We do not want outsiders to become interested in this venture. Now, gentlemen, I must take my leave of you as it's almost on the hour of one and I must be in Whitehall at two and I am dining at the Old Swan."

Samuel rose, collected his coat and his high-crowned hat from the peg on the wall and departed, leaving Robert and Henry at the door just as Tom was returning with the coach.

Before Tom could climb down from his driving seat, Henry stepped forward and grasped the side of the coach. "Mister Cavendish and I will be strolling over to the Devil's Inn for our midday meal; if you follow us in the coach, Tom, you can find refreshment for yourself and we will be returning home at four."

Later that day, after some discussion with Jane in the comfort of their home, Henry drafted a letter to be delivered to Jane's father.

To Médard Chouart Sieur Des Groseilliers

Dear Father-in-law.

I hope that this correspondence finds you and Constance in good health. If it pleases you perhaps we may have the pleasure of your company accompanied by Constance to dinner at seven on Wednesday 31st day of October 1666.

I am given to understand that you are trying to gather support for a new expedition to Hudson Bay in New France and it may be that with my connections at the Navy Office and in Whitehall I may be able to open some portals for you. These matters can be discussed after dinner when the gentlemen retire to the smoking room.

Your daughter Jane is well and looks forward to greeting you and Constance to our home.

I remain, sir,

Your obedient son-in-law
Henry.

The letter was dispatched by messenger to Constance's house in Islington where Médard Chouart was in residence. The following day Henry and Jane received acceptance to the invitation. Immediately Henry penned an invitation to Samuel and his wife and dispatched it by messenger to Samuel's home in Seething Lane.

Prince Rupert

Sunday worship at St. Mary's was over. Jane and Henry, accompanied by Robert, slowly strolled home for supper. Cook had prepared the meal and the next hour fled past as the three became absorbed in family conversation.

Finally the three rose from the table as Robert took hold of Jane's arm and said, "I think that you have made a good family home here in London. I can sense the feeling of love in this house and it comes from you, Jane."

Jane blushed and kissed Robert on the cheek then left the room to put baby James to bed whilst Henry and Robert retired to the smoking room. Henry was lighting his pipe when Jane returned; she came over and sat at his side.

He gave a sigh of satisfaction and turning to Jane said, "I was reminding Robert of your father's letters describing the wealth and richness of the furs from the area of Hudson Bay."

"Yes, I know all that, Henry, but I can't see how Prince Rupert can influence an expedition to the New World, but then I am only a woman and can't know of such matters."

"Father, I was too young to know of the Prince's exploits in the war against Parliament; what do you know of his background?"

Robert, who had recently been introduced to pipe smoking, tapped out the contents of his pipe onto the hearth, refilled his bowl and knowing he had Henry's full attention spoke softly in the manner of a storyteller relating local folklore.

"As far as I know, and this is only from my contacts at Chatsworth, Charles the First, who was executed, had a sister named

Elizabeth who was married to the King of Bohemia. They had a son who is our Prince Rupert but due to unrest, the family was forced to flee to the Netherlands where Rupert spent his childhood. As a young man he fought in the Thirty Years War and that gave him his military experience, which made him the best general in the royalist army. I am told that he was a dashing commander of cavalry; however, he had a weakness, the rank and file loved him, but he made enemies of almost every senior commander. He may have been dashing and heroic but he was impetuous. In the first major battle of the war at Edgehill, Rupert led a cavalry charge that completely routed the enemy but he pursued them beyond the battlefield and lost the chance to inflict a decisive defeat on the rebel army. He was vindicated later when he made a spectacular attack to relieve the siege at York but he again threw the advantage away when he was defeated by a parliamentary army at Marston Moor, which resulted in the loss of the whole of the north of England."

Henry had been listening intently and now said, "He seems to have had a very chequered career in the service of the old king. I hope he is not impetuous in business matters. If we are to invest, we need a firm hand at the helm."

"That is quite a naval expression you seem to have acquired, Henry, but my instincts concur with you. My aptitude for business and investment matters are poor so we shall have to tread carefully. Anyway, I will finish recalling what I know of Rupert and then you will have the full portrait of the man. After his defeat on Marston Moor, Prince Rupert convinced Charles to march from his base in Oxford and attempt to regain some of the north with an attack to relieve Chester, but Oliver Cromwell was a wily old commander and deployed his troops in delaying tactics until the army could re-muster. The king became indecisive and changed his battle plans several times; Charles even split his army to send three thousand men towards Bristol. While all that was going on, Prince Rupert attacked and pillaged Leicester with such fury that Sir Thomas Fairfax gave up his siege at Oxford and marched part of the army north to avenge Leicester. He joined forces with Cromwell at Naseby."

"You're very well versed in the events of parliament's war with the king, Papa."

"Living in Derbyshire, Jane, so far away from the city of London, can be mundane but it does give me time to read and glean reports of the changes that have taken place in England in my lifetime and it is an interest I have nurtured. Who would have thought that we'd live to witness families divided between Parliament and Royalist? Furthermore, who would ever have thought the English capable of executing their King, but they did. But I digress; the royalist army were heavily outnumbered at Naseby, initially they held a high ridge and I understand that Cromwell and Fairfax didn't want to attack across the open ground so they did what I believe is termed a 'tactical' retreat and that is when friends say that Rupert lost the battle and the King lost the war. A kingdom lost all because of Rupert's impetuous cavalier attitude, which took the better of him. He made a fatal decision to commit the inferior royal army to leave their strong elevated position to charge the enemy who were in an exposed position in that tactical retreat. Initially Rupert's forces pushed the Parliamentary army further into retreat then Cromwell's heavy cavalry wheeled round to attack the royalist flank and that was the end; the momentum of the royalist charge was broken and the superior numbers of the Roundheads routed the royalists who it is said, ran for about twelve miles. The Roundheads took no prisoners that day, they massacred all they caught; it's unimaginable that Englishmen were slaughtering their own countrymen that day."

Henry was listening with such intensity that he hadn't noticed his pipe had gone out. It was Jane who broke into his concentration.

"Civil war is so awful, Papa, it so often divides families; but we have been most fortunate that it has not divided our family, but do continue, I do love to learn history."

Henry smiled but remained silent as Robert continued, "Jane my dear, I find it a pleasure to discover that a lady is interested in such matters; but I am afraid I have almost finished about Prince Rupert. I have heard it spoken by the odd military visitor to Chatsworth that Rupert's mistakes at Naseby marked the end of royal chances to win the Civil War. Apparently after the rout at Naseby, Cromwell captured the royal baggage; in it he found letters and details of plans for Charles to enlist Irish papists and foreign soldiers to fight for him. Parliament published the letters and they caused public sympathy for the royal cause to wane. The end was now in sight and when a few weeks later Rupert was forced to surrender Bristol to Parliament; Charles withdrew Rupert's commission; I am afraid he had fallen from grace, Rupert was so incensed at the loss of his commission and the stain on his honour that he forced his way into the King's presence and demanded a court-martial. Naturally his name was cleared but he was finished as a general and he played no further part in the war. When the King finally surrendered at Oxford in 1646 Rupert was sent into exile."

Jane who had been listening with avid interest now spoke, "When mother lived in France she says it was common knowledge that Rupert was living in Paris then he went to live in Holland, but I can't understand, if he was banished by the royalists and he upset so many in authority, why is he now so popular at court?"

"A difficult question, Jane; I suppose it's because of his care free attitude to life, he never married, the ladies love him. That's proven by the fact that he has fathered two illegitimate children."

"Honestly, Papa, you men. I would be very cautious but then I am a mere woman and know nothing of these matters. However, it seems that he is a little bit impulsive and if you intend to embroil him in your business ventures, I would be very careful. Well, Papa and Henry dear, I'm weary, I think I will retire to my room."

Jane rose from her chair, bade goodnight to her father-in-law, kissed Henry on the cheek and quietly closed the door behind her.

"That's not the reason Rupert is so popular," continued Robert. "Having cleared his name by court-martial with the old king, Rupert moved his entourage to Paris where the Queen and the Prince of Wales had been sent for safety. Apparently, at the court of Queen Henrietta Maria, Prince Rupert met the accusers to his cowardice that had led to his fall from grace. Lord Digby, one accuser, was challenged to a duel but the Queen intervened and forbade them to fight but that did not deter Rupert challenging and wounding Lord Percy, the other accuser. Later, Rupert was offered the post of aide to Prince Charles who is our present king.

Well, Charles gave Rupert the command of a squadron of royal warships that had sailed to Holland for safety when the civil war ended."

Henry said, "It seems to me that Rupert is a champion of all ranks but a master at none; first he is a cavalry commander and he loses us the war, now as a fleet commander was he any more successful?"

"I fear not, Henry; it seems Rupert's naval campaigns were not a success. Rupert and his brother Prince Maurice took command of the squadron of eight warships with the intention of running supplies to the royalist garrison on the Scilly Isles and to attack shipping in the Channel. Prince Rupert was now acting as a privateer and he sold any captured ships and their cargoes and donated the proceeds to the royal coffers but then the royal court heard that Cromwell was to land troops in Ireland so Rupert now took his squadron, which was undermanned, and sailed unopposed to Kinsale in southern Ireland to support the royalist campaign. Parliament sent its own squadron of ships led by Admiral Robert Blake to blockade Rupert's fleet in Kinsale, which then allowed Oliver Cromwell to land parliamentary troops unopposed at Dublin. During a storm, Rupert and his squadron of eight ships eventually escaped from Irish waters and sailed to take refuge in a Portuguese harbour where the king promised him sanctuary. From their refuge, Rupert continued to harass merchant ships in the Atlantic. Eventually the royal squadron was blockaded in Lisbon harbour but Rupert and his flotilla again escaped to scour the sea for prizes. Again parliament's powerful squadron took up hot pursuit and now they pursued Rupert into the Mediterranean. Parliament now denounced Prince Rupert as a pirate."

"By God father, we have to admit that the fellow is audacious, but I suppose his knowledge in naval matters can only be an asset if we do decide to support Jane's father in his expedition to Hudson Bay. However, finish your account."

Henry refilled his pipe bowl as Robert continued. "After scouring the Mediterranean, Rupert escaped back into the Atlantic and sailed to the Azores before he headed down the coast of West Africa attacking and capturing several Spanish prizes, but while ashore he was wounded in a fight with natives. With his squadron now halved during the conflicts of the previous two years, realization must have dawned on him he was never going to beat the parliamentary fleet so he sailed with his remaining four ships across the Atlantic to Barbados where I believe he hoped to find shelter. When he arrived at the royalist outpost he found they had already capitulated to parliamentary authority. After taking on food and water, Rupert sailed back to Europe but in a storm off the Virgin Islands in 'fifty-two, he lost two more of his ships, one of which was commanded by his brother Prince Maurice. Now sick and exhausted, Rupert returned to Paris where I am told he was warmly welcomed at the exiled royal court but his welcome was short lived when Charles realised that the treasure Rupert had accumulated was negligible. Disillusioned and tired of court intrigue Rupert left Paris in 'fifty-four and spent the next six years wandering the continent looking for military employment. He remained a wanderer until the restoration six years ago. But you asked why he is popular at court: I can only assume it's because of his personality, his carefree love of life and adventure and that may be the one factor that will make him promote our venture to the Hudson Bay. Most of what I have told you about Rupert is gossip and hearsay that I have overheard at social functions in the shires, functions to which I have been invited but let us not forget that our branch of the Cavendish family is from the wrong side of the sheets and we will always be outsiders."

"Very interesting father; now I can add a footnote to your information, as you know, I have been investing in tobacco and Samuel Pepys at the Navy Office has been my prime friend and advisor during the last three years. He mentioned once that when Rupert returned to England after the restoration of the monarchy, he was well received by the King who granted him an annual pension and appointed him to the Privy Council with particular interests in the Navy Office and that is where Samuel will be useful if we can get him interested in the plans of Jane's father. Samuel loves to feel he is mixing with aristocracy so it may be a good plan tomorrow to introduce Médard Chouart with his title of Sieur Des Groseilliers."

Henry and Robert continued to talk as the embers of the fire glowed and died. It was almost eleven when, with a feeling that his years were catching up on him, Robert yawned and expressed his desire to retire to bed.

The French Connection

Next morning, Henry and Jane breakfasted early but it was almost eleven before Robert awoke and joined them in the drawing room, where they spent the remainder of the day discussing how far they would support Jane's father in his venture. During the course of the next two days, the subject was discussed in fine detail from social and economic angles and the effect it could have on the family if they became involved financially with the mysterious French adventurer. Eventually Henry and Robert agreed on the amount of capital investment they could risk.

The evening of the dinner party arrived; welcoming fires were lit in all the rooms. Henry and Robert had adjourned to the drawing room to enjoy a glass of Madeira before their guests arrived while Jane was putting James to bed. Just before the hour of seven, there was a knock at the door.

Tom, who was waiting in the entrance hall and was acting as the footman, stepped forward to open the door.

Jane descended the stairs after making certain James was settled for the night; having reached the bottom of the stairs, she stepped forward and extended her hand in friendship and with a brief touching of fingers welcomed Elizabeth and Samuel into her home.

Henry had also come into the hall to greet their guests. "It's a chilly night. Samuel, do let Tom take your cloaks and vestments and come and meet my father."

Henry took Samuel's arm and led him into the drawing room,

114

whilst Jane, seeing Henry was deep in conversation with Samuel, turned to Elizabeth, took her arm and speaking quietly enquired of her health

"I trust that you are feeling better today. I hear that you have been suffering of late with an abscess."

Elizabeth blushed slightly, then whispered, "It is very embarrassing, Jane, and in a very private location. I do hope you can find me a soft cushion."

Jane gave her a sympathetic response, smiled and made all her five guests comfortable. Glasses of Madeira had been poured, when the door knocker reverberated.

Moments later the drawing room door opened for Tom to announce' "Sieur Des Groseilliers and Madam Chouart"

Jane jumped to her feet and embraced Constance. "Good evening, Mama."

Henry also embraced Constance then turning to her tall broad-shouldered companion he shook Médard Chouart Des Groseilliers' hand.

Henry made the suitable introductions and offered glasses of Madeira to his guests. "There is a chill breeze on the night air, come and get warm." He took Constance's arm and led her towards the fire.

"Oh, such a fuss, Henry, we are not too cold. Médard keeps a good supply of furs for carriage journeys."

"Father, that's just what I said to you the other day; you need furs in the coach to keep out the cold when you travel home to Derbyshire."

Médard, speaking with a strong French accent, interrupted. "Sir, do not think me impolite if I offer a small gift to you, I have more than enough furs for my use whilst I am in London. I will have some sent over tomorrow. They are beaver skin wraps, which will more than keep out any of the cold you experience here in England."

"That's very kind of you, father." Jane accepted the offer on behalf of her father-in-law. "And now shall we adjourn to the dining room."

***

"Jane tells us you have experienced a very exciting and adventurous life in New France," Robert commented when they were all seated. "How on earth do you communicate with the native Indians?"

"Well, Monsieur, or may I call you Robert?"

"Robert is perfectly fine, Médard."

"To be brief, I left France just after Jane was born and took a ship to New France to seek my fortune. When I arrived it was a very bad time; one tribe of Indians called the Iroquois were waging war on the white men; their warriors were extremely savage and lurked near to the settlements. In fact, at that time it was not safe for a hunter or trapper to venture far from camp."

The door opened and conversation halted as the cook approached the table to serve the first course of fricassee oysters. When she had left, it fell on Henry to give a short blessing. "Oh Lord, we thank you for good food and the good company and God Bless the King. Amen."

"Amen." the group responded and began to eat eagerly, the silence broken only by the scrape of cutlery on plates and the occasional utterance from Samuel. Finally, Constance remarked, "That was delicious, Jane, you must ask your cook to give me the recipe."

"Well, that is a real compliment, Mama, for someone who has enjoyed French cuisine. All the recipes for tonight's fare are I believe to be found in a cookbook that is very popular at the moment called *The Queen-like Closet, or Rich Cabinet* by Hannah Wolley. I believe she is the first woman to write a cookbook."

"The recipes may be in a book but it takes a good cook to prepare them to the standard that your cook has served," Constance responded.

Cook entered to remove the dishes, in time to hear the praise; she smiled and beamed with pleasure just as Médard resumed his recollections.

"You were asking how I learned to communicate with the natives. Well, as I was saying earlier, no trapper was safe in the woods in those bad times, so I took employment as a clerk with the Jesuits. I seem to be adept in learning languages and they employed me as an interpreter. Unfortunately, my spirit soon wearied of the confines of the church and I left the order and began mixing with the friendly tribes. I learned Algonquin, Huron and even the Iroquois language. Now this may come as a shock to you, Constance, but you have to understand that moral standards in the colonies are different to those in Europe and whilst a white man may have Indian concubines, it's not considered suitable to take white mistresses and do what I did to you, so I married the daughter of a fellow trader."

All eyes now turned to look at Constance, to see her reaction to the news, but before she could respond, Henry interrupted. "I say, Médard that is a little impolite to talk of such matters in mixed company, and especially in the presence of my wife's mother."

"Calm yourself, Henry dear, the flame of my love for Jane's father expired a long time ago; although I am still fond of him, I am certainly not jealous. Médard has always been an honourable man to me and through the years has supported us financially."

Médard gave a smile and a courteous nod to Constance. "Thank you, my dear, and you will always have a place in my heart."

At that moment, conversation again stilled as the second course arrived. Cook placed a large casserole in the centre of the table and removed the lid with a flourish and proceeded to serve it onto the individual plates.

"It really looks and smells delicious. What is it?" Constance enquired.

Henry frustratingly interrupted, "It is hashed meat taken from a shoulder of mutton. Cook tells us she lays it on a gridiron by the fire until it is roasted, and then she takes slices and cooks them in a pan with claret wine, butter and little salt. But the secret is to put shallots, anchovies and capers in the pan. We have the dish frequently and it is very nutritious. Now ladies, please; enough of this talk of the kitchen, save it for after you retire to the drawing room. This delicious food needs to be eaten while it is hot then perhaps later, we can listen to more of Médard's adventures."

"Excellent idea, Henry, after the food you must go on with your story, Sieur Des Groseilliers." Henry noticed that Samuel had taken delight in using Médard's title.

With a courteous nod towards Samuel, Médard chivalrously added that good food should never be spoilt by his deliberations.

The group began to eat hungrily, and when the second course was removed by cook, Jane instructed her to delay serving the pudding course for a short time.

As cook closed the door Henry commented he was eager for Médard to continue.

"Now where was I? Ah yes, I mentioned my marriage to Hélène, the trader's daughter – incidentally, Jane, you have two half brothers in the New World… Well now, sadness came into my life for Hélène died in the harsh winter of 'fifty-two. The temperatures stayed below freezing every day. On the bad days, we lay huddled inside our quarters protected from the sub-zero wind and the drifting snow. Occasionally the sun did shine and the air you breathed put new life into her lungs and in the evening the sunsets were magnificent with their vibrant colours spanning across the bay to glisten off the ice covered rocks. In the end she was just not strong enough to survive and she passed away, I was left alone to continue fur trading while bringing up two young children, consequently in the spring of 'fifty-three, I was forced to get help and take a second wife. A young girl named Marguerite Hayet, who was only fourteen at the time of the wedding but has successfully brought up the two boys. We could not have survived without her help. Incidentally, she is the half sister of Pierre Radisson, who is with me in London. You may have heard that we are trying to gain support and finances for an expedition to the Hudson River. Well, there is not much more to tell except to say that there are vast fortunes to be made for investors in the cold harsh land the French call New France."

Médard sat comfortably in his chair and awaited the questions which he knew were bound to come.

Elizabeth was the first to speak. "That was such an interesting account, Monsieur; I felt that I was witnessing some of the hardships. Tell me, did you ever have to fight and kill any of the Indians?"

Médard smiled. "No, the warriors preferred to stalk and attack solitary hunters and I was always within a large party so usually I felt safe. My biggest danger often came from my own countrymen."

Henry and Robert burst into laughter just as the dining room door opened and cook returned to serve the final course. The dinner continued with light conversation, except from Samuel, who in the main remained silent. Henry knew Samuel was weighing up the character of the Frenchman.

Finally the ladies retired to the drawing room leaving the men alone to bring to the fore the real purpose of the meeting.

Samuel opened the conversation. "I believe, Sieur Des Groseilliers, that you are seeking financial backing for an explorative venture into the Hudson Bay? Tell me; what risks are there to ships in those waters and what resources are you talking about?"

"Well, Samuel, I hope it is permissible to address you informally; and you may address me as Médard."

Samuel beamed and nodded in agreement. Médard continued, "I know that there are vast resources of furs in the interior that can be purchased from the native Indians for a few trinkets and glass beads. When I have ventured into that wasteland, I have been a single trader with a few native canoeists, but with proper finance and equipment, I know we can take some of that trade away from the French who have treated my companions and me very badly. As for the risks to ships in those frozen waters, the main objective is to avoid the vessels becoming frozen into the sea in the first place, for the ice will crush the hull of any ship. Any vessels wintering in the bay must be of such a tonnage that they can be man-hauled onto dry land for the winter months. However, after two or three seasons and when trading is firmly established, ships could be dispatched from England in early spring so that they arrive on the Hudson River in early autumn. They could then take on their cargo and sail away before the ice and cold sets in and traps them for the winter. Of course the other big danger of sailing back to England in the winter is the Atlantic storms, but we cannot possibly plan for those."

"So, Médard, how harsh are those winters?" Robert asked.

Médard remained silent for a few moments as he considered his words. "Just imagine your coldest winter here in London; the River Thames freezes and persons can walk across the ice. When that happens, I understand street traders have in the past erected booths on the ice from which they can sell their wares. That is cold by your reckoning but Londoners can shelter from the cold in their large houses with coal fires. In New France, the rivers freeze solid; the waterfalls become majestic columns of ice. The winter sun shines occasionally and lights up the forest and makes the river ice sparkle; those are the good days but then there are the bad days when the winds come and the temperature drops so low that if a man is foolish enough to remove his mittens his hand will freeze to his hunting knife. The wind howls and snow drifts as tall as a house. I have seen wooden cabins completely covered in snow for weeks at a time. That's when it's hard and people die from exposure. It's the main reason that the natives hunt for beaver skins. Those are what I want to bring to London to sell in your trading houses."

Samuel, who had been listening carefully, said, "Médard, I have many contacts in Whitehall, and there is one man in particular who may be able to promote your venture, his name is Sir George Carteret. He is a member of the Privy Council, a Vice-Chamberlain of the Household. What is most important, he is treasurer of the Navy Office where I am employed. I meet with Sir George almost every day and he may well be your introduction to Prince Rupert, who, I believe, is also anxious to improve trading ventures with the New World."

Médard listened in silence as Samuel went on: "You must understand, Médard, that I cannot be seen to have any involvement in private ventures. My name must not be discussed at any level, but I certainly will arrange for a meeting with Sir George."

At that point Henry interceded to address Médard. "Over the last few days my father and I have discussed the matter of our possible investment in your venture, and we are willing to invest five hundred pounds each, providing you can raise support through Samuel's introductions. Now, I think we should join the ladies for a final drink."

The evening continued as a success and the party guests left for their homes before eleven.

The following day a hackney coach arrived at Henry's house. True to Médard's promise, it delivered a trunk of beaver furs as a gift to Robert.

Samuel, Henry and Robert met once more at Wills coffee house to finalise their investment plans. It was to be the last time the three would ever meet. Robert planned to return to Derbyshire and on the following Monday there was an incisive frost in the air as Tom hitched up the horses to the coach. Robert gave James a farewell hug then turning to Jane he kissed her on her cheek. He took baby James and held him for a last time then shaking Henry by the hand he climbed into the coach.

"Wrap those furs around you to keep warm" was Jane's farewell comment. With a crack from Tom's whip the horses strained and the coach moved forward on the long journey back to Ufton Manor.

It was late November, the festive season was approaching and Henry was kept busy with meetings with his fellow merchants to plan for the spring sailings to Virginia. The overproduction of tobacco three years previously had now stabilised and the merchants agreed it was time to again finance a small flotilla of six ships to collect the tobacco harvest of 'sixty-seven.

Henry and Samuel made no mention of any proposals to invest in explorations into New France. Christmas came and with it the usual festive spirit, which seemed undaunted by the disaster of the great fire. Some of the wealthier houses took food to the homeless who were living in temporary shelters in the open. A troop of mummers appeared on Newington Green to perform miming plays, which caused some merriment to lift the spirits of the village in that, cold Christmas of 1666.

***

One early morning in the middle of January; the sun was shining, its reflections glinted and sparked on the hoar frost that lay thick across the common. A single horseman had completed fifteen hours of hard riding from Derbyshire to deliver a letter from Ufton Manor to Henry.

The rider knocked furiously on the door of Cavendish House; after a few moments it was opened by Henry; who invited the messenger in for a rest and some refreshment before reading the letter.

Dear Henry.

I am sending this letter by a fast rider in the hope you will receive it in time. Your father Robert arrived home from his visit to your home in early November. He was thrilled that he had seen London again albeit in such devastation and tragic circumstances. After the journey back he suffered a severe chill and cold for the next few weeks and seemed to be over the worst during the Christmas Festivities but then on the tenth day of January he started with a fever and has taken to his bed for the last week. The doctor has bled him to no avail and I fear the worst as he is getting weaker by the day and I beseech you to hurry home as fast as possible before it is too late.

I am sorry to send this bad news and I pray you can arrive in time.

Your devoted mother
Elizabeth

Henry read the letter again then rushed into the nursery were Jane was feeding James. "My love, I fear it is bad news. I have just received this letter from mother. Robert is seriously ill with a fever and I must travel home in the hope that I am not too late."

Henry looked at Jane, unsure how she had taken the news. "Of course you must go," she said. "Do not concern yourself for us; I have the servants and friends if I have need for anything. But how will you travel, the coach will be too slow, can you manage such a hard ride by horse in the winter?"

Henry grimaced at the thought. "I am sure I can ride that hard if it is to see father again, but do not fret, my love, if I feel too weary I will stop and take a few hours' rest at an inn."

Jane packed a few necessities into a saddlebag while Henry hurried over to Miller's farm. Before he could knock the farm door was opened. "Good day, Joan," .

"Good morning to you, Mister Henry." Joan said.

Henry paused as the thought of the long journey ahead daunted him, then drawing himself up to his full height he said, "Joan, I have just received some bad news. You remember Robert my father, who visited us a few weeks ago? It seems he has taken a fever and the doctors fear for his life. I have to go to Derbyshire as fast as I can. Have you a good horse that I can purchase? Maybe when I return you could buy it back from me, with suitable recompense, of course?"

"Well, I do have a mare that the hackney cabbies sometimes hire from me if their own horse is lame or sick. I suppose you could have her. Shall we say a five pound fee and a shilling a day? If she is returned in good fettle then I will refund four pounds."

"You're an astute business woman but let's agree on it." Henry shook Joan's hand. "I will come over within the hour and be on my way."

Henry collected the saddlebags from Jane, made his farewells and then pocketing some money for his travel needs, he quickly saddled the mare. He paid Joan and waved to Jane, who stood at the front door, and then with a tear in his eye, he turned the mare to the road for Southgate.

Maintaining a steady trot and stopping to rest every two hours, he made good progress, and after nine hours it was nightfall when Henry found himself approaching a coaching inn, in sight of St Neots in Cambridgeshire. Below the inn's thatched roof swung a sign on creaking hinges proclaiming it to be The Crown. He dismounted and almost immediately a stable hand appeared to assure him he would feed and care for the mare whilst Henry rested for the night.

It wasn't a good bed that Henry was given but in his tired state he would have slept in a tree. He kicked off his boots, flung himself onto the bed and was asleep in moments.

A call of nature awoke him at four in the morning; he had slept longer than intended. After relieving himself in a slop bucket; he quickly pulled on his boots, then cracking the thin film of ice that had formed on the bucket of water that was provided, he quickly washed his hands and face and hurried into the eating area of the inn.

Henry had a hurried meal of cheese and bread and a half a flagon of ale, then after paying the inn keeper and tipping the stable hand he mounted his mare and set off on the northbound road towards Leicester.

Henry shivered in the early-morning air, and gazed upwards in awe at the myriad of twinkling stars that glittered like hoar frost on a tree. The moon's light helped him to pick his way and maintain a slow trot.

Henry rode on lost in thought, and time passed unnoticed. The first light of dawn saw the mare negotiating a bend in the track, when a sudden flurry sounded in the bushes and a solitary figure leapt out. The man had a sharpened stave in his hands, which he held pointed at the breast of the horse. Henry drew sharply on the reins, causing the mare to snort and rear.

"Throw down your bags and I won't harm yer horse," the man shouted. He sounded desperate.

Calmly and without making any sudden movement, Henry reached for the flintlock pistol in his saddle holster. He withdrew the weapon and cocked the firing mechanism. "And I won't harm you, ruffian. Now be off before I fire."

The badly armed robber dropped his staff, turned and ran off into the trees. Henry lowered the firing mechanism and holstered the pistol, then quickly kicking the stirrups, he set off at a gallop, which the mare maintained for a good mile until the horse and rider cleared the woods and they entered more open country. Henry reined the mare to a trot and then halted. He gave her neck a gentle slap with his gloved hand as he leaned forward in the saddle and spoke soothing words to her whilst his own heartbeat returned to normal.

An hour later, he passed through the village of Huntington where he and Jane had halted when they fled the plague all those months previously. Henry now increased the gait of the mare and they made good time. It was just before eleven when he reached Market Harborough but he was feeling saddle sore and weary, so he rested himself and the horse for a couple of hours.

As soon as he could summon the energy, he mounted the tired mare and set her head towards Leicester in a desperate race to be at his father's side before he passed away.

Dusk was falling as an exhausted Henry entered the outlying Derby hamlets and although only a few miles from Ufton Manor, he decided both the mare and he were far too spent and it was safer to find an inn in which to rest for just a few hours. Crossing St Mary's Bridge, Henry found himself in a maze of streets; heading the mare into the widest of the lanes he rounded a bend in Iron Gate Lane and reined in at the Dolphin. Dismounting, he led the horse into the cobbled courtyard. A stable lad ran out and took the reins. "Make sure she's fed and watered," Henry told him, "Then stable her for the night. I will want an early start in the morning."

Henry removed his saddlebag and the two pistols from their holsters. He opened the bag, carefully put his weapons out of sight of the lad, and then gave the boy sixpence. On impulse, as he turned away, Henry asked, "Been doing this job for long? You seem so young."

"Not long, sir. My father is employed here and is teaching me. My grand father, he was a stable hand here all his life." The boy began whistling as he led the mare away.

Henry entered the Dolphin and saw at a glance the flagged

floor and the stairway to a balustraded minstrel gallery from which several doors led to rooms. He approached the landlord and requested a room for the night.

"We are very busy, sir, but I do have one room vacant. I'm afraid it has a large bed for two persons so I will have to charge extra if you want it for yourself."

"That will be most suitable, but first I will partake of some of your potage and a tyg of wine."

Henry sat at a table, a large log fire was burning in the hearth and he gradually relaxed as the feeling of warmth crept into his body. When he had eaten, he took his saddlebag, and wearily climbed the stairway to the gallery

As he walked, a feeling of *déjà vu* overcame him. He reached the last door, turned the handle and entered the room; unbuckling his belt and rapier, he threw them onto a wooden chest in the corner, pulled off his riding boots, undressed and flung himself onto the large bed and immediately slipped into a deep sleep, unaware that he was in the very room where old Henry Cavendish had seduced Sylvia Leach and where Robert, who was now dying, had been conceived; a fact that Henry would never know.

That night Robert died in his sleep as Henry slept on the conception bed.

***

A sobbing Elizabeth ran into the courtyard to meet him with the news of her husband's death. "You are too late." Consoling each other, mother and son went into the family home, which now seemed so stark, silent and cold. It was completely devoid of family warmth or spirit.

Three days later Robert was laid to rest next to Sylvia his mother and Charles, his grand father, who had been the vicar at the church.

Henry stayed at Ufton for another week, during which time he discovered that in the terms of the will, Robert had bequeathed Ufton Manor to his only son with the proviso that Elizabeth had a right to live out her days at the manor if she so wished.

"At the moment I do not know what I wish," Elizabeth had retorted. "The manor has lost all the warmth that came from Robert's love. I feel so alone in such a big house. I don't think I wish to live here all alone."

"Then, mother, the solution is simple, you must travel back to London and come and live with us as long as you wish. You will have a grandchild to dote upon and Jane and I will look after your needs. We can close up the manor house and leave a couple of retainers to look after it and if he wishes, old Tom can work for me in London."

So it was agreed. Elizabeth packed a couple of trunks with clothes and a few family keepsakes, then on a crisp February morning, she took a long stroll around the outside of her home, before going over to the churchyard to say farewell to Robert.

Mother and son mounted the coach and with the mare bridled to the rear and Tom in the driver's seat, the three set forth for Newington Green and a new life.

Hudson Bay Venture

War with the Dutch was never distant and while Henry was attending Robert's funeral arrangements, Samuel was kept busy with naval matters. Nevertheless he did find time to arrange for a small room to be made available at the Navy Office for that important introduction between Sir Charles and Médard. Samuel obtained the keys for the meeting room under the pretext that Sir Charles required privacy while he was engaged in checking bills of lading. At the appointed hour, Samuel escorted Médard into the room which was furnished with a desk and four chairs. A few moments later they were joined by Sir Charles; Samuel having made the introductions then left the room, closing the door behind him.

Sir Charles and Médard sat down at opposite sides of the desk with Sir Charles explaining that his time was very limited due to his commitment to financial arrangements of the fleet for the impending threat from the Dutch navy and he would be pleased if Médard would be precise.

Médard immediately launched into a narrative about the richness of the land and waterways of New France and how the Indians had now become friendly making strong emphasis on the poor treatment the French gave to them and of the rich harvest that was waiting to be picked. By the end of Médard's discourse, Sir George was enthusiastic; he now had a first hand account that confirmed his own reports of the wealth and fortunes to be harvested from the Hudson Bay. The interview had taken longer than Sir Charles planned but after an hour of deliberations Sir

George and Médard rose shook hands; Sir George explaining he would have no trouble in gathering investors to form a merchant venturer's expedition to the Hudson Bay and he gave assurance to Médard that he would be included in the venture.

True to his word, Sir George Carteret personally involved himself in the new venture; unfortunately his involvement brought an initial setback when he undertook to procure a vessel on behalf of the merchant group, his purchase named the *Discovery* proved totally unsuitable for such a voyage and the investors had to sell it at a loss.

***

At Cavendish House 1667 slipped by, Elizabeth settled happily into her London life; she and Henry made frequent visits to the theatre and occasionally she attended dinner parties with her son and daughter-in-law. Slowly she began to rebuild a life without Robert and took a great interest in seeing London rise like a Phoenix from the ashes of the old city. The populace of London also seemed to be gaining new spirit and forgetting their misfortunes; a new spirit of hope seemed to permeate the air.

Christmas fled past with a mixture of church visits and festive merriment; but then the cold harsh winter dragged on with little shelter for the homeless.

In March 1668, Samuel had made a monumental speech in Parliament on naval matters, a subject on which he was by now the senior advisor to the government. The speech so influenced Prince Rupert that he finally took an interest and began to organize a fully financed expedition to explore Hudson Bay with the hope of finding a North West passage to India.

Two ships, the *Nonsuch* and the *Eaglet* were commissioned, the former, a small fifty foot square rigged ketch of forty three tons with an overall beam of fifteen feet that had been built in 1650 at Wavenhoe in Essex. The merchants purchased her for two hundred and ninety pounds but to conserve cash and with the help of Sir George Carteret the *Eaglet* was leased from the navy for a sum of six pounds two and sixpence. During the winter of 'sixty-seven and the spring of 'sixty-eight, both ships were fitted out for the arduous journey, their holds crammed to capacity with food, rope, clothing, guns, powder and shot. As well as a trading cargo of kettles, tools, needles, beads, tobacco and blankets and paper. For record keeping purposes a large quantity quills and ink were also loaded.

Finally, fully provisioned, on the fifth of June 1668, the two ships sailed down the Thames from Gravesend. Ten days later the ships rounded the Orkney Islands to the northeast of Scotland to head west out into the Atlantic for Hudson Bay.

Médard Chouart Sieur Des Groseilliers under the command of Zachariah Gillam sailed in the *Nonsuch* whilst Pierre-Esprit Radisson sailed on the Eaglet under the command of a naval Captain William Stannard.

Six weeks later and thirteen hundred miles west of Ireland disaster struck when both ships encountered severe Atlantic storms and heavy seas. The *Eaglet* sustained some loss of life and was storm damaged and was forced to limp back to Plymouth were she arrived in August. Meanwhile the *Nonsuch* sailed on arriving in James Bay on the twenty-ninth of September; the English had arrived on the Hudson Bay.

It was now past the conception stage and the birth of Canada was about to commence.

Samuel's Mistress

O n that fateful evening that the *Nonsuch* and the *Eaglet* had departed down the Thames on their eventful voyage which would herald the birth of a nation, Samuel and Henry had stood on the embankment of the Thames and watched as the summer breeze had filled the sails and the small boats had assisted the ships down the river before casting off their ropes. From the ships, the crews had waved and shouted farewell messages.

"A fine sight," Samuel said as they turned away to stroll back to his office. The pair continued to make small talk then suddenly Samuel stopped, grasped Henry's sleeve and said, "I must tell you, I am going on a tour tomorrow and will be away a few days. I am so excited, Henry, I have a new mistress and she is coming on my tour."

Henry turned to stare at the departing ships and said, "You are incorrigible, Samuel. Who is this latest lady, a seamstress or a maid at court?"

"No, Henry, she actually lives in my home. Her name is Deborah Willet; she is Elizabeth's maid and companion. I am going home now to put the finishing arrangements to the tour that will include the sights of Oxford and Salisbury and then on to Bath and Bristol. Of course it is a working tour and to give our journey Navy Office approval, I am taking Will Hewer my clerk to make observations on a new warship that is being constructed at the Bristol shipyards. I thought the tour would also be a good opportunity to take Elizabeth away for a few days and naturally she will have to take her companion and maid for company; to be truthful; if I get the opportunity, I shall bed Debs while we are away. She was born in Bristol and the visit to her home town will ingratiate her towards me." Samuel had confided all the information to Henry in an excited voice and now he paused for breath.

"Well, have a pleasant time on this tour, Samuel, but be cautious. You are playing with fire and you know what happened in the last fire."

Samuel laughed and slapped Henry affectionately on the back. They shook hands and parted. Back at his home, Samuel instructed Jacob his coachman to be ready to leave at six the following morning.

On the hour, the coach drew up at Samuel's door in Seething Lane drawn by two black sires; they were groomed to perfection and snorted in frustration at the halt. The travelling baggage was carried aboard and the four travellers made themselves as comfortable as possible then Jacob headed the coach out of London on the Oxford road where Samuel intended to visit the university.

"I am a Cambridge man myself," Samuel told his companions when they were seated. "I got my law degree at Magdalene College but it is always interesting to visit a fellow college."

Samuel visited the university but Elizabeth took up the remaining time during their brief stay in Oxford, consequently he found little chance to be alone with Deborah and had to be satisfied with the occasional glance and a touch of hands. He hoped that when they reached Salisbury, which was the next city on the tour, he would be able to manoeuvre Deborah into some quiet place were they could spend time to give vent to their passions.

That night Deborah lay in her bed gazing through her window at the moon; as her hand fondled her breast her thoughts were of Samuel.

***

It was a long dusty day's journey and by late afternoon the weary travellers were thankful when the spire of Salisbury cathedral came into view. One hour later the coach finally drew up at the Angel Inn and Jacob led the black sires and coach to the rear of the inn. Placing a footstool by the carriage door, he helped his passengers to alight and proceeded to unload their bags. Finally a stable boy unhitched the sires and led them into vacant stalls while Samuel escorted his three companions into the inn followed by Jacob, carrying their bags.

The innkeeper, a portly fellow with ruddy cheeks, greeted the travellers. "Good day, sir, can I be of service to you?"

Samuel looked the innkeeper in the eye, paused as he attempted to brush some of the travel dust from his coat with the palm of his hand, and said, "First to wash the dust from our throats, five flagons of your ale. Brewed on the premises, I hope."

The innkeeper confirmed that this was so.

"We also require three rooms for two nights. One room for my wife and myself plus two smaller rooms; one for my clerk and one for my wife's maid. Jacob my coachman can be accommodated, I presume, with the stable boys?" Then Samuel added, "Incidentally, can you arrange for a local coachman to be available tomorrow to take us to look at the remarkable stone circle at Stonehenge. I believe it is not too distant?"

"That can be arranged, sir, we have a coachman and I shall instruct him to come to the inn at nine in the morning."

"Right, Jacob," Samuel said. "You can look to the horses. We will not require our coach for two days, so you are free to do as you wish tomorrow but remember we shall need you the day after at eight to travel on to Bath."

That evening the four travellers dined together. Samuel entertained the group with his wit coupled with stories of court gossip. It was towards the hour of ten when Elizabeth said she was feeling a little tired.

"I think I shall retire to bed, Samuel. Will you please escort me to my room? You may rejoin the company if you wish. Goodnight, Deborah, and Mister Hewer."

Samuel escorted Elizabeth up to their room and made sure she was safely in bed, then kissing her lightly on her cheek he bade her goodnight and said he wanted to talk to Will on a few naval matters.

"Goodnight, Samuel dear." Elizabeth closed her eyes and fell asleep almost immediately.

Quietly Samuel left the room and returned to find that Will was ready to retire himself.

"Will, after we leave Bath, we must go to Bristol to take a look at the new warship that is in the docks. I shall want you to make notes about the quality of the work and materials plus the provisioning and manpower for the ship. So make sure you have adequate paper ready."

Will acknowledged that he had understood the instructions then he rose from the table and bade Samuel and Deborah good night.

"Well, Debs my dearest one, it seems we have at last only each other for company." Samuel placed his hand on her thigh and gave her a squeeze.

"Come, my Debs, I think it is past your bedtime and I must make sure you are safe in your room."

Samuel approached the innkeeper to ask for a night lamp for her room, then taking her forearm Samuel helped his mistress rise from her seat and the pair slowly made their way to the upstairs rooms guided by the flickering flame from the lamp. At Debs door Samuel paused. "May I enter your room, my dearest one? I think I would sleep better if I knew you were safe inside."

"You are a one, Mister Pepys, and that's for sure. You know an innocent like me cannot resist your charms."

Samuel opened the bedroom door and gently guided Deborah inside. He placed the lamp on a small table and turning reached out and took Deborah into his arms. He gently kissed her. Her lips parted, their tongues sought each other as she put both her arms around Samuel's neck.

Debs wore a long linen shift that served as a type of blouse. Over it she wore two skirts in the fashion of the day with the outer skirt gathered up to reveal the underskirt. Samuel slowly raised her skirts over her head and then unbuttoned her shift. Meanwhile she was unbuttoning his waistcoat and breeches, which he let fall to the bedroom floor. Naked, they stood caressing each other while the soft light from the lamp cast shadows across the room.

Samuel guided her towards her cot in the corner of the room. Gently lowering Debs onto her bed, he climbed in beside her and felt the warmth of her body as she lay next to him. He cradled her in his strong arms. They made love with urgency that released all their pent-up frustrations. Samuel climaxed too soon and as he lay by Deborah's side, he used his hand to stimulate and caress until her heavy breathing became coupled with ecstatic cries as she too climaxed. Both satisfied, they lay in each others arms for some time as the candle continued to flicker. Eventually Samuel made a move to leave her.

"Stay a little longer, my dear Samuel."

He spoke softly while dressing himself. "I must be taking my leave of you, my dearest one, we don't want Elizabeth to waken and question my absence. But Debs, always know that that I am yours in body and spirit and each night as you gaze up at the moon, remember that I your lover will also be gazing at the same moon and I shall be wanting to be with you."

Samuel gave his lover a deep passionate kiss and left Debs gazing through her window at the moon.

Samuel returned his own room to find Elizabeth asleep; what Samuel didn't realize was that as Debs was gazed at the moon in her room,, she was dreaming of their next liaison and in her dream she was again making love to her lover...

***

Elizabeth was indeed sound asleep as Samuel undressed for a second time that night and climbed into her bed.

The four breakfasted at eight and the coachman arrived promptly at nine to escort them on the tour to Stonehenge.

When they were all seated in the coach, Samuel adopted the role of guide and said, "I am taking you today to see a special place called Stonehenge. I read about this place in a paper by John Aubrey, a local antiquarian, who wrote about a site with a ring of pillars of stone that is very mysterious; nobody seems to know the purpose or the age of the stones, in fact nothing is known and everything seems to be mere speculation. Apparently some of the huge stone pillars are joined across the top with even larger stone slabs. Aubrey thinks that the stones and holes in which they sit are the works of the ancient Druids who were the priests to the Celts who were persecuted and massacred by the Romans. His paper was so acclaimed in the summer of 1663, that Aubrey even brought King Charles on a tour to Stonehenge."

The coach trundled on over Salisbury Plain; at times the track was almost lost in the open grassland. Occasionally the coachman skirted outlying farms and hamlets and it took almost three hours to travel the ten miles to the stones. The driver halted the coach and climbed down from his seat, placing a small footstool near to the door, everyone stepped down onto a small cart track.

Samuel gazed at the circle of vertical stones, and for once he was rendered speechless; finally he said, "Some very powerful people must have lived hereabouts to build such a structure."

The others in the party agreed with him and the four spent the next few hours wandering the site and gazing in amazement at the ingenuity of the ancients. It was almost four in the afternoon when the group mounted the coach and set off back towards Salisbury.

Samuel had no chance to visit Deborah's room that night as Elizabeth now demanded his full attention to her needs in bed. Frustratingly Samuel obliged.

Next morning, as instructed, Jacob had the coach ready for an early start to Bath and by late afternoon the travellers were pleased the journey for the day was over as the coach finally pulled up at the Hart Lodgings in Stall Street.

"Jacob, we shall rest the horses tomorrow as I want to visit the Roman Baths while we are in the city. Later we shall be travelling to Bristol for the day and I have hired a coach to take us, so after you have done the grooming you have a free day."

"Thank you, sir." Jacob knuckled his forehead in the manner that he had seen the naval men salute when visiting the Navy Office.

Samuel dismissed him then turned to his companions. "I intend to rise at dawn to try the hot waters of the Cross Bath. The waters will do you good, Elizabeth, and you too, Deborah, though methinks it cannot be clean to have so many bodies together in the same water. After the baths, I have hired a coach to take us down into Bristol, so I think we should all have an early night for we have an early rise at dawn."

The group left the baths soon after eight the following morning and breakfasted on cold meats, cheeses and bread at a nearby inn. Having feasted, the travellers left in the hired coach for Bristol. It was around eleven o'clock when they arrived at the Horse Shoe Inn on Wine Street and refreshed themselves before wandering the city.

"Bristol seems in every respect like another London," Samuel observed. "But it seems strange, Will. I cannot help but notice the absence of any carts for moving merchandise. Everything seems to be dragged on sledges."

"You are correct, sir. I wonder what the reason is for that."

Samuel asked a trader the question, and discovered that the Bristol authorities had barred carts from the city to prevent heavy loads from damaging the wine cellars located beneath the streets. Thanking the man, Samuel also enquired for directions to a good tavern.

"Ye be wanting The Sun on Christmas Street. The owner, he keeps a clean establishment with good food."

Samuel thanked the trader and bade him good day.

The group strolled the short distance to The Sun tavern, where having seen Elizabeth and Debs settled at a table, Samuel gave the tavern keeper a guinea for refreshments and with the owner's promise to protect the ladies from unwanted attention, Samuel and Will left to wander down to the quay where they viewed hundreds of ships moored out on the river. At the quay they found the new fifty-gun warship that was under construction by the shipwrights Bally and Furzer.

Samuel sought out and spoke to Mister Bally, "Good day, sir, my name is Pepys and I am employed by the Navy Office in London. My clerk and I have permission to be taken aboard to ascertain the manning and provisioning required when this ship enters service. Is it convenient for us to go aboard?"

Mister Bally grimaced. "You can go aboard, sirs, but watch your footings, there are still loose boards over the holds and on the lower gun deck, oh, and don't you be upsetting my workers with fancy requests from the Navy Office either."

With that warning ringing in their ears, Mister Bally turned on his heels and walked away.

"Let's get aboard, Will, the quicker we're done, the sooner we can return to the ladies."

Samuel led Will up the gangplank to commence their tour of inspection. After an hour of checking the quality of the workmanship and materials and estimating the required provisioning, Samuel was satisfied that the work was being completed to the Navy Office specifications and the pair returned to the Sun Inn only to find that Deborah had left to visit a relative. She returned an hour later with a man, "May I introduce Mister William Butts? He is my uncle and a local merchant."

Samuel offered his hand, intrigued and pleased to be introduced to a member of his mistress's family.

"I am very pleased to meet you, and this is Mister Hewer my clerk." The pair shook hands.

Elizabeth had remained seated while the introductions were being made; she now rose as Samuel introduced her to Mister Butts.

"I think we are all ready for a meal. Will you join us, William?" Samuel enquired.

"That's very gracious of you."

Deborah's uncle took a seat between Deborah and Samuel and soon a party mood developed with Samuel and William making witty conversation and keeping the group in an atmosphere of high spirits. They had all eaten and drunk their fill when William rose and still in jolly mood announced that they should walk back to the area were Debs had lived as a child and along the way he would show them some of the sights of the city.

Samuel settled his account and the party left the tavern and wandered down the quayside and passed a narrow side road named Welsh Back, William pointed to the newly built custom house with its glittering display of windows. He then led them down Marsh Street to where Deborah had been born. Samuel couldn't believe his eyes at the welcome that Deborah received. One elderly lady, who was sitting in her doorway, recognized her almost immediately and raised the word. Debs had tears of joy in her eyes at being welcomed and being recognized by some of the older residents that came from their homes to greet Mrs Willet's daughter.

The group lingered in the street awhile before Samuel heard William exclaim, "Now look sharp, we should move on. If we go through this passage we come to the rear of my house and you are all invited for supper."

So the evening continued with William Butts entertaining his niece and her employer Elizabeth Pepys while Samuel Pepys and Will Hewitt absorbed the hospitality. First they were offered wine then a servant put a large venison pie onto the table, that was soon followed by a bowl of strawberries and finally the guests were offered a fortified sherry wine that William said was Bristol milk.

137

It was well into the hour of eleven at night when William finally escorted his visitors back to the Horse Shoe Inn for Samuel to hire a coachman to drive his party by moonlight on the long road back to Bath.

Two days later, the travellers were back in London and life in the Pepys household now settled down to tranquillity but it was a brief interlude for Elizabeth, was a woman scorned, and about to unleash her vitriolic tongue on Samuel, when caught *'In flagrante delicto'* with Deborah.

In Flagrante Delicto

It was a chilly autumn evening in October. Samuel sat by the fire, with Elizabeth reading a play to him; at her side sat Deborah, her seventeen-year-old live-in companion. The domestic peace of the household was suddenly disturbed by the sound of knocking at the front door. Impatiently Elizabeth closed the book and rose, returning moments later with two companions.

"Look who has come to visit us, Samuel, we have our neighbour Joseph Batelier with his daughter Mary. He has brought me some samples of silk from his son-in-law's shop."

Samuel rose to greet his neighbour. "That is very kind of you, I am sure Elizabeth will pick out some choice colours for her new dresses. Now, Joseph, we are about to have supper, will you and Mary join us in some refreshments?"

"That's very kind of you, Samuel. By the way, I had a few hogsheads of this year's burgundy delivered last week. Would you care for me to deliver one to you, at a favourable rate, I should add?"

"That will be most agreeable, Joseph, let us now adjourn to the table."

The group retired to the dining room where they were also joined at the table by Deborah. With a lover's guile, Samuel placed himself between Elizabeth and Deborah and as the wine flowed and the conversation chanced on the current play at the theatre, Samuel let his hand rest on his knee for a moment then surreptitiously he placed his hand on Deborah's thigh. She showed no indications that she was being fondled; she was used to Samuel's groping and embraces when she was alone in the house with him. Carefully he raised the hem of her dress to feel the firmness of her thigh. At that moment the food was served and Samuel quickly removed his hand and reached for his wine glass.

It was almost nine in the evening when Joseph and Mary took their leave of the Pepys' hospitality. "I will get that hogshead delivered as soon as possible," said Joseph as they bade goodnight at the door, and then Samuel, Elizabeth and Deborah retired to the reading room

"Are you going to continue reading that play to us, Elizabeth?" Samuel asked as the three took their seats round the fire. Elizabeth picked up the play and began to read.

During a pause in the reading, Deborah enquired, "Do you want me to comb your hair tonight, Samuel?"

"That will be very good as my head is sore from wearing this wig all day."

Elizabeth rose and closed the book. She bent over, kissed Samuel on the cheek, and said, "I will bid you both goodnight for I am tired. Do not leave me too long Samuel. Goodnight, Deborah."

As Elizabeth left the room to go to her bed Debs whispered, "Goodnight, Mam."

For a quarter of an hour Samuel and Debs remained seated around the fire as gradually all sounds of movement upstairs ceased.

Samuel removed his wig, and Debs placed it on the block-stand by the door. Then she found a brush and comb and stood behind Samuel, combing his hair.

After a few minutes he grasped her hand and guided her round to the front of him. As she continued to brush his hair, he put his hands beneath her dress onto her bare buttocks.

"Oh Master Samuel, my love, do be careful, if my mistress arises and comes down the stairs, I would lose my job and you would no doubt be in severe trouble."

"Do not fret, my Debs, she is now fast asleep." Gently he caressed her with his fingers and slowly he felt her relax as she moved closer to him.

"Come, Debs, sit facing me on my knee; you can continue to groom my hair." He quickly undid his breeches to show his manhood in all its erect glory. Deborah sat astride him and as he

140

entered her she gasped. Slowly Debs began to move her thighs, pushing up and down as Samuel murmured ecstatically.

"By God, Debs, this is wonderful, don't stop, I will tell you when to dismount."

The couple became oblivious to all other movements or noises in the house and were quite unaware of squeaks from the stairs as someone descended. Debs was now moving her body at a faster tempo when the reading room door opened slowly; silhouetted in the doorway was Elizabeth in her night attire.

Deborah suddenly stood up, her skirts covered what a moment before had been her naked thighs, Samuel was not so lucky; he had just reached the moment and with his manhood still erect he was discharging onto his breeches. Luckily the glow from the fire was ebbing and Samuel hoped that when Debbie had risen from his knee and her skirts had fallen to cover her modesty, in the dim light Elizabeth had not seen the intimate details that had taken place on Samuels knee.

Samuel tucked away his now flaccid manhood and whilst rising from the chair he had used his hand to quickly wipe the fluid from the front of his breeches and just as quickly wiped his hand on the rear of his breeches as he moved towards Elizabeth, who until that moment had remained silent.

"And what brings you downstairs, my love?"

Elizabeth said nothing; she turned on her heels and went silently upstairs to her bed.

Deborah also remained silent and went off to her bedroom.

Samuel sat by the now dead fire, his bare head in his hands, and thought about the best course of action. Eventually he made his way upstairs where he undressed, slid into bed and tried to sleep.

It was about two in the morning when Elizabeth awoke him with her crying. Tears were flooding down her cheeks.

"I have a confession to make to you, Samuel," she sobbed.

Samuel opened his eyes and listened, wondering what his wife was about to say.

His hopes were bolstered when Elizabeth began to talk about her religion, a subject that to Samuel's relief had no bearing on his infidelity.

"Samuel, you have to know that I am a practising Catholic

and I can never divorce you and unknown to you I have been receiving the Holy Sacrament."

Samuel remained silent for some time while he thought of the best way to use this to his advantage. He then confessed, "Elizabeth my dearest, you must understand that my position at the Navy Office excludes me from Catholic tendencies but if there is ever a chance to support a restoration of the Catholic monarch, then I would do so."

That statement to Elizabeth in private was a statement of intent she repeated to friends and was to lead in later years to Samuel's eventual imprisonment in the Tower on suspicion of treason that was never proven and for which he was eventually released uncharged.

That night Elizabeth continued to let her innermost secrets pour forth; after the confessions the anger came forth as she raised her voice to vent her scorn at him.

Samuel tried to console her as he whispered, "I do love you, Elizabeth. It was remiss of me but I was only embracing Deborah as she combed my hair."

"Liar," she screeched. "That serpent in your breeches is for any woman but me. You are a worm, Mr Pepys, and so is your serpent. You have never made me happy in bed as you must make other women happy. To me you are useless; I have to pleasure myself at times, for you are a worthless vile man." Her voice trailed away into sobs.

Samuel lay on the bed and tried to console her, but her peaks of anger and troughs of despair went on until the first light of dawn shone through the window. Finally she fell into a deep troubled sleep from where she moaned and tossed her body in anguish whilst remaining semi-conscious.

Next morning, Samuel rose early. He tried in vain to engage in pleasant conversation with Elizabeth but she was frigid so with some discretion he beat a hasty retreat and took a barge up to Whitehall. All day his thoughts kept returning to Deborah and her future. Elizabeth had threatened to turn her out onto the streets. Samuel tried to work to obliterate the memories of the previous night's infidelity but it was of little use and he returned home to be greeted again by a hostile silence from Elizabeth and a very subdued Deborah.

The strained atmosphere continued in the Pepys' household for the next few days, with Elizabeth having bouts of silence towards Samuel followed by polite but distant moods.

For Samuel, the nights were the worst. Elizabeth would wake him in the early hours shouting and threatening to burn his private parts with a hot iron.

A week after Elizabeth had discovered the affair, Samuel returned home from the Navy Office to find Deborah had been put out of the house. Samuel made discreet enquiries as to her whereabouts but to no avail; it was as if the streets of London had swallowed her.

So the Pepys' house returned to a quieter mode with Samuel becoming the contrite husband and doing everything to please Elizabeth; he even tried to be a considerate and passionate lover but failed to arouse his wife.

She was a woman scorned.

Winter Solace

In the New World, the venturers to the Hudson Bay were about to be overtaken by the onset of winter. Atlantic storms had delayed their arrival and it was now far too late in the year to trade for furs trapped the previous winter and load them, then sail away. Consequently Groseilliers advised Captain Gillam of the urgent need to build protection against the cold weather for the stores and crew at James Bay. Immediately Zachariah Gillam set the crew to work felling and logging, the first task being to erect a temporary stockade for protection and storage. For a week, the crew slaved from dawn to dusk in a race against time for they knew that without the protection of a stockade for the stores they would not survive the winter cold. Seven days later the ship's cargo was ferried ashore and stored.

The ship was now higher in the water and could be anchored nearer to the shore. The crew began constructing a ramp from the shallow waters up onto the shore and another week of hard labour saw the ramp complete and ready to facilitate the winching of the *Nonsuch* onto the beach before she became frozen in the winter ice. That night a tired crew slept well in the knowledge that their ship was almost safe. In the morning they awoke. It was a bright dawn, the waters were calm and the trees had a glint of frost that shone and sparkled with the rising sun. After breakfasting, the crew attended a service of thanks for their safe deliverance from the Atlantic storms and were then given the remainder of the day as a rest day before the hard work began of winching the ship up onto dry land on the Monday. Evening fell all too soon; sentries were posted on the camp perimeters and the refreshed crew grouped up to enjoy a hot meal round the camp fires. A seaman produced a fiddle and a couple of sailors danced a jig while others sang. Hidden in the forest, eyes watched, the Indians wondering what strange habits these pale-faced men had brought to their land. By nine o'clock, one by one the crew were settling down to a night's sleep before a hard day in the morn.

The acrid smell of smoke from the camp fires permeated the still frosty dawn air; around the camp men stirred as gradually the settlement came to life. Fires were rekindled and food prepared before the hard day's work began. The late autumn sun was rising above the horizon as the crew under the guidance of the captain began applying vast amounts of rendered animal fats to the ramp; the fat having been procured by trade from the friendly Indians. Other crew members rigged block and tackle to trees adjacent to the ramp and now began the laborious task of slowly winching the ship onto dry land, a task not without risk of injury to unskilled hands. The crew and Indians laboured all day as slowly the ship was winched from the water and pulled up the ramp. Teams of Indian workers under the guidance of the ship's carpenter and first mate placed fifteen-foot lengths of sapling trunks to prop the hull to provide stabilizing supports and keep the ship in a relatively upright position. Dusk was falling before Captain Gillam was eventually satisfied with the ship's stability and gave the orders for the final wooden wedges to be driven under the supports to prevent undue movement of the hull when the severe cold winter winds came. The ship had been beached without accident and she was now safe.

The crew could now begin to erect a more permanent and fortified stockade. It was to be the first fortress ever constructed on Hudson Bay, and in honour of the English monarch who had sponsored the voyage, Monsieur Groseilliers named it Fort Charles.

That first winter was particularly harsh with the crew trying to keep warm during the short days and the long nights. The landscape along the coastline of James Bay had turned to ice and the temperature stayed below freezing on a daily basis. Occasionally on a clear day the sun would shine from azure blue skies and in the evening sunset, colours would show off their vibrant rays from the horizon and they would span across the bay to glisten off the ice-covered rocks. On those days the sailors watched, mesmerized by the beauty of the scene. In contrast; on the bad days, the crew lay huddled inside their quarters protected from the sub-zero wind and the drifting snow. The cold was like nothing they had experienced. If they had not prepared the stockade for shelter and defence they would not have survived, but survive they did.

The crew lived on the stores they had brought from England and on several occasions Groseilliers left the stockade to search out and to trade for frozen meat from the Cree Indians. Eventually the long dark nights eased into longer days and with them the spring brought a gentle thaw; the river ice gradually receded, the high snow drifts melted almost overnight and there was warmth in the sun again.

With the advent of spring, Cree Indians began to visit the stockade to trade furs that had been trapped during the winter months; soon the stockade storerooms were full of quality pelts, taken when they were at their thickest.

April slipped into May. The crew were getting restless for home but before anchors could be weighed and sails set for England, there were still tasks to be done to make the ship seaworthy. Captain Gillam kept them fully occupied repairing the damage that the *Nonsuch* has suffered during the Atlantic storms and the damage caused by the winter ice. By the end of May the ship was ready to be launched down the ramp where she was anchored in deeper water. For ten days, the crew were kept busy stocking the holds with the furs and on the tenth day of June, with the ship fully laden and Captain Gillam in command, the *Nonsuch* finally slipped her moorings and set sail for England.

Monsieur Groseilliers was aboard; during the winter months ashore, he had advised and shared authority with the captain but now on board the ship he was again a passenger with the prime task of writing a report for the London investors concerning the rich resources in the area of the Hudson Bay that were for the taking.

That autumn, the weather held fair in the Atlantic and with a good wind the *Nonsuch* made a fast crossing, reaching England in October.

***

During the late autumn of 'sixty-nine, life at Cavendish House settled into quiet domesticity with a well-run household managed by Jane and aided by Elizabeth who appeared to be full of joy in the helping with the upbringing of young James who was now five and learning fast from a private tutor.

In the city the Cavendish name was becoming established as a prominent family with Henry at its head, he was already a respected and wealthy man from his tobacco investments and soon he would become even richer.

The day began as any other; Henry was in the smoking room enjoying a pipe. He opened the newspaper, and read,

> *'The good ship 'Nonsuch' berthed at Gravesend on the 10th day of October in the year of our Lord 1669. She berthed with a rich cargo of furs that made some recompense for the sailors who had suffered cold confinement in the frozen land of New France during the winter of sixty eight.'*

Henry glanced at the date on the paper and saw it was the 14th October 1669. By now Des Groseilliers would have made his report to Sir George Carteret. Folding the newspaper, Henry went out and walked into Newington Green. Finding a runner at the hostelry, he gave the man sixpence and requested that he summon a hackney cab as soon as possible and have it come to Cavendish House. Henry then went home and waited.

The cab arrived within the hour, and as it pulled up, Henry put on his coat and called down the hall to Jane that he was going to visit her mother to see if Groseilliers was staying with her.

The coachman had already lowered the steps for Henry to climb aboard and immediately Henry saw that it was the Islington coachman, William Usburn, who had driven him so often in the past.

"Good morning, William," Henry said. "Will you convey me to 6 Hoxton Square in Shoreditch? You may remember it is where you left me when you cast a wheel all those years ago."

William helped Henry inside the cab and closed the door, remarking that he remembered the incident well and knew the destination.

It was an hour before the cab reached Hoxton Square. When

147

Henry dismounted and knocked at the door he was elated to find Constance at home. Dismissing William, Henry embraced his mother-in-law, entered the house and closed the front door.

"Come into the drawing room, Henry. How are Jane and my grandson?"

"They are both well and Jane sends her love. She says you must come and visit us soon. It is good to see you, Constance; we have been neglecting you of late but now my mother has departed back to Derbyshire perhaps we shall have more time to spend with you. It has been a very distressing time for her, as you will appreciate."

Constance nodded and thanked him for his offer.

"Now, Constance, I believe that Médard Chouart has returned to London from his expedition to the Hudson Bay; is he by chance staying with you, because I need to see him as soon as possible?"

"He has a room here in the house, Henry. I will go and see if he is in."

Constance left the room and returned a few minutes later with Groseilliers.

"*Bonjour, Monsieur.*" Henry courteously greeted Médard Chouart in French. "Welcome. It is good to see that you are safe after such a hazardous sea journey."

They shook hands and Constance invited them to sit.

Henry spoke first. "You are certainly looking well, Médard, considering the rigors of the harsh winter. I presume the voyage was a success, but have you written your report for Sir George Carteret to that effect?"

Groseilliers laughed. "Now, Henry, you would not want me to betray the contents of my report to you, would you? All I can say is that if you invest in your wife's father, you will not be misguided."

Constance, who had been listening, smiled at the jibe to her Parisian love affair while Henry smiled and understood the subtleness of Groseilliers' comment but did not pursue the matter any further.

The three sat in conversation for another hour with Médard describing the voyage and the winter conditions that the crew had endured. Finally Henry rose and bid farewell as Constance escorted him to the door.

"Promise to visit us soon, Constance," Henry remarked as he embraced her and left to find a cab.

***

A week passed and Henry again saw nothing of Samuel, although he had heard from friends that to compensate for his infidelity he had taken his wife to Paris for a tour. Then Henry received a letter from Samuel suggesting a meeting to discuss new developments for investing in the Hudson Bay venture. The letter suggested the pair meet at The Cock alehouse.

When Samuel arrived, he had the appearance and look of a very worried man. As they took their seats at a corner table, Henry was perturbed and asked, "Are you ill, Samuel? How was your trip to Paris and how is Elizabeth?"

"I'm a worried man, Henry, we arrived home three days ago and Elizabeth has already developed a fever. She has taken to her bed and I have summoned the doctor, but I must confess I am worried for her health. But for now I need company so enough of my troubles, let us enjoy an evening and catch up on all the news."

Samuel summoned a serving girl. "We will each have a medium-sized lobster fully dressed and served with a bottle of white wine."

"It's a favourite tavern for me, Henry. Many has been the night when I have eaten, drunk and joined in the merriment, and you may not be aware of it, but over the last few years I have been keeping a diary of all my observations and the effects that the restoration, the plague and the great fire have had on my life. I have even recorded my dalliances with some fair ladies and even my fumbles with this landlady Mistress Knipp get a mention, but I regret the diary must now come to an end. My eyesight is not what it was and I fear that if it fails any further I may not be able to carry on at the Navy Office. I suppose I am fairly well off, as witnessed by the fact that I have recently had the expenses of having to invest in a coach and a pair of black sires to transport Elizabeth and myself to various social occasions. The real reason for the expense is that since Elizabeth discovered my dalliance with Deborah, I have had to be more attentive to my wife. Thankfully my existence at home has gradually become more peaceful

149

since Debby was put out of the house, but I do feel a sense of guilt over her demise as I was the one who encouraged the relationship. And now with Elizabeth's fever I am even more tinged with guilt."

"I am so sorry to hear all this, Samuel. I had learned about your wife's discovery, but as for your failing eyesight, you seem to be unimpaired in going about your normal day-to-day routines. However, I suppose the writing by candle and lamp light is the problem."

"Ah, no matter, Henry, I thought I would mention it to you so that you can understand how important the Hudson Bay investments are for my future. I must have a good source of income in case I am forced to give up work due to loss of sight. But now, to more serious matters. With your father's death, are you willing to invest what would have been his share in the venture?"

"I cannot foresee any problem with me raising the extra capital," Henry confided.

"Good, because the report that Groseillier has given to Sir George Carteret was all that he promised."

Henry remained silent to the news; the hints Groseillier had made at Constance's home had been factual after all.

Samuel continued, "The good news is that Sir George has managed to arouse the interest of Prince Rupert who is an admiral, and the Prince visits my office quite often. It is rumoured that the king himself is also interested. Now do you remember when we first met back in 'sixty-three; you had a letter of introduction to Sir William Cavendish, which opened doors for you?"

Henry nodded.

"Well, I believe you also had other letters of introduction and one was to your distant relative, Edward Montague, who just so happens to be a distant kinsman of mine. Since the Restoration he is in favour with the king and he is now a Knight of the Garter with the title of the Earl of Sandwich. I see a lot of him at the Navy Office; he is a naval administrator who has distinguished himself at sea as a fighting admiral."

Samuel paused and took a drink then continued. "Montague has the king's ear and if I can introduce you at the Navy Office, Edward may be so minded to also press our case for this expedition. I know Prince Rupert is enthusiastic and another voice in

Whitehall can do no harm, so have you still got that letter of introduction, Henry?"

"I never discard anything that may be useful, it will be somewhere in my writing bureau."

"Well done. Then if you can come before noon to the Navy Office on the first Monday in the New Year, I know that Sir Montague will be there to oversee some details for a new warship. Now drink up and let us enjoy an hour or two of merriment and join in the singing. As I said, I particularly like this establishment. As I intimated, the landlady Mistress Knipp is very good to me, if you know what I mean." Samuel gave Henry a dig in his ribs with his elbow. "In fact, many is the afternoon she has consoled me."

"Samuel, you are a rascal, I would have thought you had learnt your lesson after Elizabeth caught you with Deborah."

And so the pair talked and occasionally joined in the singing. It was towards midnight when they left The Cock. Samuel, who was a little unsteady on his feet, summoned a sedan, while Henry took a handsome cab back to Newington Green.

On the second day of November, Henry received a note from Samuel that read,

> Dear Henry,
> I beg to inform you that since we last met, God has afflicted me by the sickness of my wife, who, from her coming back to London, hath laid her under a fever as severe as at this hour to render her recovery desperate. I fear for her life.
> I am, Sir
> Your most obliged and dear friend and Servant.
> Samuel Pepys

Eight days later, Elizabeth died at the age of twenty-nine. Henry and Jane attended the funeral at St. Olaves Church in Hart Street, which was within walking distance of Samuels's home in Seething Lane.

***

The New Year dawned before Samuel returned to the Navy Office. As arranged, Henry presented himself at the office at eleven on the pretext of enquiring if the navy had any ketches that were no longer in service and could be bought by private investors. He was welcomed by a saddened Samuel, and was taken into a meeting room where his friend had prepared a portfolio of obsolete ships that the navy were prepared to sell.

Henry seated himself and Samuel began by describing the basic specification for three of the ships. "I think I should ask Sir Edward Montague to give us a few moments to advise you on the seaworthiness and suitability of these ketches for Atlantic seas."

Samuel rose only to return a few moments later with the admiral; Henry stood stiffly whilst Samuel introduced him as Mister Cavendish. Sir Edward offered him a hand, then with the three seated the admiral gave Henry some expert opinion as to the seaworthiness of each vessel.

When they had completed their discussions, and just as Sir Edward was about to take his leave, Henry said, "Thank you for your kind and valuable advice, Sir Edward. Incidentally, I believe that we are distantly related. My father gave me a letter of introduction to you before he died but I have never felt the cause to present it to you, sir, as I have made my own way in the world."

"And very commendable it is, Mister Cavendish. So Robert Cavendish was your father. I don't recall ever meeting the gentleman but I do know William Cavendish exceedingly well. You may not know it, but at the Battle of Marston Moor back in 'forty-four, I commanded a parliamentarian regiment of foot whilst you're relative William Cavendish, or to give him his just title, the Earl of Newcastle, led his own regiment of foot known as the Whitecoats. They made a heroic last stand during that battle but Prince Rupert made a mistake in dividing his cavalry. It cost the King the battle and eventually his head. The Earl of Newcastle was a fine leader, unfortunately we were on opposing sides, but that is all in the past, we all made mistakes and as you know I am now a staunch Royalist. So tell me, why would a merchant trader be interested in purchasing three naval ketches? Is there some money-making venture in the offing of which I am unaware and from which I could benefit?"

Samuel glanced surreptitiously at James before speaking, "I have heard rumours in the office, Sir Edward, that an adventurer named Médard Chouart, Sieur Des Groseilliers has returned to London from the Hudson Bay and has made a favourable report to Sir George Carteret but I am not privy to such confidences."

"And rightly so, Samuel, it would not do for all and sundry to be privy to what could be confidential information favourable to the government. So, Mister Cavendish, you haven't answered my question. Why are you interested in purchasing three naval ketches, which you yourself state must be of such seaworthiness as to be able to brave the Atlantic storms?"

Henry hesitated, realizing that he had almost accomplished his task of arousing the interest of Sir Edward Montague. "I have to admit, Sir Edward, that I do have some access to information that will benefit my trading interests. You see, the adventurer Médard Chouart, of whom Mister Pepys has heard, is my wife's father. I have met with him since his return from New France, and what he tells me leads me to believe that there are vast fortunes to be made in the Hudson Bay area."

"Well, thank you for being honest with me, Mister Cavendish. I am not without influence at court and if I can press home a case for the government to support the exploration of this new land for trade then be assured I will do so. Now, when you are seeking some investors in your venture, please give me the opportunity to avail myself by some investment."

"Certainly, Sir Edward, and thank you for the promise to press the case for our venture to the correct persons."

Sir Edward rose to leave the table, making apologies for his exit. "Now I must return to naval matters. At the moment, we may be at peace with the Dutch but I fear that a third war may take place and the navy needs to be better equipped with more funding from Whitehall."

As the meeting adjourned and Sir Edward departed, Henry was pleased he had managed to obtain some help in choosing suitable ships while presenting his case well. Sir Edward went away with the knowledge that he was privy to knowledge that could increase his wealth while Samuel said nothing, knowing his financial future was more secure.

***

The spring came and Elizabeth grew restless, expressing frequently the desire to return to her family home at Ufton Manor where her beloved Robert lay at rest.

Early in April she realized her ambition. Tom took leave of Henry's employment, hitched the pair of horses onto the family coach and with Elizabeth's trunks on board, drove out of the city and climbed the hill at Southgate. Elizabeth glanced back at the rebuilding in the distance and remembered Henry remarking a few days earlier that over two thousand new houses had been built in the last few months and that trade was getting back to normal but for Elizabeth she was going home, to Derbyshire, to her Robert.

***

After Elizabeth's departure, family life settled down in the Cavendish home. James progressed well with his lessons and Jane and Henry resumed their social life, which had been neglected after the death of Robert.

All the hard work done by Samuel in promoting, albeit surreptitiously, the exploration of the North West Passage and the area of Hudson Bay now bore fruit when in May, the good news came that the king had given a Royal Charter titled, *'The Governor and Company of Adventurers of England trading into Hudson's Bay'* to promote exploration for a North West passage to India.

Prince Rupert was appointed as the governor of the new company, which was formally named The Hudson Bay Company and several members of Parliament and the aristocracy, including Sir Edward Montague, joined as shareholders in the "Company of Adventurers". Henry and Samuel each invested five hundred pounds, the latter as a sleeping partner.

Unfortunately, fate was to intervene and Sir Edward would not to live to benefit from his investment.

Re-united

Ayear after Elizabeth had tragically passed away and almost two years since Deborah was turned out of the Pepys' home, in the December of 1670 Samuel and Debs met completely by chance.

Samuel was visiting a naval officer in Whitechapel and as it was only a ten-minute walk to Seething Lane, he decided to stroll back to his house. He was passing Angel Alley, deep in thought, when walking towards him he saw what he perceived to be a heavily pregnant young woman; he couldn't believe his eyes, he stopped as his eyes swam in a torrent of emotional tears, it was his lost love.

Quickly wiping his eyes dry, he stopped to greet Deborah, "Good day, my fair Debs." Samuel made a shallow bow at the demure but pregnant lady. "I see you have found yourself a husband?" More a question than a statement.

"Why yes, Master Pepys, I have been wed for all of a year and to a young clergyman named Jeremiah. I am now Mistress Wells. And how are you, Samuel, and your dear wife?"

A look of sorrow crossed Samuel's face as he explained that it was almost a year since Elizabeth had died of the fever.

"Oh, I am so sorry, Samuel, I had no idea." In a moment of gentleness her hand briefly touched his arm. "You must be feeling very lonely without Elizabeth to comfort you."

"No matter, Debs, but thank you."

Samuel and Deborah continued in conversation for some time and as they parted, Deborah promised to contact him if she was ever in need.

The request for help came just prior to the Christmas festivities when Samuel received a letter at the Navy Office from the Reverend Jeremiah Wells.

Dear Sir,

We are pleased to inform you that God has blessed my wife and I with a daughter. Mistress Wells gave safe deliverance of our daughter named Deborah on 14th Day of December 1670.

Whilst I am conveying this good news to you, may I humbly make a request? My wife, Mistress Wells, informs me that she was in the employment of your departed wife and she hathe requested that I beg you to use your influence at the Navy Office for me to gain employment to serve God and the King as a naval chaplain.

I am, Sir

Your most obliged and humble Servant.

Jeremiah Wells

Samuel read the letter; re-read it, then finally placed it in a drawer for his attention in the New Year. Over the festive period, Samuel gave some thought to its contents and the request from Jeremiah Wells for a naval post. Samuel realized that with her husband at sea the opportunities would give him an opportunity to renew his relationship with Deborah and he was torn between his conscience and the desire in his loins for his lost love.

Eventually in the spring Samuel finally salved his conscience on the grounds that he was providing employment for Deborah's family and he made arrangements for the Reverend Wells to be duly employed as a ship's chaplain.

Meanwhile at Cavendish House, Jane and Elizabeth were keeping in touch with the exchanging of news letters. Jane wrote how London was being rebuilt at a phenomenal rate with rows and rows of houses completed each week and how proud she was that James was growing fast and beginning to master some basic Latin and how clever he was becoming at his mathematics. Elizabeth responded with news of country life and how she was caring for the family grave but how lonely it was in the manor house and how she missed her family in London.

In another letter, written during the July of '71, Jane described how thrilled James had been when Henry took them to see the new Guildhall and the Royal Exchange and how they drove past Pudding Lane, which was rumoured to have been the source of the Great Fire. Henry had pointed out the work on the foundations for a huge monumental column designed by Christopher Wren and to be constructed of Portland stone. When complete it would be two hundred and two feet tall and would have stairs on the inside all the way to the top. Henry had told James that it would commemorate the fire. James being a boy asked if Henry would take him to the top when it was built. I told James of course his father would but then we told him it will be some years before it is completed.

Jane continued to correspond with Elizabeth and so the family kept in touch all through the year and into 'seventy-two.

Meanwhile, at the Navy Office; to help with the loss of his wife, Samuel kept himself busy absorbing his time with navy matters and consequently his meetings with Henry were infrequent, but in the February of 'seventy-two they met briefly. Henry was pleased to see Samuel had regained some of his spirit after his sad loss.

"Hard work usually distracts the mind in such times," was Samuel's retort. "But it's not just the hard work, Henry; I have found my Deborah and occasionally I seek solace in her arms when I invite her to visit me in Seething Lane. She is married now of course but with her husband employed as a ship's chaplain and away for lengthy periods, she is rather lonely, so we comfort each other; and I must say the hard work is necessary as the navy has been neglected of late. We may be equipped with ships but the treasury is most reluctant to invest in victuals; if war comes, I fear that we shall be ill prepared in men and supplies but I shall do my best."

That was his final remark to Henry on the subject. Samuel left Henry to make his way home wondering if the merchant fleets would be safe if war came.

Samuel's hard work did come to fruition when he eventually obtained funding from the treasury to organize and supply the fleet for the inevitable third Dutch war and for three months Samuel redoubled his frantic efforts to prepare the fleet. During that time Henry saw very little of Pepys.

157

Samuel's fears of war finally materialized as hostilities broke out in March 1672 when an English flotilla attacked a Dutch convoy of ships trying to reach a Dutch port.

In Paris, diplomatic envoys from Britain continued to work hard to align the French and English as allies and by the middle of May, the English fleet had set sail. For the moment, the pressure on Samuel now eased and he took time to socialize with Henry.

***

It was a late spring evening; Henry had taken a Sedan chair to *The Cock* alehouse where once before he had met Samuel for supper. The pair had arranged to meet for supper and during the course of the meal, the effect of the war was raised and how it could affect their trading ventures and profits.

"You realize, Henry, that our Virginian tobacco may well be at risk this year as this season's batch is due to arrive within the next few weeks but if the Dutch intercept any of our flotilla, we could lose it all to the Dutch merchants."

"It could cost us dear," said Henry. "If we lose even half of our merchantmen, it will seriously lower our capital for more investment into the Hudson Bay venture."

"That is certainly true, Henry, but putting our financial risks aside, what worries me most is the fact that England may be at risk. We have a combined British and French fleet of ninety-eight ships anchored off the Suffolk coast at Sole Bay with James the Duke of York as Admiral of the fleet and our friend Edward Montague, the Earl of Sandwich, as second in command but I fear the French Admiral Comte d'Estrees may not be up to his appointment of being in charge of the French contingent."

"For the sake of England and our profits, we can only hope that the Dutch can be defeated," Henry commented. "Otherwise all our trade routes will be in danger. Now let us eat and enjoy the evening for it may be some weeks before we can meet again."

True to Henry's prediction, it was the middle of June before they managed to meet again and on this occasion it was at Wills coffee house. Henry was the first to arrive and had just ordered a coffee when Samuel appeared.

"Let me order your coffee," Henry remarked as Samuel took his seat. "How goes the news of the war, Samuel, do you think we have anything to fear for our ships? They are due to berth in

158

a few weeks' time."

"I have excellent news, Henry. We have had a great victory at sea but it is saddened by the fact that our friend Edward Montague, the Earl of Sandwich, was killed in action. Apparently he went down with his flagship the *Royal James* which; according to accounts, he refused to abandon. He died a hero; it is sad, I know, but I had to tell you."

Samuel paused. "I am told his body was recovered from the sea several days later and he will be buried in Westminster Abbey."

"It is indeed sad news, Edward was a very good friend to me and must be a great loss to the admiralty; and to you as well, Samuel, however, the battle was won. Do you have any reports?"

Samuel took a sip of his steaming coffee that a waitress had placed before him. "Well, as I mentioned, the Anglo-French fleet was under the command of the Duke of York who was the Lord High Admiral; his flagship was the *Prince*, our deceased friend, the Earl of Sandwich commanded the *Royal James* and that cowardly villain, Vice Admiral Comte d'Estrees had the *St. Philippe* as his command ship. Comte d'Estrees and the French fleet were supposed to follow the battle plan as determined by the Duke of York."

"So what did the French do that seems so cowardly?" Henry asked.

"They sailed away out of the battle, leaving the English to fight the Dutch alone. It must be said that the Dutch fleet under the command of Michel de Ruyter, who is the Dutch Lieutenant Admiral, fought a valiant battle but the action of the French leaves me feeling very dispirited and distrustful towards any future alliances we make."

Samuel paused and sipped his coffee, which by now was cooling. "It appears that the battle began at dawn on the twenty-eighth of May. A French frigate that had been one of the scouts searching for the Dutch fleet returned post-haste to Sole Bay to raise the alarm with the news that the entire Dutch fleet was hot on her heels. That caused immediate confusion as the duke's flagship the *Prince* was still careened and taking on fighting men and ammunition. I must say, Henry, it was embarrassing, it took some time to float her and by the time that was achieved; and the combined Anglo-French fleet of ninety ships had put to sea, the Dutch fleet was on the horizon. The battle plan was for the French squadron to take the vanguard but in the confusion of setting formation, they found themselves placed at the rear. It was then, as I said previously, that the French sailed away and took no part in the rest of the action. With the Frenchies now running, the seventy Dutch ships outnumbered the Duke of York's division by two to one and the fighting that followed was brutal and intense. The Duke of York's flagship the *Prince* was of course an obvious target and from the start she was struck by several Dutchmen and attacked by fire ships. She was hard pressed."

"It seems that the Dutch are indeed tenacious opponents," said Henry. "I don't think I could ever have the courage to be aboard a man-of-war."

"And there is more," continued Samuel. "By the afternoon the decks of the *Prince* were swept by musket fire and her hull and rigging so badly damaged that she could no longer function as a flagship so the Duke was forced to transfer his flag to the *St Michael*. She then came under such a ferocious attack and was so severely damaged that the Duke and his staff were again forced to change flagships; this time they took to a barge and were rowed through the thick of the action to the *London*. It was about that time; during the heat of the battle, that our friend the Earl of Sandwich, on his flagship the *Royal James*, encountered his own problem. His ship was rammed and brought to a standstill by a small Dutch vessel that got snagged under the bowsprit; she then became a prime target for the Dutch fire-ships. It is on report that Edward fought on and remained in command of his ship and showed remarkable courage and aplomb by pacing the quarterdeck with his fellow officers until the flames drove them over the side and into the sea. It was then that Edward was drowned. The *Royal James* sank shortly afterwards following a huge explosion. Then with the sun setting and in the failing light apparently the Dutch received news of the possible return of the French fleet and they withdrew. The battle finally ended at sunset but I have to tell you, Henry, losses on the Allied side were heavy with the loss of the *Royal James* and many of our ships damaged but the Dutch also suffered severe losses. It was a very bloody battle. Even now, three weeks later, bloated and rotting corpses are still being washed ashore."

Henry sat in silence for a few moments, then said, "A truly great victory, Samuel, but at what a price. I suppose England is safe and our shipping lanes are secure?"

The pair sat in subdued conversation for some time before taking their leave.

Five weeks later, the tobacco-laden ships of the summer harvest began to arrive in the port; of the seven ships owned by the London merchants, five arrived over a period of seven days, a sixth limped up the Thames a week later but the seventh, a small ketch named the *Robert*, failed to reach port. Presumably she was lost at sea during the Atlantic crossing. Henry was particularly saddened; he had named that ship in honour of his father. He had now lost both Roberts.

Samuel falls from Grace

On a cold but sunny January day in 1680 Henry kept his promise and escorted a sixteen year old James on the arduous climb up the three hundred and eleven steps to the balcony of the Monument that gave a view of the new London.

Christopher Wren's Monument to commemorate the Fire of London had been completed three years previously but James had been studying hard and Henry found he was always busy with his financial trading ventures and there just hadn't been time, but today, as the cold winter air chilled their breath, the scene before them proved that the wait had been worthwhile.

Looking towards the Thames they could make out the movement of skaters on the frozen river, whilst further to the south a beautiful winter scene of the undulating South Downs covered by snow and illuminated by a weak winter sun lay like a picture before their eyes.

"It's like a scene from a painting by the Dutch artist Hendrick Avercamp," James commented.

Henry turned to stare at James. "Who on this earth has a name like Hendrick Avercamp, and who is he and how do you know about him?"

"Oh Papa, you're so out of date with modern art. He is, or I should say was, a deaf and dumb Dutch painter who died about forty-five years ago. He was the most brilliant exponent of painting of the winter landscape. I have read about him in one of my art studies."

Henry mused on the information and added, "Well, store the

facts away in your brain, James, education is never wasted, although I don't know when you will ever need that in our business."

Henry looked around the landscape then pointed to the place were the old St Paul's had once stood. "I'm afraid, James, I shall not live to see the new cathedral, but you must come up here some day with your children to marvel and show them the skill of those master craftsmen and builders."

Henry's prophetic statement was to come true sooner than expected; he would not live to see the new cathedral, and it would be another twenty years before it was completed.

Slowly descending the stairs, the pair walked some distance then stopped at a coffee house. During the course of conversation, James remarked that he hadn't seen much of Samuel since the death of Elizabeth.

"He hasn't become a recluse or morose, has he father, he is in good health, isn't he?"

"No, there is nothing to worry about, James, he is in good health, but there are worries about his future. You may recall your mother and I talking about Samuel entering politics."

"I do seem to have heard you mention it, father."

"Well, before Elizabeth died, he became the first Member of Parliament for Castle Rising in Norfolk. Then this year he changed his constituency and was elected to represent Harwich, but I fear that he has been disgraced and has had to resign his seat."

"Oh dear, what can he have done, to be so disgraced? I always considered Samuel to be an honourable man."

Henry agreed but added, "I fear it is a serious matter, he has been arrested and sent to the Tower. He may be accused of selling secrets to the French and if proven he will be charged with treason. I don't believe the accusations for one moment but they have to be investigated. We are all praying for him to be released without charge."

Henry and James finished their coffees and took a hackney carriage back home were they found an agitated Jane waiting for them.

"Its bad news, I fear, Henry; a fast rider has just relayed a message from Ufton Manor. It seems Elizabeth has taken a chill and is not too well. The doctor is calling each day but I think we should go post-haste in case the worst happens. We don't want her to pass away without her family around her, do we?"

Urgent preparations were made and Henry, who now owned his own coach and pair, gave orders for the baggage to be packed and loaded onto the coach. Adequate furs to ward off the cold were placed on the seats and with a reliable driver in charge, Henry, Jane and James departed on a three-day journey up into the midland of Derbyshire, finally arriving at Ufton Manor on Wednesday the twenty-sixth of January to find a frail, weakened Elizabeth, in bed, being attended by her doctor.

"I fear the worst, Henry," the doctor explained. "Your mother has taken a very severe chill. You know she was always head-strong. She was begged not to go out to your father's grave on Christmas Day as it was exceptionally cold but she insisted. She even knelt in prayer at the graveside. I fear it was too much for her and she has developed a fever which is taking all her strength. It can only be a matter of time."

Elizabeth died peacefully in her sleep on the fourth of February 1680 with her family at her bedside,

During the following week Henry and Jane visited Mister Jones of Middleton and Jones, the family solicitors in Chester-field, to make arrangements to ensure the finances were in place for continuance of the payments to the retaining staff and also to make arrangements for the continued upkeep of Ufton Manor.

It was the middle of February before their affairs were in order and the three travellers laid flowers on the family graves, closed up the manor house and headed south to Cavendish House in Newington Green. On their return they received the good news that Samuel had been released from the Tower without charge but he had decided to move from Seething Lane to a house in Buckingham Street that stood a few yards from York Stair Water-gate and gave him direct access onto the Thames and the ferry-men who offered fast transport up to Whitehall.

During 1682 life for the Cavendish family returned to nor-mal. The financial prosperity of the family was assured, with the revenue from the tobacco and fur trade increasing in spite of the death of Prince Rupert who was their Hudson Bay sponsor.

Prince Rupert had died at his house in Spring Gardens, Westminster on nineteenth of November 1682 and like most British dignitaries was buried in Westminster Abbey. Irrespective of Samuel's recent fall from grace, the very fact that he was released without charge was enough for him to be invited to attend the funeral service and for him to continue in his employment at the Navy Office where he frequently came into contact with James the Duke of York who had distinguished himself in the war with the Dutch as the Lord High Admiral.

Now as 1682 drew to a close, the Duke was Samuel's ear at court, enabling Samuel to continue to advise James on their foreign investments.

Life is a See-Saw

Two days before Christmas 1683, London was enveloped in the coldest period in living memory. The Thames was frozen to a depth of two feet and by New Year's Day, the weather was so severe that hundreds of traders set up shops on the ice. Ten days later, the ice became so thick that traders lit fires on the ice and were roasting meat on braziers; a complete miniature town centre was created out on the ice. The populace no longer used London Bridge to cross the river as coaches, carts and horses crossed over on the ice. Some coachmen plied their trade offering trips between the frozen ferry landing stages from Westminster to the Temple. However, the carnival atmosphere was soon to change as the severe cold went into February.

In the forests around London, trees were split by the great freeze, birds and fish were frozen to death. Herds of deer perished in the arctic cold.

Although there was a good reserve of wood in the cellars at Cavendish House, fuel for the fires became too expensive for the poorer people. James and his associates found themselves donating money to the churches to help the poor and sick from freezing to death.

With the prolonged cold another problem manifested itself. There was very little breeze, and the consequent lack of air movement meant that smoke was hindered and the air at street level became so polluted that the populace could scarcely see across the narrow streets. The foul smoke-polluted air filled the lungs and breathing became difficult and the elderly and sick began to die in the streets.

In the middle of February it began to thaw but the thaw was short lived and the river froze again. Now London was facing a real health hazard. It had always been considered unsafe to drink water, especially the river water, and so beer was offered as the safe staple refreshment. But now, due to a lack of water, breweries had to close. Then just as food and fuel supplies were becoming critical, nature released its icy grasp and the mini ice age siege of London of 1684 was relieved when at the end of February barges again were able to traverse the waterways.

Life for the Cavendish family was a continuous seesaw of emotions from the low depression cast with losing their bene-factor Prince Rupert, followed by the winter depression of the arctic freeze. Then the seesaw tilted and their spirits rose with the warmth of the summer of 1684 and life returned to some normal-ity.

Henry and Samuel began to reap the benefits of their invest-ments in the Hudson Bay, but then the seesaw crashed down into depression when on the sixth of February 1685 Charles II died, an event that threatened their whole scheme of investment.

Samuel and Henry met to discuss the effect the king's demise would have on future expeditions to the Hudson Bay.

"I really am concerned, Samuel, the royal patronage given by Charles was crucial in expanding our trade in the New World. The new monarch may not be as favourable. What is your opin-ion?"

Samuel thought for a moment or two before responding. "I am sure that when the Duke of York is crowned as king, he will be just as enthusiastic to promote the exploration and develop-ment of trade. The death of Prince Rupert a couple of years ago didn't affect the venture, so I hope that we shall still receive royal blessing."

The couple continued to discuss the issues for some time, which did little to allay Henry's fears and when the pair parted, he wore the crown of a worried business man.

Towards the end of May Henry again met Samuel, who was by now ecstatic with news.

"I have been appointed Secretary of the Admiralty and with that position I shall be a canopy bearer at the forthcoming coronation of James II. The coronation has been arranged for the twenty-third of April. I think that day is chosen because it is St George's day and it is hoped in official circles that it will herald in a new era of prosperity for our country. You and Jane have been good friends to me through the years and so I have used my influence to obtain seats for both of you in St Peter's chapel in Westminster."

Henry was almost as excited as Samuel and embraced his friend. "I know you to be discreet," Samuel continued, "and I know I can trust you, Henry. When my wife Elizabeth died, she died as a practising Catholic. My own faith is also disposed towards Catholicism; however, due to my employment within Whitehall, I cannot let it be common knowledge. I know that when King Charles was dying he reverted and died a Catholic. Now that the Duke of York is to be king, I think we may see a return of Catholicism in England."

"But surely Parliament won't allow that."

"You may be correct. We must wait and see what our new king advocates but I fear we may be in for some tempestuous times, Henry."

It was in 1688 that Samuel's fears came to pass. To prevent a reversion to Catholicism, William of Orange invaded England; King James II fled to France, Parliament absolved his reign and invited the Protestant William and his Queen Mary to take the English throne.

Meanwhile at Cavendish House, James was slowly handling more of the family business interests and now at the age of twenty-four, he was an eligible batchelor who had caught the eye of wives of some of the London merchants who were looking for suitable spouses for their daughters.

The Walters were a family of the original Virginia merchants. The head of the family, Oliver Walters, owned a modest stone-built residence in fashionable Islington, where he lived with his wife Frances, and Constance, who was the elder of their two daughters. She was eighteen years old with hazel eyes and chestnut coloured ringlets framing an angelic face and had a countenance that seemed to bring a sparkle to the eye of James whenever Henry and James called at the Walters' home.

Lately James had taken to calling without the presence of

Henry, and during the summer of 1688 Oliver and Frances noticed there seemed to be a mutual attraction. A distinct possibility of a suitable match for Constance had arrived on the scene.

Henry and Oliver discussed the possibility and both agreed to discuss the matter with their wives before broaching the subject to James and Constance. After a meeting of the parents all agreed it was a suitable match and there was no objection if James and Constance were agreeable. James and Constance were approached individually as to their own feelings on a betrothal.

James welcomed the proposal but tried to remain aloof from showing too much enthusiasm in front of his own parents.

At the Walter's household, Oliver and Frances summoned Constance into their drawing room. Frances opened the conversation.

"Do come and sit beside me on the sofa, my dear. We have a matter to discuss with you."

Constance demurely took a seat keeping her knees together as she had been taught. She let her hands rest comfortably in her lap and waited for her mother to continue.

"You are now of an age when we should be seeking possible suitors for you and we have noticed a mutual attraction between you and the young Cavendish boy; James is his name, is it not?"

"Yes, Mama."

"Your father and I have discussed the matter and also with James's parents and if you are agreeable we have no objection to a formal arrangement for you both to be betrothed. How do you feel about the proposal?"

Constance greeted this announcement with cries of excitement coupled with displays of affection to her mother and papa. The betrothal was announced for friends and family to attend a wedding planned for the following year.

Early in June of 1689 the happy couple were joined in wedlock at the church of St Mary Aldermary in Bow Lane. The church had previously been destroyed in the great fire but was now rebuilt by master craftsmen to the design of Christopher Wren. Samuel attended as guest of honour but sadness fell on the Cavendish home when a week after the wedding Samuel's honour and good name was once more besmirched. He was again arrested but this time on suspicion of Jacobite tendencies for the restoration of a

Catholic monarchy.

Again the charges were dropped for lack of proof but it was felt that Samuel's declining health had partially influenced Parliament.

Privately Samuel's friends knew that he held more allegiance to the deposed Catholic King James, whom he respected for his ability on naval matters, than the incoming protestant William of Orange, and although Samuel was relieved to have been released without charge, he decided it was finally time to retire from government office.

So the emotional seesaw continued within Cavendish House with the joy at Samuel's release followed by the sadness of his retirement, which was followed by joy when Constance gave birth to a son whom they named Charles. Constance repeated the process in 1691 when she was again safely delivered of a child. This time it was a girl whom they named Annabel.

Henry and Jane now had a full life and took all their pleasure from their grandchildren.

Even the sad news that Queen Mary had died from smallpox passed almost unnoticed by Henry, although Jane did remark, "Well, it doesn't give much hope to the poor people, does it, that the Queen with all her wealth can be struck down with the disease at the age of thirty-two?"

All Henry said was, "*C'est la vie*, my love, *c'est la vie*," as he continued to read his newspaper, which contained one item of commercial news that did arouse his interest and was to cause some excitement among the merchant traders.

Henry read that the government was to found a Bank of England to become the national bank for the country and handle the money business of government and the national debt.

The seesaw of life for the Cavendish household was now stable, and remained in equilibrium for the next three years, a situation that would have continued except for the fact that the winter of 'ninety-seven was again extremely harsh. Not as harsh as the big freeze of thirteen years previously but still very harsh.

It was a cold sunny February day; Charles and Annabelle awoke to see that a heavy fall of snow lay on the green. The sun sparkled on the icicles dangling from any suitable appendage including the branches of the deciduous trees. The snow glistened on the ground.

"Can we build a snowman, a big one with a carrot for his nose?" Charles cried excitedly.

"And two stones for his eyes," Annabelle added.

Armed with a suitable spade, Henry took young Charles and Annabelle onto the green to start a mound of snow. The three kept working, piling the snow until there was a mound about five feet in height. They had worked for about an hour, their breath vaporizing on the still morning air.

Henry paused in the work and rested on the spade. "I'm getting too old to be doing this," he said, and at that moment, tightness seemed to grip his chest, and he felt his vision revolving as he fell to the ground.

"Papa, Papa, do get up, please get up. Are you unwell?" Annabelle shouted as she ran to his still form that lay in the snow.

Charles also shouted in alarm.

At that moment Constance and Jane came running from the house. They had been watching from one of their windows as their family played in the winter sun and had seen the incident.

A crowd of onlookers surrounded Henry's still form. Four men lifted him and slowly carried him back into his house. Jane fought back the tears as Charles and Annabelle clung to her skirts. A doctor was called but Henry aged sixty was pronounced dead.

Samuel sent his condolences as soon as he heard the news and called the following day to enquire if he could help the family in their time of grief.

"Where are you having Henry interred?" he asked.

"We thought we would take him back to Ufton Manor. That is where all his family are buried and he did grow up in that part of the country," said James, who was now the head of the house and took charge of the affairs.

So arrangements were made for Henry's coffin to be returned to his birthplace to be buried in the Cavendish family plot in the tranquil churchyard where Sylvia Leach had first met her lover, all those years ago. James and Jane accompanied the cortege whilst it was agreed that Charles and Annabelle would stay with Constance in Newington Green.

Arriving at the old manor house, James and Jane found it looking a little neglected. It had been virtually unoccupied for almost twenty years since Elizabeth had died in 1680. Henry had visited his family home once a year since his mother died but had taken little interest in its maintenance. Now James found that the property was in need of substantial repairs. After the retainers had lit extra fires in all the rooms, James and Jane settled down to making arrangements for the interment.

A service was held two days later in the family church, followed by Henry's interment in the graveyard alongside his parents Robert and Elizabeth and his grandmother Sylvia Leach. Henry had come home to rest.

A few days later, James was talking to his mother in the library. "Mother, we need to arrange for younger staff to be employed here at the manor. The three staff that have been retained over the years are now getting elderly and we should make arrangements for their welfare and replacements."

"You do whatever you think is right for them," Jane answered. "Have you also assessed the repair work that needs to be done? The old roof is beginning to allow rain into one of the upstairs rooms."

"You are right, mother, the property will have to be maintained or sold. But remember, the old manor house could one day be a home for Charles or Annabelle if they ever decide to leave London and settle for a rural lifestyle."

So it was agreed to finance the repairs and after consulting with the family solicitors Middleton & Jones in Chesterfield to arrange financing for renovating the old property, James sought the advice of Michael Jackson, a local guildsman, who promised to visit Ufton Manor the following week to make extensive notes of the renovations and repairs that James wished to implement. A few days later, with the new staff employed, Michael and his young journeyman Noelius Ellison arrived at the manor to take instructions for the restoration work.

"Don't you be worrying, sir. We shall do a good job. Young Noelius is a good lad, he tries it on occasionally, as all lads do, and he fails to follow the plans occasionally, but I keep an eye on him. I usually give him a few sharp kicks of his backside plus a stoppage of his visits to the Peacock and he's soon back to getting a good job done."

Noelius kept his eyes lowered to the floor but James thought he had caught a flash of hatred in the eyes at Mr Jackson's comment's but knowing the restoration work would be completed under his watchful eye, James agreed to the work to go ahead.

The following day James and Jane returned to London.

The spring of 1698 slipped into early summer without any major incidents. James was kept busy organizing the provisioning of the fleet of merchants' ships that were to leave London to transport commodities to the planters in Virginia in exchange for the season's tobacco harvest, but a major problem had arisen that was causing rising costs to the investors. The problem lay in a shortage of labour to harvest the tobacco crops. The cause of the labour crisis was the increased demand for tobacco resulting in plantations expanding further up the Potomac River into virgin territory. The expansion caused a demand for field workers who were willing to do the hard work. The demand exceeded the supply from the colonies or from England and a solution had to be found quickly. It had to be a solution that would provide a cheap inexhaustible workforce to the plantations. The solution was an expansion of the slave trade.

Bristol and Liverpool on the western seaboard of Britain seized the opportunity to become the prominent trading ports. It was a solution that was to affect the traders in London, who were about to suffer a decline in their profits.

Shipshape and Bristol Fashion

For ten years Edward Lloyd's coffee house in Tower Street was fashionable with a clientele who were mainly merchant traders. It was an establishment that was destined to become a world famous name in shipping insurance. The proprietor Edward Lloyd didn't partake in any of the investments, but he had two assets: he served excellent coffee and he had access to the nearby Navy Office where Samuel Pepys spent much of his career. Consequently, news of shipping movements was on display daily in Lloyds.

On numerous occasions Henry Cavendish had taken James to Lloyds and it was there that James had met a leading member of the Royal African Company, a Mister Edward Colston.

Colston was born in Bristol but had lived in London for many years and had a flourishing business trading in cloth, wine, sugar and slaves but now the loss of the trading monopoly caused by Parliament cancelling their Royal Charter was a severe concern. Edward Colston arranged a meeting with other merchants to discuss a solution to the crisis and for London to continue to provide slaves to the colonies in the New World. A private room at Lloyds was booked and on a late May afternoon in 1698 the members of the Royal African Company and James Cavendish and other representatives from the initial families of the Virginian Merchant Venturers attended the meeting.

Colston had travelled by river boat down the Thames from his home in Mortlake in Surrey. He rose to his feet to address the meeting and a hush fell over the assembled merchants.

"Gentlemen, I am Edward Colston and we are here today to discuss possible measures that we can take to counter the loss of our monopoly in the colonial slave trade. I know that some of you have invested in the tobacco plantations of Virginia. As you may know, my investments have been in the sugar plantations but we are all going to suffer if we cannot get an unlimited supply of cheap labour to harvest the crops, and that supply is slaves from the African coast. As you are aware, the Royal African Company was given its charter by Charles II and we have all benefited from that monopoly of slave trading, but now due to pressure from the Bristol and Liverpool merchants, Parliament has deemed it wise to abolish that charter and we are going to face increased competition from those sea ports. Gentlemen, I put it to you to make suggestions that we can implement to resolve the problem."

With that speech, Edward remained on his feet to seek some response from the traders.

James rose to address the general assembly of merchants. "I am James Cavendish and it seems to me that with Bristol and Liverpool lying geographically on the west coast of England, and London lying to the east, it is logical to assume that now our monopoly has been broken, Bristol and Liverpool will become the prime trading ports in England and as merchants we must seek investments in those cities."

Turning to address Edward Colston, James continued, "I understand, Edward, that you originally came from Bristol and so your family will have business contacts in that city. Am I correct, sir?" Edward nodded in affirmation. "Then, gentlemen, I propose that a representative selected from the Virginian Merchant Venturers, and Edward as a representative for the interests of the Royal African Company, visit Bristol to discuss entering into some association or investment with our Bristol competitors."

At that moment Edward Lloyd entered the room with a tray of refreshments and heard the end of the proposal. Placing a large tray of coffees onto a table, he said, "Excuse me, sirs, but I couldn't help but overhear that a group of you may be going to Bristol to enquire about shipping of slaves to the colonies. I have it on good authority that a ship owned by a Mister Stephen Barker named *The Beginning* is being fitted out as the first slave ship to depart from that port. I thought the information may be of use to you."

175

"That information will be most helpful in our enterprise. Thank you, Mister Lloyd." James sat down.

Some merchants added the viewpoint that a possible visit to Liverpool would be profitable but eventually the meeting voted that primarily a delegation should visit Bristol.

Edward Colston rose again from his seat to address the gathered merchants. "So it is agreed gentlemen, James and I will travel to Bristol and report back to you in a month's time."

***

The day before Edward Colston and James were to travel together to Bristol, James met with the now ageing Samuel Pepys who grasped James' hand and said in a beseeching tone, "Remember, James, I have commercial interests in making sure that we maintain our investments. If you need to register any of our ships in Bristol, I think you should know that when I visited Bristol some years ago with my beloved Deborah, her uncle showed me a new customs house. It was built for the newly appointed King's Officer to the Port of Bristol. If my memory serves me correct, it was located in a place I believe was called Welsh Back."

Samuel paused for breath then continued, "There may be a slight problem for you to register as a ship owner in Bristol. I have it on good authority through the Navy Office that the authorities for the Bristol port will only allow Bristol born personages to register ships in that port. But I am confident that you will overcome that problem."

Pay on the Nail

The Tudor mansion house in the Surrey town of Mortlake lay silent; Edward Colston closed the front door and approached his carriage; Henry the driver took Edward's travelling bags and stowed them away, then opening the door he assisted Edward to climb aboard.

"Down to the river, Henry," Edward instructed. "You need to find me a waterman to ferry me across to the northern bank."

Half an hour later Edward's coach came to a halt. Edward peered out and saw the river with wisps of early morning mist rising from the shimmering water as the early morning sun began to break through to shine and glint on the water. Occasionally a brown trout broke the surface to snap at a fly, all was at peace with the world. Nothing moved, Edward noticed a landing stage whose timbers rose from the placid waters like dead sentinels guarding a silent road. A ferry boat was moored but abandoned.

Henry climbed down. "I'll find you a waterman; you just sit in the coach, sir." He returned minutes later and opened the coach door to assist Edward to disembark. "I found one, sir, he was in the Sitting Goose ale house; he's called Ned; he were having a rest as he says trade was a bit slow this early in the day. He will be along in a minute."

Henry unloaded Edward's travelling bags and escorted him onto the landing stage where the ferry boat was moored.

Ned the waterman appeared moments later as Henry took his leave and Ned carried Edward's bags aboard.

Edward climbed aboard unassisted and took a seat while Ned

slipped the moorings, then using the oars, the waterman eased the boat out into the mainstream of the river; slowly the boat picked up speed as the current took hold and Ned oared his boat towards the Chiswick waterfront. Easing the boat into the landing stage, Ned jumped ashore and moored the craft safely. He then helped Edward onto the landing stage. Edward paid the waterman sixpence then gave a penny to a boy to find him a coachman to drive him the two miles to the Kings Head in Turnham Green, where it had been arranged for James to meet him with the Cavendish coach.

***

At five o'clock on that same June morn over in Newington Green; the butterflies fluttered in the long grass, and overhead swallows swirled, swooped and dived as they fed on the early morning swarms of summer insects in the meadow at Miller's Farm.

The elderly Joan Miller, who owned the farm when Henry had moved into the village, had passed away twenty years previously. The new owner had retained the name of Miller's Farm and Henry had made an agreement with him for the housing of his coach and the stabling of his horses. Time had also seen the demise of old Tom who had died in 1670 and been replaced by a younger coach man named Ben McQuire. He too was now approaching fifty. He had a wife name Vivien, who worked in the house as serving maid. She had been a buxom wench in her younger days; Henry had often remarked she would have not been shamed alongside Nell Gwynne.

Today Vivien was helping Ben harness the pair of mares to the Cavendish coach. She had risen early and helped put a final polish to the coach. Now she waved goodbye to Ben as he went to collect James from Cavendish House; leaving Vivien to walk back to another day of her servitude in the Cavendish household.

"Take the Chiswick road," James instructed Ben as he climbed into his coach. Arriving at the King's Head, James and Ben refreshed themselves with a brief wash from a water butt. Inside the Inn, they discovered Edward Colston was waiting for them to join him for a late breakfast; after which, with Edward on board, they drove off on the Bristol Road. For the first few miles the road was fairly well maintained but then the old packers' track became

178

badly rutted and the journey became exceedingly uncomfortable.

By the end of the first day a weary James, Edward and Ben pulled into an inn at Reading.

Ben retired to the stable boys' quarters to groom the horses and have his supper while James and Edward partook of the local fare in the inn and after sharing a bottle of claret they retired to their rooms for a good night's sleep.

Making an early start the group travelled for two days with overnight stops in Marlborough and Chipping Sodbury and on the third day, tired and travel weary, they finally arrived in the bustling seaport of Bristol.

Ben slowly drove the coach along the cobbled quayside and stopped at the corner of King Street. In a row of five cottages, the centre one, larger than the others, had a sign proclaiming it to be *The Llandoger Trow*

Ben climbed down from his seat and opened the carriage door for James and Edward to descend onto the cobbled quay. Stretching, the pair looked around and took in the scene. At least fifty merchantmen were moored in the basin; farther out in the mainstream of the river James saw a naval frigate. All along the quayside people jostled with barrows laden with goods being transported to and from the ships. Everywhere it was a hive of activity with sailors mingling with the port workers. Slinking along the side of the cottages James saw a mangy dog with a torn ear.

Entering the inn, James found a middle aged well built man wiping the top surface of a serving bar.

James approached the man and enquired about rooms for Mister Colston and accommodation for himself and his coachman.

"I 'as a room with a bed and cot in it for you and your driver," said the landlord, "and there be room for Mister Colston at the rear if that suitable, sir."

"Are you the landlord of this establishment?" James asked

"Indeed I am, sir, Jim Hawkins is the name.

"Well Mister Hawkins, we are sure the rooms will be fine, could you show Ben were he can stable the horses?"

The landlord assured James that he would get the horses stabled nearby and the coach could be put into the yard at the rear of the inn.

"Will you be staying with us for long, sir?" Hawkins enquired.

"Probably a week if our business is settled quickly and perhaps you can help us; we are looking for a gentleman named Stephen Barker who, we believe, owns a ship named *The Beginning*. Have you any knowledge of were I can find him?"

Edward cut into the enquiry. "Oh, and any knowledge of members of the Bristol Society of Merchants Ventures would be useful." He opened his purse and put a half sovereign on the table just out of reach of Hawkins. "I will pay handsomely for any reliable information."

Having given a display of his intended generosity, Edward picked up the half sovereign and put it back in his purse.

"I am sure I can assist you, leave it with me, kind sirs." The landlord touched his forelock then took his leave.

Edward and James ate at the inn that night whilst Ben went over to the stables to check the horses were fed and groomed. Then he joined some of the other drivers at a nearby ale house for supper and a pint of cider before making his way along the quay to his room at the Llandoger. He was just two ships' lengths away from the inn when a cloud obscured the moon; for a moment the wharf was plunged into darkness except for a glow of lamplight from an opened door, Ben quickened his pace, but he never heard the sound behind him as his head exploded in a myriad of dancing stars and he fell to the cobbles.

His assailant quickly pocketed his cudgel, rifled through his victim's pockets. Finding only a purse with a few silver coins, the thief stood up, planted a hefty kick into Ben's back, and took to his heels. Moments later a pair of sailors, returning to their boat, found the body lying in a pool of blood on the cobbled quayside. Turning the body over, one felt for a heartbeat,

"He's alive," he shouted as he gently moved him against a house wall while his mate went into the Llandoger Trow for some assistance.

James and Edward were sitting at a corner table discussing the days activities and their plans for tomorrow when the door burst open and a seaman ran into the room shouting, "Help, there is a man lying outside, he's been attacked and robbed."

The landlord hurried over to the sailor and the pair went outside to see what could be done. Jim Hawkins immediately recognized Ben and hurried back to the inn where he found James.

"Sir, I believe your coachman has been attacked and is lying injured on the quay." James and Edward rose and pushed through the small crowd that was now gathering.

Taking in the scene James knelt at Ben's side and felt for a heartbeat. "At least he's still alive," he said to Edward.

"Can we lift him gently and get him inside?" asked James and the two sailors carried Ben into the inn.

"There is a barber surgeon who serves on one of our boats. He lives nearby, I can ask him to come," offered the older sailor.

"That's extremely kind of you, my man," responded James. "Meanwhile can we get him upstairs and onto the cot in my room?" Edward and James lifted Ben under his armpits and manhandled him up the stairs whilst the sailor departed. The excitement over, the crowd began to disperse.

Ben's still form was lying on the cot when the surgeon barber arrived. After a brief examination he concluded that his patient hadn't any broken ribs but could not comment on when or if he would regain consciousness, nor if brain damage had been inflicted. But as a precautionary measure and to allay any blood forming on the brain, the surgeon suggested that he bleed the victim with leeches. An hour later, with Ben still lying unconscious, the surgeon departed with assurance of his return the next morning to check if there was any change in his patient's condition.

As Edward bade James goodnight and retired to his own room, it was a sad and worried James who undressed and climbed into bed that night.

***

The sun was beginning to shine through the window when James woke. He had not slept well; it had been a restless night. James threw off his covers and climbed out of bed; stretching and rubbing the sleep from his eyes, he went over to his servant's cot. James smiled; inwardly pleased that Ben seemed to be sleeping normally and some colour had returned to his cheeks. Bonehead McQuire, James thought, his nickname seems to be well earned. He didn't disturb Ben as he crept out of the room and went down into the yard at the rear of the inn to fetch a bucket of water from the pump.

Returning to his room he washed his hands and face, by which time he noticed that Ben was stirring as if coming out of a deep sleep. James took a damp cloth over to him and gently wiped Ben's brow with the cool damp cloth. Ben gave a moan and slowly his eyelids fluttered open. His eyes seemed glazed, and then they gained some clarity as they focussed. Finally he tried to raise himself onto one elbow.

"Just you lie back," James said. "You have had a bad experience and are very lucky to be alive. I was just thinking, you must have a thick skull." James jested in an attempt to make Ben's plight more durable.

"I was attacked, Master James, I never heard 'em creep up on me."

"I think they may have stolen your purse, as it was not on your person when we found you. Did you have much money on you?" James asked.

"No sir, just a couple of six penny pieces and a few penny coins, you know sir, just enough to buy me an ale or two."

At that moment the barber surgeon knocked and entered the room. "Well, my lad, I am pleased to see you are sitting up and seem to be recovering from that assault. You know it was quite a nasty knock to your head. But I don't think you will be in need of my services any more."

James escorted the ship's surgeon downstairs.

"How much do I owe you for your services?" James asked.

"Pleased to help, there is nothing to pay; I only helped an injured man in his hour of need."

"That is most Christian and charitable of you." James paused as a thought entered his mind. "I must apologize but I am unaware of your name, sir?"

"I am Mister Rosewell, Surgeon Barber and my premises are in All Saints Lane, just around the corner. It is a brief walk from here and near to the trader's market in Corn Street."

"Then, sir, you may very well be able to assist us further. You have associates in this city and you are also a navy surgeon. My friend Henry Colston and I are in Bristol to attempt to meet some of the Bristol Society of Merchants Ventures and also to discover if a ship named *The Beginning* has departed to the Americas yet."

"I may be of assistance on both matters," Mister Rosewell responded. "Near to my premises is Corn Street, and there are a few coffee houses where traders meet. In one of those, I am sure you will find for whom or what you are searching. As for the ship, *The Beginning*, I believe she sailed last week, but I understand that Stephen Barker, her owner, does frequent this inn on occasion. If you require it, sir, I have a few customers from the merchant fraternity and I may be able to give you an introduction."

"That's very kind of you, Mister Rosewell." James thanked the surgeon with assurances that they would call on him later that morning. They shook hands and parted company.

James returned to his room to find Ben out of bed and on his feet.

"Ben, just be careful, you should be resting. Are you feeling well enough to get out of bed?"

"Aye, sir, I will be all right with some cold water on my face and then some food in my belly."

Carefully the pair made their way to Edward's room. They then took hold of Ben's arm to help him descend the inn stairs. A few sailors and quayside workers were already partaking of early morning refreshments. Ben, wishing to maintain a servant-to-master status, sat separately from James and Edward and ordered a platter of bread, cheese and an onion and a flagon of ale. Having eaten he rose with a little more assurance and steadiness.

James rose from his table and went over to Ben and said, "Now, Ben, you have a rest today. You've have had a nasty knock to the head."

"Thank yer, sir, but I shall just look to the horses, sir, and then I will clean the coach. I shall not be wandering off today." And with a touch to his forelock Ben took slowly took his leave.

"He's made a good recovery from that blow to his head," Edward said. "These lower classes must have thicker skulls than us. It's a sad fact, but I hear that such blows to the skull may affect their descendents; we can only hope Mister McQuire's descendants will not be too badly affected."

James made no comment, whilst inwardly contemplating a side to Edward Colston's nature of which he had been unaware. The pair finished their breakfast and enquired of the landlord if he had any news from his enquiries.

"I do indeed, sir. That ship you was asking about, *The Beginning,* that was her name, I believe, well, she set sail middle of last week. She had a cargo of woollen cloth, pottery, jugs bottles and pewter jugs and bowls. She was also carrying other small tradable items such as pipes, tobacco, glassware and beads. I believe she is bound for the Ivory Coast of Africa. As for the Merchant Venturers, I am told they assemble to discuss trade and shipping news at one or two of the coffee houses on Corn Street."

"Well, thank you for your information." Edward opened his purse and passed a half sovereign to Hawkins.

"Come along, James, we have business to discuss this day."

The pair left the inn and made their way on foot along the quay until they reached All Saints Lane. Looking into the distance James saw the red and white striped pole protruding above the surgeon barber's shop. Mister Rosewell was standing in the doorway.

Slowly the pair strolled up the lane.

"Good morning, sirs." Both James and Edward raised their canes to touch their foreheads in acknowledgement of the greeting. "I am experiencing a lack of customers today. My son is learning the trade and he can stand watch for me."

Mister Rosewell shouted instructions into his shop; then closing the shop door, the three continued the walk up onto Corn Street where facing them they saw a pair of four-storey houses and a church. On the south wall of the church, a colonnade had been built. A sign proclaimed it to be Tolzey Walk.

The walkway was thronged with people, some transported in sedan chairs, others strolling. Amidst the casual buyers and urban dwellers, porters hurried by carrying anything from a set of books to a few papers for delivery to the merchants and traders. Located at the entrance to the colonnade were four waist-high brass pedestals at which traders seemed to be haggling and dealing.

James noticed that money or promissory notes were placed on the flat top of the pedestals. Before James or Edward could ask, Mister Rosewell in a deep Bristolian accent said, "See them brass short pillars with flat tops, they be called nails, they be. Him there, he be very old, then him there is from Queen Elizabeth's time. He was given by a Bristol merchant Robert Kitchen who died about

1594. Those other two, well they be younger nails, only about fifty year old they be, 'im there, he has the name John Barker on his rim. He was a wealthy merchant and was our mayor before old Charles lost his head to parliament's axe-man. Before the restoration, in the old days, merchants used to bring the nails to market each week and do their business deals on them, but now they are permanent fixtures here in the colonnade. 'To pay on the nail' has become the expression."

"Well, you learn something every day," James retorted. "I often wondered how that saying came about."

"Well, my dears this isn't finding you the meeting house for the merchants," and Mister Rosewell led Edward and James away towards a small coffee shop.

At Mister Rosewell's suggestion, the three took a table near the rear of the establishment, "This way I can see who is entering, and when I see one of the gentlemen I am looking for, I will introduce you."

James ordered the coffees, and just as it was being served, Mister Rosewell rose from the table and spoke to a man who had just entered the establishment. After a few minutes, the pair approached James and Edward. "Gentlemen, may I introduce Nathanial Day who owns a number of ships and I think he may be able to help you."

Edward Colston rose and shook Nathanial's hand. "Do be seated, Mister Day. May I offer you a coffee?"

Nathanial nodded and took a seat alongside Mister Roswell who finished his coffee and then rose.

"Well, sirs, I will be leaving you now, I have left my shop for too long."

With a farewell handshake to James and Edward he left the three merchants to discuss business.

Slave Traders

Nathanial sat quietly; his face wore an almost pained expression of boredom as he listened whilst Edward explained that he and James represented the London merchants. "We have trading interests in the Virginian tobacco plantations but we are experiencing a labour shortage and now we have lost the monopoly to trade in slaves, our situation can only worsen."

At last Nathanial spoke. "So what makes you think that we Bristol merchants will want to help you and your type from London? For all too long you have held the monopoly and now it's been broken when Parliament listened to our demands, now you come here asking for our assistance. I think not, Mister Colston and Mister Cavendish. Furthermore, for your information, we have a Bristol statute that only allows persons that are Bristol born to buy and trade from our port so I could not help you even if it was in my nature to do so." With that fiery statement Nathanial Day rose, raised his cane in mock salute and said, "Good day, gentlemen."

James looked askance at Edward as they watched Mister Day exit from the coffee house. "Do not worry, James, my family heritage is something of which our Mister Day is unaware. You see, I was born in Bristol and moved to London to become a merchant but I still have family connections here. I think our next step is to apply for a port licence and then we can report back to our fellow investors in London to see what they want to do next."

James said, "Before we departed from London, I met with a

186

good family friend who told me that when he visited Bristol some years ago, he remembers seeing a customs house in a place called Welsh Back. Perhaps we should visit Mister Rosewell for directions?"

James and Edward finished their coffee and headed off down All Saint's Lane where they found Mister Rosewell in his shop just finishing the shaving of a customer.

"Ah, Mister Rosewell, we wonder if you can help us in a further matter. We have to find the king's customs officer responsible for the port; we believe he may be located at somewhere called Welsh Back. Can you direct us to where we may find this officer?"

Mister Rosewell smiled, "That is not a problem, I know that he has a lot of waterfront to patrol but your best hope is to return to the vicinity of your lodgings at the Llandoger Trow, then walk back onto the quayside. The quay itself is named Welsh Back, the custom house is a very ornate building with gilded framed windows. You can't miss it; anyone in the area will point out the customs officer, as they all try to avoid him, if you know what I mean."

It was late afternoon; the summer sun was already casting long shadows on the quayside when the customs official finally arrived back at the custom house after completing his duties around the incoming ships of the day. James and Edward had been waiting for almost two hours when he arrived. Edward Colston introduced himself as a Bristol born citizen and explained that he had been a member of the now defunct Royal Africa Company with its own slave ships that were registered in London.

"As a Bristol born citizen," Edward said, "I wish to apply for the registration of two new London built ships to become Bristol registered."

The official looked at the ornate timepiece on the bureau in his office and commented, "Mister Colston, it is already late afternoon and the negotiations with the licensing authority may prove to be lengthy. May I suggest we all meet back here in the morning so that I can consider your case and consider if you comply with the regulations for a licence."

Next morning Edward and James arrived at the customs house and the negations recommenced. Edward explained that it was a new venture and to satisfy the Bristol authorities they would convert two new merchantmen into slave ships by putting three decks into each cargo hold and with the Port of Bristol's approval, the ships with Edward Colston and James entered as joint owners would be sailed from London into the Bristol port for conversion. After three hours of negotiations the port authorities were convinced that Edward was a genuine local businessman and the appropriate licences were issued.

That evening Edward Colston and James Cavendish returned to the Llandoger Trow very happy men; they had successfully completed their business and tomorrow they could report back to the London merchants with the news of the successful outcome to their expedition. After an early breakfast, James and Edward settled their accounts and thanked Jim Hawkins for his help and hospitality.

The jubilant pair arrived back in London on Wednesday the twenty-fifth of June 1698 after an uneventful journey. Rather than travel up river to his Surrey home in Mortlake, Edward accepted an invitation from James to stay overnight with Constance and himself in their Newington Green home. The following day Edward and James made an excursion to Lloyds coffee house and placed announcement notices that a meeting of the merchants would be held on the following Tuesday afternoon.

On the appointed day, a mixed group of twenty prominent merchants attended the meeting and on arrival each was escorted into a private room by Edward Lloyd where they found Edward and James sitting at a corner table. When the company were all seated and the door finally closed, Edward rose to give his report to the expectant audience.

"Gentlemen, as you know, Mister Cavendish and I visited Bristol to determine if the London merchants could benefit from trading from the port of Bristol; at first our proposals were dismissed out of hand and we were informed that only Bristol born patrons are permitted to trade and register ships in Bristol. As I was born in that fair city, I have taken the liberty of registering two new vessels with James Cavendish and myself as joint owners; we named the ships the *Bristol Trader* and *Virginian Trader*. What I propose is that we use those two ships as a base for a new investment and any of the merchants attending this meeting may invest in the cost of buying and converting those two ships to suit the slave trade. For those of you that are unaware of the accommodation on a slave ship, I will explain briefly; the standard deck in the holds of our trading ships gives a head room of sixty inches for the crew. On slave ships the holds are divided with an additional deck so that headroom is reduced to thirty inches to accommodate the two hundred slaves on each ship. We do that so the capacity of the cargo space is fully used. Now this conversion work will take time and be costly therefore I propose that as we are funding a pair of ships, we should make it clear to both captains that the profit from both ships shall be considered as a joint profit. Those measures will ensure that if we lose one ship on the crossing or if there is a large loss of slaves through disease, then we all share in the loss as well as the profit. Is that agreed?"

The merchants discussed the proposals and finally agreed to the drawing up of draft proposals for the formation of a new company to trade from the Port of Bristol. Edward Colston and James each took twenty percent of the shares.

James made the mental note that he had the intention of letting Samuel Pepys have a substantial portion of his share.

Two weeks later the *Bristol Trader* and the *Virginian Trader* sailed from London to Bristol and the conversion of the two ships, which would take three months, was underway. With the winter approaching, the investors voted to delay the first voyage of the *Bristol* and *Virginian* until the March of 1699, and it was towards the end of February when James wrote to Edward Colston.

Dear Edward,

As you are aware we have a great deal at risk if our Bristol investment fails and therefore I intend to visit Bristol at the end of this month to oversee the provisioning of our two ships on their first voyage and also to confirm with the captains that it is a joint venture and the sale of goods from both ships will be considered as one in total. I invite you to join me but I shall not deem it amiss if you refuse my offer.

I am, Sir

Your most obliged friend.
James Cavendish

Edward responded with a letter to the effect that he had prior engagements and he would leave matters in the capable hands of James.

***

The journey for James to Bristol was uneventful and he again took lodgings at the Llandoger Trow.

Jim Hawkins the landlord greeted him as a returning customer.

The following morning after a good night's rest, James walked the short distance along the quay where he sought out Captain Speers of the *Bristol* and Captain Peters of the *Virginian* and boarded both ships to briefly check that they were in fact well loaded with Gloucestershire woollen cloth, plus caps and hats, waistcoats and jackets and weapons to trade to the African slave traders, then he and the two captains retired to the Llandoger Trow to discuss final business.

When the three were seated, James confirmed that the captains both understood that it was a joint venture with the profits and losses from both ships considered as one in total. James also made sure that both captains had their cargo manifests for the sale of goods to the African traders plus a sum of gold coins to the value of two hundred pounds each. James then informed Captain Speers and Captain Peters that he intended to protect their investments by recruiting a doctor to sail on each of the ships. The captains welcomed the proposal and the three shook hands and parted company with James's assurance he would return with details of the appointment of the doctors.

James ventured out onto the quay and walked the short distance to the shop of Mister Rosewell the barber surgeon who had befriended Edward and James on their previous visit.

"We have two slave ships sailing this week and I think it would be a good investment if we had a doctor on each ship to tender to the needs of the crew. The doctor should also care for any of the slaves that fall sick; they may be cheap but each death is a loss of profit. Can you recommend any such doctors? Maybe you know of persons who have fallen on hard times or are in disgrace and wish to leave Bristol and would be willing to undertake such a voyage?"

Mister Rosewell thought for some time. "I have to mind a

190

couple of such men who may be willing to undertake such a task. One is Doctor Roberts; he lives in the district of St Pauls. I do know that he has a shrew for a wife and I think he may take the opportunity to escape her vicious tongue. The only other that I can think of is a Doctor Price who lives in Redland. He is under suspicion by the authorities for aborting his sister-in-law's baby; she died, and if it can be proven he may face the gallows. It is rumoured he was the baby's father. You could try those two."

James thanked Mister Rosewell and left to attempt to recruit the doctors. James first took a coach to Redland. As with most city coachmen, he knew his area; he knew the location of the brothels and he certainly knew of Doctor Price.

James told the coachman to wait and nervously James mounted the three steps to Doctor Price's front door. Knocking heavily, James waited; eventually the door was partially opened by a middle aged woman who appeared to be in a highly nervous state.

"You're not from the authorities, are you?" the woman asked.

"Certainly not, madam. My name is Mister James Cavendish from London and I have a business proposition which necessitates that I speak to the doctor."

The door opened wider and James saw a bespectacled man standing behind the woman.

"I am Doctor Price, do come in; please state you business then go quickly, we have enough trouble at the moment."

James entered the hallway and spoke of his need for a ship's doctor for a voyage on a slave ship to the colonies. "We expect the ship to return in the autumn of this year. Would you be willing to undertake the task?"

"What are you willing to pay for my services?" Price enquired.

"We will pay your wife ten guineas when you sign on and another three guineas when the voyage is complete. If you do not return, she will still be paid the three guineas."

The doctor's wife looked apprehensive but then said, "It is better for us both if you go away; at least I know you will not face the authorities and maybe the noose. I know you did my sister wrong but you are still my husband. I think you should go."

Doctor Price shook James by the hand and agreed to be at the Llandoger Trow that evening.

James bade the doctor and his wife farewell then took his coach down into St Pauls where the coachman said he knew where to find Doctor Roberts.

The outcome of that meeting was also successful, although James did beat a hasty retreat when the vitriolic tongue of the doctor's wife lashed him as the doctor grabbed his medical bag and made a quick escape to join James in his coach.

James stood on the quay and waited. Finally he escorted the doctors aboard their allotted ships before returning to his room at the Llandoger Trow.

Trade at the Llandoger was slow that night, and after James had eaten, Jim Hawkins the landlord, found time to engage in conversation with James.

"Sir, I seem to remember when you visited my inn last year with the other gentleman." Jim Hawkins hesitated as he tried to remember the name, "A Mister Colston if I remember correctly, you were enquiring for information about the Merchant Venturers."

"That's correct." James said.

"Well its seems just a coincidence, but I know you are from London and when I was a young man, I sailed on a merchant venturers ship from London. The ship was named *The Prince.* I remember it was harsh conditions, we sailed for Jamestown in Virginia and brought back tobacco. It was a hard life and not for me, I made a decision to change my life and here I am, years later an innkeeper in Bristol. I only mention it because I hear that you are making a move away from London and trading from Bristol, well good luck to you Mr Cavendish. Bristol has been good for me and I shall end my days but….."

James noted a look of sadness had come into Mister Hawkins's countenance as Jim continued, "….. my son and his wife and my grandson young Jim Hawkins want to move away from this city life; they are buying the Admiral Benbow at Black Hill Cove down in the south west."

During the next two evenings James managed other discussions with Mister Hawkins about sea life and the colonies.

Two days later James watched as a pair of small boats towed the *Bristol* and *Virginian* out into the main river channel to wait for a fair wind to take them down the Bristol Channel, then James turned, retrieved his baggage from the inn and took the coach back to London.

Living Cargo

Thirteen days after departing from Bristol, the *Virginian* and the *Bristol* made landfall off the African coast. To avoid the deadly fevers affecting white men on that coast the ships anchored offshore and as it was dusk, the captains signalled they would wait for dawn when the Arab and black slave trading canoeists would paddle out to begin transporting the trading articles ashore.

As the first rays of the sun broke the surface on the horizon and the early morning grey skies turned to a myriad of pinks, the golden yellows made scattered reflections across the calm waters of the sea. To herald the new day the fiery orb of the sun rose majestically towards the heavens announcing another hot scorching day. Silently and stealthily from the shore the canoes came, paddled out on still waters.

For two days the canoes ferried to and fro heavily laden with articles of clothing, woollen goods and weapons all for trade for the living cargo that was to come aboard.

The crews and the ship's doctors were lucky for this voyage; the *Bristol* and *Virginian* were new ships, there was not the inherent stench that always pervaded the air for a mile downwind of any slave ship. The second voyage would be different, for despite the cleaning out of the holds after the ship had discharged its human cargo, the smell would permeate the ship's timbers until she was sunk or burnt.

With the holds empty, the same canoeists became slave traders and began ferrying their captured black brothers out to the ships. The first to be transported were the male slaves, who were manacled and forced into the lower decks. Hour after hour the canoes ferried the human cargo that had been snatched from their villages; each canoe having as many as ten subdued captives. For three days, the male slaves were taken on board and forced below decks into the larger holds on the lower decks, then for a further day the canoes transported the women and children, who were segregated from the male slaves. The women tried to comfort their children as they too were packed between decks. Finally with two hundred humans stowed as living cargo aboard the ships and with the trading manifest entered into the logbook of each ship, they set sail on the twenty-fifth of March for the New World.

They were only three weeks into the middle crossing, and still in early spring when the ships encountered heavy seas. The ship's portholes were covered during the storm to stop the ingress of seawater and the crews did not have time or the opportunity to clean the slave decks. The smell became unbearable. After fourteen days of bad weather, Doctor Price on board the *Virginian* refused to go below to tend to the sick; slop buckets were no longer available and the slaves were now forced to void their bladders and bowels and to lie in their own excrement and urine as the captain battened down the hatch covers to keep the stench from pervading the rest of the ship. Gradually the conditions in the holds got worse with very little fresh air to breathe. Each day the crew tied rags over their noses to make quick visits to hand out the meagre food rations of one bowl of gruel and one bowl of water to each slave before beating a hasty retreat back into the fresh air above decks.

After four weeks into the voyage the bad weather cleared, the heavy seas abated but the ships had lost sight of each other.

On board each ship, life followed similar routines; crews formed bucket brigades to try and swill out holds. During that month at sea, twenty slaves on the *Bristol* had died and their bodies had been thrown overboard. The *Virginian* fared a little better with fifteen dead slaves thrown into the ocean. The trading losses were recorded in the ships' logs.

Aboard the *Bristol* Captain Speers used the period of fair weather to give the slaves an airing and gave the order for the women and children to be brought onto deck for a time. At the end of the time on deck Speers allowed three of the females who were unencumbered with children or babies to remain on deck.

It was May, in mid-Atlantic, and with the dark seas and low horizon, dusk fell early, and by lantern light throughout the long night, the crew abused and raped the three hapless women. By dawn one of the females was dead, one was so badly abused she died within the hour and the third was forced below decks in a state of shock into the confines of the stinking fouled hold.

The two dead females were thrown overboard, their deaths recorded in the ship's logs as due to sickness.

Later that morning with the fair weather continuing, Captain Speers gave the order for batches of twenty male slaves to also be brought on deck and given an airing.

The *Bristol* and *Virginian* had both sailed from Africa on the same tide and until the storms had struck had remained within sight of each other. Now during the fair weather there was no sighting from either lookout as to their sister ship.

The *Bristol* and *Virginian* sailed on in solitude, neither aware if the other had survived.

Chesapeake Bay

The sunrise was sending slivers of red and golden arrows darting across the rippling waters of Chesapeake Bay. From the wharf at Jamestown early risers saw the herald of a beautiful day as the *Virginian* was sighted, her sails silhouetted against the sun giving the appearance of a glass ship sailing on a mirrored lake. But as she neared land, the familiar stench of a slave ship wafted ashore and the spell was broken.

It was noon on a late day in June 1699 before the *Virginian* finally berthed. Immediately Captain Peters ordered the covers from the holds to be lifted and the manacles that secured the stinking black living cargo to be removed. Sequentially the rows of unfettered slaves emerged from the black hell holds, crawling out into the daylight; some cringed in fear, most were uncertain on their legs, but all shielded their eyes to protect them from the glare of the daylight.

Eventually, a total of one hundred and seventy slaves that had somehow survived the ninety-day passage across the Atlantic were unloaded onto the wharf and were again manacled; the males and females and family members were segregated and led to wooden buildings. Once inside they were given buckets of cold water to wash the filth from their bodies and were provided with basic cloths for clothing before being led away to separate buildings where they ate and slept on floor mats until a market auction could be arranged.

Meanwhile Captain Peters set the crew to work to cleaning out the holds to try and relieve some of the stench of urine and excrement that now permeated the timbers; but it was an impossible task, the smell was now an integral part of the slave ship and would remain until she was destroyed.

Seven days after the *Virginian* berthed and unloaded her cargo, the *Bristol* limped into harbour; she had sustained severe damage to her foremast due to an unexpected and exceptional shift in the wind during another squall when only three days from landfall.

Captain Speers had commissioned running repairs at sea and now as she limped into Jamestown, Captain Peters stood on the quay watching the battered ship making landfall and wondering how many of the crew and slaves had survived the crossing.

When the slaves were unloaded, washed and clothed, it transpired that of the original two hundred, only one hundred and fifty-four had survived. On the voyage three crew members had also died of disease or accidents at sea.

As did Captain Peters, Speers now set the crew to work to cleanse out the holds and after a few days the odour from both ships began to diminish slightly.

The captains now appointed agents to act on their behalf to arrange the sale of the slaves. Posters were printed and displayed in Jamestown announcing a slave market would take place on the second Saturday in July. On the appointed day, plantation owners came into town to examine the merchandise for health and fitness; the male slaves were still segregated from the remainder, which meant that families were parted, destined never to see each other again.

The bell on the church tower struck noon as the hapless blacks were paraded on a raised platform and the bidding started. The first to be auctioned were the healthiest males, who sold at the average price of fifteen pounds. Next to be sold were the females; those with infants of less than four years were sold as a pair, and then came the sale of the remaining older children followed by the elderly or sick. With the last elderly slave sold for one pound, the sale was concluded and each captain took a copy of the bill of sale arising from the auction.

There had been a total of three hundred and twenty-five slaves that had survived the voyage on the *Bristol* and *Virginian* and the auction had raised a total of four thousand three hundred and seventy-five pounds, which the captains now divided equally to present to the owners when the ships made a final berthing in Bristol.

Satisfied with the revenue raised, Speers and Peters set the crews to work to restore their ships to a seaworthy condition after the stormy Atlantic crossing. The crews were hard pressed to complete the repairs before winter fell and it became too cold to work. The crews worked from dawn to dusk and it was late into the fall before repairs were complete to the satisfaction of each captain.

About the same time that the ships repairs were complete, the tobacco crop for the year was all harvested; it was late October and the plantations were kept under constant visitations from representatives of the thirty or forty ships that were anchored in the river estuary. For three days Captains Speers and Peters, along with a dozen or more other captains, were ferried out to the wharfs on the plantations to make purchases of the tobacco harvest. By the fourth day, with negotiations completed for the purchasing of four hundred hogsheads at a cost of ten pounds each and the plantation owners agreeing to store the Colston and Cavendish tobacco crop until the spring when it would have had time to be properly dried and casked and ready for collection, Speers and Peters sailed back down to Jamestown to a safe anchorage for the winter.

With the advent of December, the first snows began to fall and the crews of the ships settled down in stockaded compounds to endure the harsh cold winter that was made slightly more comfortable with plentiful supplies of meat and vegetables supplemented with the occasional large Canadian goose that was in plentiful supply as a resident fowl on the river.

Winter faded quietly away as March roared in with its strong winds, then after a week they diminished until at last came a day when the sun shone weakly and a fair wind began to blow. Activity now broke out as Jamestown came to life, the crews of every ship raced to load their ships and be the first to set sail.

Urgency became the order of the day. Captains urged their crews to even more speed to be the first to catch the tide and set sail for home; the prize to get the best possible price for their cargoes on the Bristol market.

The *Bristol* and *Virginian* were not the first to set sail, but they were not the last; of the thirty ships that had anchored up for the winter, four were destined to sink on their voyage back to Bristol, Liverpool or London.

The *Bristol* and *Virginian* both made safe passages with the *Bristol* making the faster crossing, arriving seven days before the *Virginian*.

Goodbye Mister Pepys

The Bristol quay was alive with activity. Clerks and agents mingled with shipping merchants and sailors while amidst the throng a single customs official and shipping agent stood in conversation. The agent engaged in the conversation had been appointed by Edward Colston to administer the formalities to get custom clearance for the cargoes to enter the Port of Bristol. The custom official inspected each bill of lading the captains had presented to the agent; the official then escorted the captains to the custom house where the tax papers were completed to the satisfaction of the agent and a tax of one thousand pounds per ship was imposed.

Captains Speers and Peters returned to their ships to pay their crews and to organize the unloading of the cargo of tobacco. On the quay, the agent escorted the two doctors to a small room at a nearby inn; that he rented, and which he liked to call his office. The agent attempted to persuade the doctors to sign on for another year of service on the ships but he had not foreseen the emotion that was bottled inside Doctor Roberts, who now drew himself up to his full height, something he had not been able to do in the cramped and confined conditions on the ship, and the agent received the full fury of a year's pent-up anger. "Sir, my wife may have a vicious tongue and be a shrew by nature, but on that voyage I have witnessed abominations, cruelty, murder and I would prefer to live in torment with her for eternity than spend another day on a slave ship. Good day and good bye, sir."

The stunned agent paused before turning to Doctor Price and

201

asking if he would sign for another year. Price responded in a milder manner. "I think my problems at home may be over, so I must decline your offer." Doctor Price took his money leaving a shaken agent to sit down at his table to prepare a report of the transactions and send it post-haste to London.

Doctor Price returned to his wife in Redland, who greeted him with the good-news that there was to be no action from the authorities for the alleged aborting of his sister-in-laws baby.

A week later, Edward read the agent's report and then sent it to James to read in the privacy of his home. Two days later, Edward and James met at Lloyds and posted a notice to inform traders that a private room was booked for a joint meeting of the investors to be held on the twenty-second of May 1700 to report on the accounts from the two Bristol registered ships the *Bristol Trader* and the *Virginian Trader*.

***

Edward rose to his feet to address the meeting and a hush fell over the assembled merchants.

"Gentlemen, it gives me great pleasure to inform you that the *Bristol Trader* and *Virginian Trader* both made successful crossings and returned safely. A combined total of three hundred and twenty-five slaves that survived the voyage to Virginia and an auction raised a total of four thousand three hundred and seventy-five pounds. The captains made a purchase of four hundred hogsheads of tobacco at ten pound each which has been sold on the Bristol market. I will now pass round the profit and loss account sheet for your perusal whilst I sit and enjoy a cup of Mister Lloyd's fine coffee. We will discuss future plans in fifteen minutes."

Applause broke out; Edward sat down while James rose and handed out the account sheets.

Accounts of the Bristol & Virginian Trader 1699 Tobacco Season

	Costs	Sales	Nett
Initial provisioning of ships with woollen goods and trading implements (which we then exchanged for four hundred slaves)	300	300	
Purchase of four hundred slaves	300		
(Death of seventy five slaves) Sale of three hundred and twenty-five slaves		4,375	
Purchase of four hundred hogsheads of tobacco at £10	4,000		
Selling of four hundred hogsheads of tobacco at £45		18,000	
Payment of Captains & Crews		200	
Payment of ships doctors of 26 guineas plus agents fees of 13 guineas making total of £40	40		
Gross £	4,840	22,675	17,835
Nett Profit £			17,835

After the fifteen-minute period had elapsed, Edward rose and again addressed the meeting. "Gentlemen, as you can see from the balance sheet, the initial venture into trading from Bristol was a success and returned a profit, but we cannot take all the profits. This time we were lucky, both our ships returned but we must invest in more ships in case of losses at sea. Can I recommend that we re-invest twenty percent of our profit for future expansions?"

A general discussion took place and the merchants agreed with Edward Colston to purchase another four vessels. The slave trade for Edward Colston and James was about to blossom and flourish.

James wondered if he had just mounted a whirlwind.

***

Doctor Roberts, who had been aboard the *Bristol* and had witnessed Captain Speers condone the rape and murder of the female slaves, was a troubled man. A few days after he arrived home he drafted a letter to James Cavendish and explained what he had witnessed. James read the letter and he too was uneasy. It was different now, times were changing. When old Henry Cavendish had invested in the tobacco trade, the plantations had been worked by immigrants but that supply of manpower had been inadequate and long gone. James knew slaves had to be used, it was a commercial fact but he had been unaware of the barbaric trafficking and his conscience was troubled. He finally realized he was buying and selling human flesh.

When James next met Edward Colston he showed him the letter and on Edward's advice, James decided to take no further action against Captain Speers, but James was still plagued by his conscience and confided to Constance, "What worries me is the fact that when I pass the business over to Charles, his and Annabel's inheritance will have been made on the suffering of these people. What can I do, Constance?"

Constance was not usually short tempered, but on this instance, she may have had visions of changes to her comfortable lifestyle. She turned and snapped at James, "I think that you should heed Mister Colston and ignore the matter…"

And so for a time being James buried his conscience as he and Constance settled back into their comfortable lifestyle.

James increased the Cavendish investments in the Bristol-based merchant venture as the investors purchased another four ships.

***

It was an idyllic time in the Cavendish house; Charles and Annabel were both learning fast. James made monthly reports to his old friend Samuel; and life should have continued along those lines, but in 1700 Samuel could no longer live alone without care and he decided he would live at Clapham Common in the home of Will Hewer, his loyal clerk from the Navy Office all those years before.

Samuel was sitting in a high-backed chair in his room at Will Hewer's house. It was a Monday morning; Samuel glanced at the calendar on his desk, it was the 22nd of May 1701. At that moment Will Hewer came into the room and made an announcement. "Samuel, we have worked in the Navy Office for some years, and it may interest you to know that Captain Kidd is to be hanged tomorrow at Execution Dock in Wapping. I intend to see that rogue swing. Would you like to attend the execution?"

"I fear my strength would fail me, Will, but you go and tell me all about it when you return."

Samuel waited tensely for news of the events of the execution and it was late on Tuesday evening when Will returned. As they sat at supper, Will recounted how Kidd was taken from Newgate, together with a pair of condemned Frenchmen, in two horse-drawn carts. The carts were guarded and led by a Marshall from the Admiralty. "You would have enjoyed the spectacle, Samuel; the marshal carried a silver oar; as you know, it is a symbol of the Admiralty's authority. I was informed later by one of the marshals that as the procession approached the Tower of London down to Execution Dock in Wapping, it was quite clear to the large crowds that Kidd was far from sober. In fact he was so drunk that the Chaplain from Newgate prison was shocked into venting verbal disapproval."

Samuel interrupted. "You can't expect a fellow to have his neck stretched and remain sober. I had great respect for his naval capabilities and I think I would get drunk in his position."

"Well, I had a good vantage point near to the gallows and heard Kidd utter a warning from the gallows to all ship-masters to learn from his fate. Then a rope was placed around his neck. As you know, Kidd was a large man and as the cart was drawn away from the scaffold, the rope broke, leaving Kidd floundering in the Thames mud whilst the other condemned men swung at the end of their ropes."

"An undignified ending to a one time servant of the Navy Office, but do continue, Will."

"Well it was obvious that Kidd was still very drunk and now covered in mud, he had to be helped to his feet and man-handled back on to the gallows for a second time. The disapproving chaplain was still in attendance and praying. Somebody produced a new rope; it was hastily thrown around Kidd's neck and he was eventually hanged."

"I suppose he will be left at the rope's end for the customary three tides to cover his body?" Samuel enquired.

"I believe so. That will be completed by tomorrow after the symbolic triple drowning, and then I understand his body will be taken to Tilbury Point and placed in a gibbet as a warning to others."

"God rest his soul," Samuel added and the pair continued with their supper.

For the next hour the conversation drifted into reminiscences of their working times at the Navy Office before Samuel retired for an early night.

Death Stalks in Threes

For the citizens of London there was little escape from the dust and the myriads of flies as the summer months of July certainly earned its name *'flaming July'* that year and it was during the height of the heat wave that Jane collapsed and died. Once more James and Constance with their children Annabel and Charles accompanied Jane's coffin to the family graveyard at Ufton Manor where she was interred alongside her husband Henry.

At last the heat wave gave way. The warm mellow autumn of golden hues turned to red as if in remembrance of the inferno that had been the summer heat. Soon the cold frosty mornings began as gradually winter crept in. All too soon the Christmas festivities came and went.

James made frequent excursions out to Clapham Common to keep in touch with his old friend and make Samuel aware of any social gossip and court news.

On one such visit in February of 1702 James found Samuel in his room, seated in his favourite high-backed chair with woollen blankets around his legs to ward off the winter cold. Will Hewer had lit a fire and as James entered, he noticed a marked deterioration in Samuel's health. James took a seat and they sat in silence for a few moments gazing in contemplation out onto a frost covered garden.

Samuel spoke first. "James, I think I shall be lucky to see another spring. It's been a good life. I have served three monarchs, and I got our navy in good order and for that I am pleased."

"You have indeed, but that is defeatist talk, Samuel, you have survived other illnesses, remember your kidney stones?"

"I do indeed but then I was a younger man. I admit my mind is still active but the flesh is weak."

"You will probably outlive our present monarch and that is a fact. Have you heard that King William has sustained a severe injury in an accident that that may well end the Stuart dynasty to the British monarchy?"

"An accident, what happened to him?"

"It seems that he was out riding when his horse stumbled on a molehill. The king fell badly and broke his collar bone."

"Oh, how the mighty can be brought down by such a small creature," was all Samuel could say.

The pair conversed for another hour of old times; the events they had witnessed in their lifetime, the plague, the fire of London and the rebuilding of London, then James bade Samuel farewell and promised to return in a few days; when he did, it was with the sad news that the king's condition had deteriorated so badly it was obvious that he was unlikely to survive the accident.

"His demise will be no great loss to England," Samuel muttered. "In fact after his orders to attack the Jacobites in Scotland, I think many a sympathiser will be drinking a toast to *the little gentleman in black velvet*. You know, James, it's a curious fact of life that even a little creature like a mole can unseat a king."

James left Samuel to return home, and next morning the citizens of London awoke to learn that King William III had died. James looked at the date on his calendar; it was the seventh of March 1702.

Samuel's health was now seriously declining although his mind was still very active and he still took great interest in James's accounts of their investments, but on the twenty-sixth of May 1703 he passed away. Ten days later at 9 o'clock on a warm summer evening Samuel was interred alongside his wife Elizabeth at St Olave's Church.

James and Constance attended to pay their respects to a very old family benefactor and friend.

As if with a whimper, half a century of Cavendish family associations with Samuel Pepys came to an end.

To show the esteem in which the state held Samuel, the funeral service was conducted by the Archbishop of Canterbury and the Bishop of London.

For the house of Cavendish it was a turning point in the family fortunes; a few days after the funeral, and after many hours of self-deliberation James made a decision. Calling Constance into the drawing room and making sure she was comfortable, he said, "My dear, I have deliberated and I keep reflecting on Doctors Robert's letter about the slave conditions on that voyage. My conscience will not let me continue to profit from the selling of slaves and therefore I am selling my assets and will no longer be investing in the tobacco trade. In the future we shall rely on the investments we have made in the Hudson Bay."

With that declaration of intent to Constance, James held a meeting with the London merchants and informed them of his intentions to sell his Virginian assets and re-invest in the Hudson Bay.

Samuel's death caused some contacts and sources of information that James had within the government to vanish. He was of course a wealthy man and he began to consider leaving the city and moving his family back to Derbyshire.

Then at about eleven in the evening on the twenty-sixth of November 1703 a catastrophic event occurred that hastened the decision to make a move; the catastrophe was a hurricane that hit the north coast of England and swept the sea waters up the Thames. The river rose and flooded parts of Westminster. All the shipping on the river from London Bridge down to Wapping and Limehouse, with the exception of four ships, were broken from their moorings and thrown onto the shore; upwards of four hundred ferry boats were lost and more than sixty barges were driven on the tidal wave to run foul on London Bridge, while above the bridge, hundreds more vessels were either sunk or damaged, but the greatest loss fell upon the navy that was anchored offshore in the North Sea. Thirteen warships sank and upwards of fifteen hundred seamen were drowned.

When the full extent of the damage was known, James discussed the situation with Constance who understood his concerns over the loss of life and damage to trade to the London merchants but said, "In principle, my dear, I think it would be nice to move the family back to your ancestral home but Charles and Annabel are approaching an age where in five or six years' time they could benefit from the London social calendar and it would be better if you delayed our move so that the children could obtain a foothold into London society."

Having curtailed his interests with Virginia through the merchant venturers, his losses were not as great as some of the merchants and so James maintained his investment in the Company of Adventurers to Hudson Bay in order to replace their shipping losses from the hurricane.

***

Seven years passed as in the blinking of an eye, the dome was finally finished on St. Paul's cathedral. England and Scotland became part of the new nation of Great Britain.

It was a changing world and in that changing world, there stood Constance, an ever attentive mother, casting an eye for suitable suitors for her offspring.

Going Home – Outroads

Charles' voice had broken; he was reaching puberty, he had developed spots on his face and he was self-conscious. About the home he was morose and argumentative with his parents and James realized that it was time for the young man to broaden his outlook on life and for him to be gradually introduced into the world of commerce and the Cavendish family business. For the next three years Charles accompanied James to meetings with other merchants, and he escorted James when they visited warehouses to check on the commodities suitable for sale to the colonies.

At the age of twenty he had taken a minor role in attending business meetings at Lloyds and was already enthusiastic to follow his father's footsteps and expand the family fortunes.

On a winter evening in February of 1710, James and Constance were sitting in the library; a log fire burned in the grate, Annabel was playing the harpsichord and had just completed a difficult rendition of a simple melody. Charles had sat and listened in a veiled attempt of brotherly interest accompanied by bored silence. James rose and poured a glass of claret for each of them then he motioned for Annabel to join them as Constance commented, "That was very nice, my dear, but father and I have something we wish to discuss with you both."

James coughed, sat down and said, "Mother and I made a decision a few years ago that when the time was right we would acquaint you both with what we feel is the mistreatment of the slaves on slave ships. The evidence I have and which proved a

211

life changing factor came in a letter from a Doctor Roberts who served on a slave ship. I received the letter about ten years ago."

James now handed the letter to Charles and Annabelle. Silence descended on the room as they read of the rape and murder of the women and the brutality and filth aboard the slave ships. In silence Charles folded the letter and handed it back to James; Annabel had tears in her eyes.

"So now you know why our family sold our investments in the Virginian tobacco trade and re-invested in the Hudson Bay. You also remember our dear friend Samuel?"

James paused as Charles and Annabel nodded. "While he was alive we felt duty bound to stay by him in London but when he died in 1703, I promised your mother we would stay in London for another seven years until you both reached an age where you were on the social scene in London and could make a decision. Those years are now passed and this year we will decide if the family is going to move back to Ufton Manor in Derbyshire. Now, Charles, you have an insight into our financial world, how do you feel about moving and travelling back here to London twice a year to protect our interests?"

Charles remained in thought for a moment then looking at Annabel for some support but finding nothing in her manner he replied in a totally unexpected manner. "Sir, I have visited the home of Samuel Clarke, one of your merchants, and I have discovered that he has a very agreeable daughter named Charity. I have been meaning to speak to you father, about my future with this young lady and I would ask if you will speak to her father on my behalf. If it is agreeable and I marry Charity, then it would be most suitable if she moved with us to Ufton Manor. It would also be beneficial to our business if her father would act as our agent here in London and what better connections could your agent have than to be my father-in-law?"

Constance smiled and agreed that James should meet with the Clarke family. Introductions between the families were not deemed necessary as James knew Samuel as a fellow trader and shipping agent.

James and Samuel Clarke met and James explained in detail his plans to move his family back to the ancestral home in Derbyshire. Samuel Clarke agreed that if a betrothal was arranged, neither he nor his wife would object to Charity living at Ufton Manor after the wedding. Samuel also agreed that he would help protect the Cavendish shipping interests and act as their agent on the proviso that Charles visited London at least twice a year to advise on the Cavendish wishes.

In the spring of 1711, with the winter furs from Hudson Bay safe in the London warehouses, Charles and Charity were joined in wedlock at the church of St Mary Aldermary in Bow Lane.

It wasn't a sunny day; friends and relatives were sitting in the church before the ceremony listening to the strains of the musicians quietly playing a selection of cantatas.

Charles waited nervously for his bride to arrive and James was engaging him in conversation to help calm him. "You know, this is the church were your mother and I married back in 'sixty-nine, I hope you have as many happy years with Charity as I have had with your mother. She was pure when we married, I trust Charity is also."

"Father, how could she be any other? We are always chaperoned and tonight we will enjoy our union for the first time."

At that moment the mood of the music changed. Charity on the arm of her proud father entered the church wearing a wedding dress of pure white silk. The gown trailing on the stone floor emitted a sound like a rustling restless wind as the silk slithered across the stone floor as the bride walked sedately down the aisle.

Her father had obtained the material at a bargain price through a merchant trader of the East India Company.

***

The spring flowers bloomed and died, summer fruits ripened and were picked in the orchards as Charles and Charity continued to enjoy their honeymoon period of marriage with passionate nights of love.

Annabel however was showing little interest as a London socialite; her interests seemed to be more in reading and art. Consequently James and Constance began planning for the sale of the family home in what was still a rural but very fashionable area of London.

"I think we are moving at the right time," James commented to Constance a few weeks later. "These rural surroundings will not survive another decade, the city expansion is beginning to absorb the outer villages and I am afraid our village will disappear into a part of the city."

But the plans to sell Cavendish House were delayed when in 1712 Charity announced she was pregnant and it was decided to await her safe delivery before submitting her to the trauma and upheaval of a family move.

In the spring of 1713 Charity gave birth to a daughter whom they named Elizabeth.

Then finally the move was put into operation with the better pieces of the family furniture and the heirlooms packed and loaded onto horse-drawn carts ready for transporting to Derbyshire. The day finally arrived in August 1713 when House of Cavendish made outroads and the family left their London home that Henry Cavendish had purchased almost fifty years previously to begin their new life at Ufton Manor.

Elizabeth Cavendish was going home...

Epilogue

Although *The House of Cavendish—Outroads* is a work of fiction, many of the characters that you have met in my novel are factual historical figures and some are briefly described below:

Samuel Pepys was naval administrator and a Member of Parliament, who had no maritime experience but rose by patronage, hard work and talent for administration, to be the Chief Secretary to the Admiralty under both King Charles II and subsequently King James II.

Barbara Villiers was the wife of Roger Palmer, Earl of Castlemaine. She became King Charles's mistress in 1660, while still married to Palmer, and whilst Charles was still in exile at The Hague.

William Usburn was an original licensed London hackney coachman.

George Vicars – Tailor at Eyam

William Mompesson – Eyam church leader

Des Groseilliers – Hudson bay fur trapper

Radisson – brother in law to Des Groseilliers

Mr. Rosewell, Surgeon Barber with premises in All Saints Lane Bristol,

Middleton & Jones Solicitors Chesterfield, Derbyshire

Lightning Source UK Ltd.
Milton Keynes UK
06 September 2010

159503UK00001B/30/P